After You Died...

MELINA LEWIS

Print ISBN: 978-1-54393-070-2

eBook ISBN: 978-1-54393-071-9

Contents

For my husband and children,
you are my everything

Introduction

The Seven Stages of Grief [1]

First introduced as the five stages of grief, defined by Elizabeth Kübler-Ross in her 1969 book 'On Death and Dying', the stages of grief are known as the emotional stages a person would experience as a terminally ill patient or as the result of the loss of a loved one. Kübler-Ross noted later in life that the stages are not a linear and predictable progression, but may be cyclical [2]. Additional stages and variations have been developed by various organisations and psychologists over time.

---

1 Based on the Seven Stages of Grief Social Work Tech | Ignacio Pancheco. Available at http://socialworktech.com/2012/11/13/the-seven-stages-of-grief/

2 Kübler-Ross, Elisabeth; Kessler, David (June 5, 2007). «On Grief and Grieving: Finding the Meaning of Grief Through the Five Stages of Loss». Scribner. Retrieved November 27, 2016 – via Amazon

After you died...

After a traumatic event, such as the death of a loved one, people are forced onto a journey. Often experienced in seven stages, they set out on this journey to face everything they were and everything they will become.

Shock and Denial

Stage 1

A numbed disbelief occurs after the devastation of a loss. A person may deny the reality or gravity of their loss at some level to avoid pain. Shock provides emotional protection from being overwhelmed all at once. This may last for weeks

Chapter 1

Tshepo

It had been raining.

In heaving gusts, the wind shattered raindrops against windows, doors, trees, cars, in fact anything it could. Like a fish-wife gone mad in the night, the northwester thrashed out at the world, bellowing an angry torrent from the heavens. Then almost as if a door had been closed on her fury, the storm came to a complete stop. Time seemed to stand still, as raindrops slowly slid down leaves and gutters, before draining towards the ocean below.

The wet hillside road was slick with water, shimmering beneath street lights that still cast their eerie yellow glow.

A taxi picked up speed as it hurtled down the slope towards the main road intersection; the bass of the kwaito music jolting it from side to side, shaking every rusty bolt in the speeding vehicle.

This wasn't the usual route that Tshepo took. This morning the boss had come down hard on him, saying his numbers had dropped in the morning commute, and he needed to pick up his return trip time to Masiphumelele. The boss wasn't a man who wasted time, and Tshepo knew that if he didn't make up the cash, he'd find someone else to fill his driving seat, quicker than you could say 'wololo'.

He'd decided to take the bumpy mountainside route, in between the rich people's homes, even though none of the other taxi drivers came this way. Tshepo was certain he could use this route to beat the other drivers back to Masiphumelele, and back into the boss's good books.

Pushing around 100 km/hr down the last slope, to give him the edge on time,

Tshepo leant across to turn up the volume on the retrofitted boom box. When he looked up, she was already all over his windscreen.

In slow motion his windscreen began to shatter and eat up her face; her long blonde hair seemed to fill the entire front of the car, tiny drops of blood suspended in the air.

Then she was gone.

The taxi spun in great heaving ovals, over and over again, until the world tilted and fell over. The sound of metal grating on tar screeched across the small village of Fish Hoek, ending the silence after the storm.

The sounds from outside Tshepo's head came and went in waves. He tried to open his eyes, but warm liquid poured into his eyes. His left arm was pinned under his body, useless. With his right arm, he clumsily tried to wipe his eyes, smearing blood across his face as he tried to see.

His leg under him was caught. He tried to move, but the pain shot through his entire being, making him sweat cold rivulets. He stopped trying to move.

He tried to wipe the blood again; this time he could see.

He was still in the boss's taxi – it was totally fucked. The boss was going to kill whatever was left of him for sure this time. Shattered glass and steel surrounded him.

Then he saw her.

Her face was white, like a ghost. With hair pulled back tightly away from her face, her large dark eyes were like black holes. Her lips, tight and trembling, looked as if they were holding back a terrible message. She stared at him a second longer. Then, as if the wrath of all man's demons had entered her soul, she let out the most harrowing scream he'd ever heard, shaking the broken glass around him.

'You killed her! You fucking crazy bastard. You killed her and now she is dead, you stupid fucker!'

She didn't stop to breathe; she just screamed for what felt like an eternity, until eventually men in luminous clothing dragged her away.

Reappearing, the luminous men spoke to him through the wreck, asking his name and telling him to stay calm. One even crawled in and covered him with a blanket, but he couldn't stop shivering. Then without warning, the metal started to shriek and move.

'What's happening? Tell me what's happening,' cried Tshepo.

The men explained that they were using the jaws of life to get him out safely. The roof of his metal cage stretched open and the men stepped inside.

'Don't worry Tshepo, we'll get you out,' they said, but they couldn't with his leg still trapped.

Then more men came. Like a rugby team set for a scrum, they shoved into the taxi to lift it just enough for the others to pull him free. He tried to look down at his leg, but turned away as he saw the flash of horror cross the paramedic's face. Shivering uncontrollably, Tshepo was lifted onto a trolley bed as the paramedic shoved a needle in his arm. 'Don't worry, you'll be fine,' they reassured him.

The public hospital was two roads away, but every jolt and bump of the ambulance felt like it was driving over boulders. The pain exploded through his body as they hit each bump.

It all felt so hazy, but the paramedics' words found him, different voices jumbled into one another.

'He fokkin killed that chick,' said the Afrikaaner, 'this is bad guys, did you see his leg? It's way stuffed. Serves the stupid bastard right.'

'Shut up guys, he isn't out yet; he can hear you and will sue the shit out of us for something or other.'

'With what money is he suing anyone? This guy's going to get shot by his taxi boss for crashing that death trap of a vehicle anyway. Don't know why we're even bothering with this.'

Eventually it stopped, it all stopped: the voices, the pain, the ambulance.

False Bay Hospital's emergency room was bright and quiet. Pre-dawn Monday mornings were pretty easy going. The weekend's chaos had come and gone by then, and the staff could breathe before they finished their shift. After the handover at 7am, the morning shift would deal with Monday's influx of sick babies, cardio clinic and old folks who'd slipped on the bath mat that morning.

'Ag bladdy hell Shani, are we out of sugar again! Sheesh that matron is tightening our belts for us,' shouted Sister Marie.

The stout nursing sister liked nothing better than cup of sweet tea before she finished her round. Turning around to continue her diatribe against the matron, Sister Marie couldn't believe that the paramedics were hauling a body into the emergency rooms.

Shit, she thought to herself. All she wanted was a cup of sweet tea and to end her shift. After pulling a double shift on the weekend, she was dog tired, and in no mood for a huge case to deal with.

During her first shift, a granny had vomited peas down the back of her uniform. That meant a change of clothes (so two outfits to clean at home, not just one). Mid-second shift, she'd tried to warm up a near-dead bergie, after he'd spent too much time in the rain and wind. When he'd woken up, he'd tried to wrap her in his arms and kiss her; the stench was more that she could bear and it was her turn to nearly vomit on him. Shuddering at the thought, Marie snapped into focus.

'Ok boys, what's this all about?' Sister Marie demanded from the paramedics.

'This doos taxi driver just killed a runner Marie,' stated the medic flatly.

'His leg is shattered and probably the hip too, so he needs to go straight into emergency and probably surgery. Anyone around?'

'Dr Yusuf is busy, but she should be done soon. Bring him in and we can stabilise him. Shit man, is the runner really dead?' asked Sister Marie.

The paramedics nodded as they hauled Tshepo into the emergency room, and lifted his small but solid weight onto the bed. 'That's bad hey, who's the runner?' asked Sister Marie.

The paramedic they all called Venter, a 6-foot monolith of a man, who hated everyone but was a well-respected paramedic, looked squarely at Sister Marie with eyes cold, 'A woman Marie, this oke's made a fucking big mistake!'

Sister Marie shook her head and turned her attention to Tshepo. The paramedics had sedated him, which she was glad for. The leg on this guy was a definite amputation – crushed bone, jeans and flesh mixed into one gory mess at the start of his thigh.

As his vitals started to beep across the screen, his heart rate started rising which caused his blood pressure to drop. Something was wrong; Sister Marie called over her shoulder for help. The medical officer in charge had been freed up and came over.

Dr Yusuf looked at the mangled leg and felt into Tshepo's pelvis, her thin, bony finger carefully prodding into his hip. Usually calm and professional, she winced and swore under her breath.

'He needs to go to Victoria Hospital ASAP; we can't deal with this here. Give him fluids, wrap him up as best you can and then let's send him. I'll speak to the paramedics to call the helicopter. We need to move fast or we'll lose him,' said Dr Yusuf, before turning to speak to the paramedics. Sister Marie fixed her attention back to her patient. Feeling the adrenalin rush through her body, she busied herself with trying to save the man's life.

It was well past the end of her shift when Sister Marie watched the helicopter take off from the helipad, at the back of False Bay Hospital. She'd managed to stabilise the taxi driver just enough. Praying silently to herself, she hoped that he'd make it to Victoria Hospital and they'd be able to save him. As the downwind from the helicopter whipped up wet leaves around her, she hung her head and walked back into the hospital. It was time to go home.

When Tshepo woke up, his body began to shiver. For one long cold second he thought he was back in the shattered taxi carcass. With exhausted blinks he tried to see where he was, straining to focus on anything. Eventually, the once-white ceiling came into focus. Tilting his head towards his chest, he could see the end of the steel bed.

Around him were other beds, with other bodies in them. Nurses moved in between the beds, noisy machines wailing all around him. He was in a hospital, of that he was certain. His body broke into another shiver, his mouth was dry and his throat ached. He tried to swallow and ended up groaning from the pain. A nurse came into view, looked at him, and then checked the noisy machine above his head.

He turned his head to her and tried to speak, but his speech was garbled.

'Shhh, you're a lucky boy wena. Don't speak yet. Just know you are alive ne,' she said.

He stared at her.

She was older than him, with hair braided in rows along her head. She seemed to have a kind face, but he was scared she may be pretending. He'd heard how nurses abused patients in government hospitals - drowning them in hot baths, shouting or physically abusing them. The Daily Sun newspaper had described the rampages of over-tired nursing fraternities at length in a recent article.

He began worrying that this nurse might want to kill him because he had overcharged her on a taxi trip. Maybe he'd made her sit in front and count the money, and she hadn't liked that. Maybe he'd made her sit five, instead of four, along a row in the taxi. She looked slim; it could definitely be that.

Oh God, he prayed, please don't let this nurse kill me because I am a taxi driver. I only did it for the money.

Tshepo closed his eyes tightly, caught up in a world of patient-killing nurses, and didn't see the doctor approach. He only realised he was there when he heard him speaking to the nurse.

'I see he is awake. Has he said anything yet?'

Tshepo opened his eyes and could tell he was a doctor. He was possibly the tallest man he'd ever seen: skin as dark as ebony, and definitely not South African. He had an authority about him that made the nurse stand straighter.

'He tried Dr Kabaya, but I told him to stop speaking. After all the intubation in theatre, it's going to be rough going,' responded the nurse.

Dr Kabaya mumbled to himself. He nodded his head and looked over the chart. The machines continued to wail above Tshepo's head.

'His vitals are good, and he doesn't seem to be allergic to anything. Suppose he is pretty young. Does he know about the leg?'

His leg, what did this doctor mean about his leg? Then he felt it: the undeniable throb of drug-smothered pain coming from his left leg. He shuffled to look down at his leg, but couldn't see anything because of the sheet. Looking further along the bed towards the end, he tried to see his toes. The sheet moved as he wiggled his right foot; then he wiggled his left, but nothing happened. Beseechingly, he looked at the nurse and the doctor. They looked at each other, and then seemed to breathe deeply in unison.

The doctor spoke: 'I'm Dr Kabaya. You came in two days ago with a serious injury to your left leg and pelvis, after a car accident. The damage was very bad and you broke your pelvis in multiple places. I am very sorry to say, the damage to your leg was irreversible and we were forced to amputate. It was what we had to do to save your life.'

Tshepo's initial panic turned into overwhelming claustrophobia. Everything slowed down and he felt as though someone was sitting on his chest. Words continued to come out of Dr Kabaya's mouth as he moved around the bed, each step long and slow.

The doctor lifted the sheet gently. 'I am so sorry my friend, but you will heal well. You are young, and we will give you crutches to take home with you. We could only save half the thigh, but this is better than having to cut at the hip. Unfortunately your hip was a mess, and we had to reconstruct it,' he said. Pointing to the leg and hip, he continued: 'You will have to stay in hospital for at least another four weeks. False Bay Hospital will rehabilitate you,' explained Dr. Kabaya.

Tshepo heard the words as his head craned forward, his chin nearly touching his chest. He could see the bloody stump where his left leg used to be. The stump's wound was covered, but seeped pink liquid. The exertion and sight of his stump made Tshepo faint. His head dropped back and his body relaxed.

Dr Kabaya was still explaining the merits of his surgery on the leg, when the sister interrupted him: 'Doctor, he's out. I don't think he's taking this well. I will speak to psych about what meds I can give him to help him a bit, that ok?'

Dr Kabaya seemed perplexed that his patient could have fainted at the sight of his surgical prowess. Non-medical people were always so weak at the sight of a little blood, he told himself.

'Yes do that, and make sure Dr Naidoo at False Bay assesses him when he is there,' he said looking down at Tshepo.

'Ok, well, you take it from here. I need to finish this round, still got clinic to deal with after this. Keep an eye on the antibiotics and possible sepsis; we can't be too cautious. He gets transferred back to False Bay in a few days for recovery. I want him to be in good condition when he goes,' he stated, before turning to the next patient.

When Tshepo awoke he was met with a smiling nurse, standing almost over his face. He was convinced she was definitely going to end his life, and would have fainted again, had it not been for her placing a small piece of ice on his lips.

Enkosi thixo[3], he thought to himself. The cool melting ice slipped into his mouth, soothing his throat and making his eyes roll with relief. He grumbled for more, and she continued to slip ice onto his parted lips. As his mouth and throat cooled, his mind began to clear; he was now a one-legged man. Tears began to stream from the sides of his half-closed eyes, down the side of his face and into his ears. His chest sucked deep gulps of air and he shook as he cried.

The kind nurse sat beside him and continued to place small pieces of ice into his mouth, even as he spluttered and sobbed. The snot that ran down his face was wiped away, as she softly sang a sweet lullaby that mothers sing to their children: 'thula thula thulam twana….' Her melodic voice helped to ease the sobbing, and eventually Tshepo heaved one last sob and fell into an exhausted sleep.

After a few days, Tshepo was moved back to False Bay Hospital. He didn't remember much of the return journey. He knew it was in an ambulance; he knew there were people who sat with him and spoke to him. He knew the ambulance shook and swayed, resulting in bolts of pain in his hips and back. He tried to succumb to the drowsiness, but the motion of the ambulance left him grinding his teeth and clenching his fists from the pain. He remembered that eventually it had stopped. After being jolted out of the ambulance into the bright blinding light of day, he was pushed into the grey building and drifted into nothing.

Tshepo's pain medication was reduced, milligram by milligram, until he was awake for longer stretches of time, and was able to feed himself. Being awake meant that the reality of life as a one-legged man began to set in, leading Tshepo into a dark world of self-pity. He begged for more painkillers from the nurses, who just shook their heads at him. Consciousness afforded him no hope; the days slipped into one another and Tshepo no longer knew the day or date.

One morning as he heaved his eyelids open, a policeman stood at the end of his bed.

Tshepo's body ran cold. Why was the policeman by his bed?

Without so much as a greeting, the officer launched into how Tshepo was going straight to jail as soon as could get his ass out of bed.

'Just because you buggered your leg, doesn't mean that you aren't going to

---

3   thank God

spend some time in prison for manslaughter!' the officer told Tshepo, a smirk on his face.

Tshepo's heart stopped beating. It was as if the officer had punched him in the chest and stopped his heart with those words. He saw it happening in front of his eyes again: the hair, long and blonde across his windscreen, the glass shattering, the tiny drops of blood floating all around, and the other girl with big eyes, screaming and screaming. She had said it then; it must be true, he had killed her friend.

He hadn't really understood what she meant then, but now he did. The drugs couldn't mask it anymore. He had killed a woman with the boss's taxi. He had lost his leg, and was going to jail if this officer had anything to do with it. He was so fucked, and he prayed to die.

Maureen

When the noise of the wind and rain had stopped, the sudden silence woke Maureen with a start and she reached over to Chris's side of the bed. The cold sheet under her hand told her he wasn't there. 'Disappointed, she drew her body back to her warm side of the bed.Why did he do this to her? To their marriage? Why wasn't he back yet?

Chris had arrived back from his offshore job that morning, earlier than expected. Usually it was six weeks on and six weeks off, but this time he had come home two weeks early.

He had scared her half to death with his unexpected arrival. She'd been in the shower admiring her lengthy armpit, fanny and leg hair, dreading the upcoming wax appointment with that demonic beauty therapist, when Chris had come crashing in through the door.

The steam had hidden his face so she wasn't able to see who it was. All she knew was that a large man had walked into her bathroom while she stood there naked.

Nearly slipping on her Crabtree & Evelyn shower gel that fell from her hand, she screamed until Chris opened the shower door and shook her while shouting:

'Relax babe! It's only me!'

Once she heard the voice, and opened her eyes to see his face, she stopped screaming. Jumping into his arms she buried her face into his chest.

'Jeez baby, who the hell did you think I was? This is Fish Hoek remember, safest place in the Western Cape. No-one is going to come barging in on you and take you out your shower. It's not bladdy Joburg you know,' said Chris drawing her out of the shower, switching the tap off and holding her close.

Her wet body drew dark marks onto his clothes. 'But, but, you're home early,' stammered Maureen.

'I know right, SURPRISE!' grinned Chris with glee.

She just stared up at him, big blue eyes wide.

Chris was home. Early. She needed to sort herself out before he noticed.

'I'm so glad it's you, I missed you,' she mumbled into his chest.

Chris was rather pleased with his little surprise. As his wife's wet body hugged him he could feel those fantastic tits, he'd paid for a while back, push up against him. He slid his arms down to her tight behind and gave each bum cheek a firm squeeze. Her body pressed into his firmly.

Yes, it certainly was good to be home.

He lifted her up easily as she squealed with delight, and took to her bed.

Frantic and almost desperate after six weeks of longing, the sex was fast and intense. Chris slumped into the bed next to Maureen as he caught his breath.

'Welcome home baby,' purred Maureen, stroking his chest. He grinned back at her.

'How about a good cup of coffee, same as usual baby?' she said as she slid off the bed and pulled her silk gown tightly around her. Chris rolled onto his side and grabbed his mobile from the bedside table, his back to her and looking at his phone.

'Ya, thanks. Actually no, make me a flat white. It's a big thing in London,' he said.

Maureen raised her eyebrows and walked down the stairs. Was he serious, she thought to herself? A flat white from a Nespresso machine? Shaking her head in annoyance, he always came back from London with some ludicrous ideas and 'this is what they do in London' comment.

It was all good and well for him to stop over in London, from whatever godforsaken place he'd come from, and sip on a flat white in some hip cafe. But he seemed oblivious to the fact that Fish Hoek was a one-horse town, that had only recently discovered cappuccinos.

She thought briefly about googling how to make a flat white with a Nespresso machine, then thought better of it and made a cappuccino. She'd drunk a flat white at the French deli yesterday and couldn't tell what the hype was about; it tasted exactly the same to her. No doubt Chris would be just as clueless. He came from the East Rand like her: fancy up to a point, the rest money had to buy.

As the machine did its work and filled the kitchen with the aroma of coffee, Maureen spied herself in the reflection of the double oven. She smiled; Chris would be pleased, if he actually looked at her long enough. She had been working out every day at the gym. Between the classes and her personal trainer, she was looking incredible.

She ran her hands down the sides of her body and felt good. Luckily her hair colour had been redone two days ago. It was redder than Chris liked, which was why she'd gone early. They could never get it right at the salon, but at least none of the grey was showing. She spotted her mobile and quickly called the beauty therapist, insisting on an appointment that afternoon. She was probably their best client, so they'd make a plan.

On the upstairs en-suite balcony, Chris and Maureen Klaasen sat and drank their coffee. The temperature was warm enough, but there was a cool nip in the air, and the mist across the water seemed to be bringing a change in the weather.

Holding her warm cup under her nose, Maureen looked out across the valley as she breathed in the smell of coffee mixed with the salty air. Maureen glanced down at the houses of Fish Hoek. Despite her distaste for village folk, she loved her view from the mountainside. On clear days you could see all the way across False Bay to Gordon's Bay, the beautiful mountains framing the entire peninsula. The space from her balcony made her feel free. As she gazed across the icy blue water and thin line of small waves that tumbled onto the stretch of creamy sand, she sighed, wondering why he was home early.

'Isn't this great baby. So good to be home,' said Chris, taking a sip of the cappuccino and smacking his lips loudly.

'Just like the London flat white baby, cheers,' smiled Chris as he saluted Maureen with his cup.

He seemed happy to be home and updated Maureen on work, and the guys on the rig, the problems and the weather. She smiled and nodded back, making sure to take mental notes of the name, job and marital status of each of his co-workers. Chris spent so much time away, that his co-workers were his friends and family.

If Maureen wanted to be able to talk to him about anything, it was best she understood his life on the rig and got it right too. When he had finished his update, she gently broached the reason for his early return home.

'That's what I forgot to tell you; the rig has been bought over and there were some changes. Some of the guys got sacked. But luckily for me, I got promoted. More mula, less time offshore. Couldn't believe it, but I guess they finally figured out I was the one doing most of that stupid Aussie's work anyway. He got retrenched, said Chris, holding up his two fingers in mock air quotes either side of his face.

Maureen sighed audibly in relief. She'd been starting to think that Chris may have been 'retrenched' too. There had been rumours amongst the offshore wives. Only one of the women she knew had actually said that her husband didn't have a job to go back to. Chris's early return had made her worry he'd been sacked too.

Now that she knew everything was as it should be, she stood up and straddled Chris's lap. A naughty grin spread across her face.

'How about we go out for dinner to celebrate? And then come home for some fun?' she asked, filling his view with her breasts.

'Maybe tomorrow baby, I'm shattered. I'm gonna lie down, catch a kip. The guys are organising drinks at the Lizzy, so I'm gonna head there after. You know how it goes,' he said, winking at her breasts then looking up at her, 'besides, we have four weeks baby. No need to rush. Been a great start already'.

She clenched her jaw as he lifted her off his lap and put her aside. Grabbing the coffee cups, she stomped downstairs, slamming them on the kitchen counter.

How could he!

The guys always came first, the Lizzy second and then her. Luckily they didn't have a dog, or that would have come before her too, she thought to herself!

The Lizzy was the affectionate name for the Elizabethan Pub, a local bar at the end of the main road in Fish Hoek. It sold 2-for-1 double brandy and cokes between five and seven. If the guys had enough of those by 7pm, the bar could count on having them there for the rest of the evening.

She ground her teeth as she packed the coffee away and slammed the kitchen cupboards closed. After clanging everything in annoyance she decided to go and try to convince Chris to have dinner with her.

Maureen found him fast asleep. He had slept through her kitchen tantrum, which was not surprising really, as his life on a rig made him immune to noise. She sighed again, wondering to herself if having him home every four weeks would actually be a good thing?

He always slept for hours when he came home, so Maureen grabbed some lunch, made Chris a plate and left it on the counter for him. Then she went out to stock the fridge and get rid of that pesky body hair.

Chris really hated it if she wasn't as hairless as a newborn. Luckily he hadn't complained earlier; desperation had obviously made him less discerning.

He always said that he left her with a platinum credit card, to use to make sure she always looked good. He worked hard and he wanted his lady to be beautiful.

This used to make her feel special. Now it just freaked her out. Having to maintain perfect looks was a big ask when you lived on your own and did pretty much fuck all in the day. Chocolate and coffee had become her crutch. The odd cigarette now and then had also been a lifesaver, but only when Chris was away. He hated it when she smoked and she dared not risk him catching her.

Maureen spent the afternoon at the salon. Lying on the therapist's bed, she patiently waited as her body hair was removed or tinted, depending on where it was. The therapist's room was quiet, except for the droning of classical music and the odd panpipes song. Wondering if they were ever going to change the music, she made small talk with the therapist. She chattered on about how Chris had surprised her, and that was why it was an emergency hair removal situation.

The therapist, a twenty-something-year-old from Retreat, commiserated with Maureen as she systematically ripped the hair off her body, never flinching as Maureen's skin reddened. The smell of the wax filled the room and although an electric blanket was warm under her, Maureen began to feel cold and edgy.

Perhaps it was worry that the therapist might botch her eyebrows: by either plucking her one brow too ferociously, or by leaving the tint on for too long. Luckily she had none of these beauty disasters, but Chris being back early had thrown her. Especially the way he had barged in on her in the shower. He loved toying with her, always trying to freak her out. The morning shower incident had definitely succeeded in making her feel unsettled. As she tried to push the feeling away, she told herself she was being silly.

After her appointment, Maureen headed to one of the two malls in the Southern Peninsula, situated between Fish Hoek and Noordhoek, and central to most of the surrounding neighbourhoods.

Longbeach was a strip mall with all the basic large retailers one needed, plus the smaller vet, clothing, décor and odds and ends shops. This was a functional mall and it brought together a motley crew of locals: From the endless stream of retirees on pensioners' day and wild and wooly hippies dragging their children in tie dyed t-shirts, to the horse owners of Noordhoek in their jodhpurs, in stark contrast to the slightly overweight mothers with two or three snotty children in tow.

With her daring red hair, gorgeous figure, skinny jeans and clinging top over her slightly too perfect breasts, Maureen stood out from the usual mall clientele, and caught the eye of most people mooching their way through the mall. You could tell she wasn't a local. She dressed up and put make-up on to come to the mall. Maureen just put the cold stares and rubber necking down to the backward nature of small-town folk. She had no idea why they couldn't even try and dress up a little bit. One day she'd even seen a woman in her stokie slippers in the mall. After that, she'd driven to Constantia Mall for her groceries for three weeks, until she'd gotten over the horror. She'd come from a middle class area, and had worked hard on perfecting her look to fit in with the well-heeled members of society. Maureen wasn't going to let her perfectly manicured look go, just because everyone around her didn't care how they looked.

Maureen chose all of Chris's favourite foods, and found some extra delicious goodies he was sure to love. She slowly meandered through Woolies, popping expensive dips and desserts into her trolley.

On her way out of the grocery section, she spotted the lingerie department and couldn't help but head over, just to see what was there.

As she passed the children's wear, she overheard a mother trying desperately to convince her primary school daughter that another pair of gold pumps was not required. The little girl was explaining to her mother that every girl needs many shoes, at which point the mother rolled her eyes and threw the pumps into the trolley.

The scene reminded Maureen of herself and her mother. She missed her mom, who was back in Johannesburg. She would try and visit her when Chris left. He didn't get on with his mother-in-law, so there was no need to rock the boat. Chris liked to mock how her accent changed when she spoke to her mother:

'Sounding like a real East Rand chick again baby,' he'd say, knowing it annoyed her to be seen as middle class. She'd worked hard to improve her standing, and even before Chris had come along, she'd crafted her career, her look and her accent.

There was a new arrival in the lingerie section: a cream corset with red ribbons laced through, suspenders and a chiffon cream shawl. With her red hair, it was perfect. She grabbed her size and paid at the counter, trying hard not to go red in the face as the cashier lifted it up to admire it, casting knowing looks at her fellow employees.

As she left the mall, she felt the cold northwester wind and saw the ominous grey clouds rolling in; the weather had changed quickly since the morning. Typical Cape Town, she thought to herself, four seasons in one day.

It was late afternoon by the time Maureen got home. She unpacked all the food, put some champagne and craft beers in the fridge, and hurried upstairs to put on the new lingerie. It fitted like a glove. She spent some time admiring her figure in the mirror, sliding her hands over her corseted body. She couldn't wait to see Chris's face when he saw her in this outfit.

He had obviously gone out. The bed was made, navy style, and his motorbike wasn't in the garage. She was sure he'd just gone out on an errand and would be back before meeting up with the guys. But he hadn't popped back in and there was no sign of him. She called him, just to make sure he was ok, but he hadn't answered any of her calls. Just one WhatsApp.

'We discussed this, I'm out with the guys, give it a rest baby. I'll see you later.'

After half a bottle of champagne on her own, the sun long set and the sky dark, Maureen eventually collapsed into bed, the wind and rain howling around her.

When she woke up, the wind and rain had stopped dead. Chris still wasn't home. Feeling like her head was the weight of a rock, she'd hobbled to the bathroom and taken two ibuprofen to deal with the headache. She stared back at herself in the mirror. Her careful make-up was smeared across her eyes, her blow-dried hair a nest around her face. Feeling desperate and sorry for herself, she burst into tears. Sobbing so hard, her petite frame shook violently as she slid to the tiled floor, hugging her knees.

He always did this, every time, yet she always thought he wouldn't do it again. He just didn't care about her; he cared about drinking with his friends and staying out all night, and never coming home on time.

He always did this to her. Asshole.

She stopped crying and pulled herself up using the ball and claw bath to steady herself. She walked unsteadily towards her cupboard, digging her way through her coats, towards the back where she found her hidden cigarettes in her ski boots. Extracting herself from the cupboard, she walked to the balcony and threw the doors open. The air was cold, and she felt her skin prickle. Her chiffon shawl flapped uselessly.

Quietly, like an apparition she stood there in the dark, alone.

Maureen lit her cigarette and sucked so deeply that it burnt half way down. In a long exhalation, she blew out the smoke, filling the air in front of her with grey smog. The first cigarette was finished.

She lit another.

Holding her chiffon lingerie closer for warmth, she sucked hard on the second cigarette. Then she heard the sound of feet, running feet and voices.

It took her a while to see them. Four women were coming down the hill, puffs of warm breath above their heads and voices lifted in laughter.

Happy runners.

She couldn't quite hear what they were saying, but they seemed to glide over the wet road with ease. She wanted to hate them. Look at them; they had friendship, health, great bodies and each other. She couldn't stand their very existence.

She sucked on the second cigarette, harder than before. Waiting for the rush of nicotine, she imagined what it would be like to be with them.

Her train of thought was interrupted by a beat, a low thud thud of bass. The bass was getting closer and closer, and then it was right there.

The taxi flew past in a white light and enveloped the blonde girl, spitting her out before turning and crashing on its side. It spun round and round and then came to a halt, screeching as the metal scraped against the tar.

Maureen blinked.

What had she just seen?

Her arm became limp and she dropped her cigarette. She leant over the balcony and looked along the road. The three girls were standing and looking around in shock, then one seemed to wake up and run towards the blonde on the tarmac.

'Oh my God, oh my God,' was all Maureen could hear her utter, over and over.

Without realising that she was doing anything useful, Maureen's body fetched her mobile and called Valley Emergency Services.

Calmly, she heard her voice explain what had happened and give the address. Then she put the phone down, opened her front door and walked outside.

Awesome foursome

Tanya always arrived first. Her shiny black Fiat 500, that she couldn't really afford, was always parked perfectly in the same place under the light. She was standing next to her car warming up. Petite with an hour glass figure and just enough bosom, she knew what she had and always looked well put together. Even at 5:30am she had all the right spandex and accessories one would need for an 8.5km run through Fish Hoek. Her blue-black hair was pulled away from her face and her head band revealed her sharp nose, angular cheekbones and green speckled eyes. She checked her watch again. Did they always have to be late? she thought to herself.

She stomped her feet and jogged on the spot in frustration. She stopped jogging to reprogram her running watch. As she finished, she looked up and saw Claire driving into the beach parking area. As Claire pulled up in her 'reliable Renault', she flashed such a warm, friendly smile at Tanya, that she couldn't help but smile back and instantly forget she was peeved at her friends.

Claire had this magnetic effect on people: tall and a little too skinny, with long blonde hair that always whipped around her head, and an enormous smile that could lift anyone's spirits. Tanya couldn't understand why Claire didn't make her life easier and work in a private school doing speech and hearing therapy, versus working in the local township school in Masiphumelele. She could be making a packet of money in a private school, but not Claire, money didn't drive her. Claire bounded out of her car like a Great Dane puppy towards Tanya.

'Hey Tan, so sorry I'm a little late, I got up early to finish off some work for some CPD points I need for this year, and got sucked in. Please say you'll forgive me?' said Claire, as she made big eyes at Tanya.

'Honestly Claire-bear, how could I be mad at you? It's those other two dawdlers that drive me nuts. Did they sms and say they were on their way?' asked Tanya. She hugged Claire and then stood back and folded her arms across her chest.

'I left my phone at home so can't phone and wake them up! They are utterly useless. They would just sleep their lives away if we didn't get them out of bed,' fumed Tanya. Kate and Liz worked in the valley and didn't have any idea what traffic to town was like.

As Claire was about to try and call Liz, Tanya stopped her. Liz, followed by Kate, was driving into the parking lot. Kate could see Tanya's face from a kilometre away, and knew she was angry because they were barely five minutes late.

That girl really needs to chill out or get a decent shag, thought Kate to herself. Surely Tristan, Tanya's boyfriend, wasn't that bad in bed? Kate braced herself as she stepped out of the car. She was sure she was about to get a mouthful.

Luckily Kate was driving behind Liz, leaving Liz at the receiving end of Tanya's ice cold greeting first, followed by a sharp 'Well let's get going, I have to be on time this morning, got a review with my boss at 9am.' Tanya turned on her heel and started the run.

Starring wide eyed at Tanya and pleadingly at Claire, Liz grabbed Kate's arm and followed behind Tanya and Claire, who would now set the pace and make sure that Liz and Kate worked hard for their tardiness.

Liz wasn't feeling all that awake this morning and so had made a cup of tea to wake up before the run. This had caused her to lose track of time and be late. As her legs moved sluggishly, and the tea sloshed in her stomach, she realised that her body actually ached. She'd seen nine patients yesterday, back to back. Each one had felt like she was massaging more than just their aches and pains, but their life's problems. She'd decided to become a physiotherapist to deal with physical problems, not emotional ones.

But over the years, she'd come to realise that a lower back muscle strain meant money issues or other worries, shoulders carried the whole family's problems, knees and ankles gave way to when it was time to slow down. There was no way to separate physical and emotional problems in people; they came all mixed up together.

'Wake up Liz, where are you?' Kate burst into Liz's thoughts.

'Nothing, just thinking about my day yesterday. Nine patients, all intense, it was so long. I'm shattered. How are you?' she said looking in front of her, trying to keep up.

'Sheesh Liz, that's hectic. Don't do that to yourself, just say no to those patients. They can wait a day, surely?' questioned Kate.

'It's not that easy to say no when they are begging you, Kate. Anyway, it's done and today will be slower. What's up with you?' Liz asked.

Kate grinned and Liz, still struggling to maintain the pace, gave Kate a sidelong glance. 'I'm good. A little late because I had to kick that surfer we met last week, out of my bed to get here,' revealed Kate.

Kate's grin broadened into a triumphant smile that spread from ear to ear, as an open-mouthed Liz nearly tripped. 'Kate, he is like 22 or something. Surely you didn't?'

Kate liked to sleep with surfers. It was her thing and she didn't mind their age.

Liz personally couldn't think of anything worse: the shabby hair, usually unkempt and not quite clean, the car that smelt like a wet dog lived in it, and the constant hustle to find the best waves. Liz couldn't figure out why Kate hadn't grown out of surfers.

'He isn't 22, he's 24!' Kate said in a slightly defensive tone.

'That's still almost a decade between you and him Kate! Does he even know what to do in bed?' Liz asked in mock shock.

Kate had felt quite good about her latest conquest. The young surfer had cruised into the deli a few weeks back, and Kate had been enjoying the look of him since then. She had managed to strike up a surfing conversation, which she was now a professional at, and he had invited her to watch him surf in Kommetjie.

He was a great surfer, and she just couldn't get enough of watching him pull his wetsuit down to his waist, and expose his lithe, ripped body. Kate feared that she would probably never get enough of young surfers. Luckily she was sexy enough, and her curves definitely kept the boys interested. But she couldn't really compete with girls in their early twenties anymore. They were young for one thing, they hung out at different places and liked music that Kate couldn't bear to listen to.

She felt like her time to enjoy young surfers was going to come to an end, so she had to get all the surfer action she still could. Besides, she wasn't making anyone do anything they didn't want to. What really annoyed her was that Liz was a little right. Sleeping with young boys did mean you had to take the lead in the sack, which Kate didn't mind doing. That way she got what she wanted, but at the same time there was a small part of her that wouldn't mind something more mature.

'Whatever Liz. You're just jealous because you didn't get any last night,' jabbed Kate in an attempt to redirect the attention from herself onto Liz.

'Seriously Kate, I would rather have no sex than have sex with teenage boys, it's just wrong,' responded Liz, who wasn't getting any.

Kate and Liz caught up with Tanya and Claire as the two leaders slowed down to cross the busy main road. They waited for a break in the early morning traffic to head towards Echo steps, a steep staircase up the mountainside. At the top, they'd run along quieter roads that weaved between an eclectic assortment of a few distinctive modern homes, many derelict cottages, and mostly 1970s and 1980s double and triple storey homes that covered the mountain of Fish Hoek.

As the friends started the climb up the old concrete stairs, the ground squelched beneath their takkies. Brushing their wet leaves on heads and arms, the canopy of branches stretched across part of the stairway, cooling the steam coming off their bodies. At the top of the stairs the path took a sharp right angle, before turning a corner and heading up a road that climbed up at a 45 degree angle for a kilometre. The walk up the stairs had them all gasping for breath. Even Tanya and Claire had to gulp a few extra breaths at the top, before they began their slow run up the inclined road.

As they reached the end of their climb, Kate swore quietly under her breath 'Fuuuuck I hate those stairs.'

Tanya's wolf ears heard Kate and she couldn't help but roll her eyes.

'Seriously Kate, it's part of getting fit: it's not easy, you have to work at it. It's not like lying on your back and enjoying the pleasures of you know what!' she hissed.

Tanya's mouth puckered as though she had tasted a lemon.

Kate was dumbstruck. Tanya was an insane prude and openly offended by Kate's nonchalant approach to sex, having as much of it as she could, with whoever took her fancy. This statement was, however, a cut too deep for Kate and she glared at Tanya, pushed past her and started the run up the hill.

'Jeez Tan chill,' mouthed Liz as she ran after Kate. Tanya turned to look at Claire to ratify her mean words, her eyebrows raised in alarm. Claire's large eyes and slightly open mouth told her that she had definitely gone too far this time. Tanya felt defeated and slightly guilty. She looked straight ahead at the back of Kate and Liz and ran after them.

When it came to Kate, Tanya couldn't stop herself. She loved Kate's bubbly hippie-like appearance, so different from her own, and her total disregard for norms and standards in life. But when it came to the way Kate totally threw herself at all kinds of men, well mostly surfers, she just couldn't stomach it.

Kate was really striking and turned heads, so why would she do this to herself? Why couldn't she just find one decent guy? Why did she have to degrade herself like this? Tanya had overheard the banter between Kate and Liz, and it instantly made her blood boil. A 24-year-old this time! It was so demeaning; it was time someone told her. Everyone was thinking it anyway, so why did they just nod and smile and laugh at her filthy habit? According to Tanya, Kate needed to grow up!

Tanya powered up the hill with Claire at her side. Claire had become mute, keeping her eyes on the road and focusing on each footfall. They could hear

Kate's breathing up ahead; she had gotten so mad that she'd shot up the hill at a pace way beyond her body's capability. Tanya's superior fitness enabled her breathing to stay pretty consistent, even up the steep incline.

Claire seemed completely unfazed, which wasn't unusual. The girls were convinced it would take a snarling Rottweiler and Mr Jobes chasing behind Claire for at least 10kms to really get Claire to actually break a sweat.

The thought of Mr Jobes made Tanya chuckle, and as they reached the summit of the hill, she shouted to Kate and Liz up ahead,

'Remember Mr Jobes.'

It worked.

The friction that Tanya had created with her tongue was wiped away by the memory of Mr Jobes. As soon as Mr Jobes was conjured up from the recesses of Kate and Liz's minds, they spluttered and very nearly tripped themselves up.

Claire pretended to vomit, and they walked for a few metres to catch their breath.

Mr Jobes had been the girls' high school Biology teacher. Tall, yet stooped in the shoulders; a confirmed bachelor who shuffled around the school in old brown shoes from the 1950s, with polish so thick they must have weighed a ton. He'd been at least over sixty when he'd taught them, and his thick rimmed glasses made his goldfish eyes appear even larger. Add to that the propensity of old men's ears to keep growing, as the rest of their body shrank, not to mention the hair sprouting from his ears and nose.

He had been an incredible teacher, despite his comical and sadly rather stereotypical appearance. This would have been all good and well, if it hadn't been for his inability to hide his absolute adoration of Claire. On the first day of Grade 10 Biology, the four girls had walked into class and all, except for Claire, had noticed how Mr Jobes's mouth had fallen open when Claire had walked in. From the age of 15 years old, Claire had been nearly 6-foot tall and drop dead gorgeous.

The boys their age had been half her size for most of high school, except for the first team rugby players, whom Claire found repulsive and dim-witted.

Mr Jobes had been totally enchanted by her. He had managed to barely pull it together to take that first Biology class, and eventually got used to seeing her.

But he adored her, and it was very obvious to all around. The kids used to tear strips off Claire at all times, and it was just too easy. Poor sweet Claire hadn't deserved it, but her height and beauty made her an easy target for the plain, quick-witted girls in every high school classroom.

Claire, Tanya and Liz had quickly made friends at Fish Hoek High School. Smart and bordering on nerdy, they'd found themselves in the same classes and just clicked. When one of the popular girls had been teasing Claire about Mr Jobes, Kate had stepped in and told her to shut it or she would rat on her about smoking behind the gymnasium. The girl had threatened to rat on Kate for the same offence. Kate had just laughed; Kate's mother didn't care if she smoked or got detention, but popular girl's mother did. That had sealed the deal for the three smart, pretty nerds, and Kate was one of them. They called themselves the 'Awesome Foursome' and never looked back.

The four women picked up their running pace and lengthened their strides down the hill. The image of Mr Jobes and the antics of high school spilled out of their memories, leaving them gulping for breath as they ran and laughed. The morning air was cool after the rain and their breath hung in puffs above them. As Kate finished recalling another 'Mr Jobes moment' as she liked to call them, she shot a glance at Claire and said, 'Oh Claire, where would we be without you to keep us laughing?'

Claire never answered.

A flash of white removed her from where she had been next to Tanya. Metal screeched along the tar and then everything was quiet. In an instant, Claire had been removed from their run.

It was as if she'd been plucked off the earth by a giant hand. Gone.

Kate, Liz and Tanya found themselves standing dead still. Three women, in the middle of the road, dumbstruck and unable to comprehend what had just happened. Their blank faces turned to each other; their feet moved in uncertain steps and they looked around them.

Then they saw her. She was lying on the road.

Her silky hair lay free around her head. Her eyes were wide open and unmoving. Her body lay neatly, but her arms and legs were twisted in unnatural angles, like a discarded Barbie doll that had been contorted beyond her moulded ability.

Liz, usually slow to act, ran to Claire first.

'Oh my god, oh my god,' she kept saying.

Tanya and Kate jerked to life and followed.

'Claire? Claire? Can you hear us Clairie?' Kate whispered as she bent on the wet tar next to Claire, shards of glass poking into her knees and shins.

Claire's immaculate face was speckled with fragments of glass and spots of blood. Liz was desperately looking for a pulse on Claire's limp arm, then she put her head to Claire's chest, barely feeling the shattered glass cut into her ear and cheek.

Nothing.

She frantically tried to feel for a pulse on Claire's neck, pressing her fingers in just under her chin, first on one side, then the other. Tanya and Kate held their breaths as they watched Liz. In a last attempt, Liz gently pushed Claire's shoulder,

'Claire? Claire?'

She knew it was useless. Shaking her head mildly at first, and then with more vigour, Liz began to drone,

'Oh no, oh no, oh no.'

Tan gripped Liz's shoulder, 'What do you mean Liz?' she dug her fingers into Liz's shoulder 'I don't know what you mean?' said Tanya.

Liz began to sob incoherently. Tanya shook her, 'Liz, what the fuck is going on? What's wrong with Claire?'

Kate stared at Claire's once perfect face.

Claire was gone.

Claire's eyes always sparkled; it was the sparkle she had noticed the first day she'd met her in high school. No matter where they were, or how Claire was feeling, she always had sparkly eyes.

Now the sparkle was gone.

Tanya's frantic shaking of a moaning Liz brought Kate back. She looked up at Tanya.

'She's dead Tan. Our Claire, she's dead.'

Kate's words were gentle and true, yet they slapped Tanya in the face, cold and hard.

'What? Claire's dead? Fuck, who did this, who did this?' Tanya demanded, becoming hysterical.

Tanya turned and headed towards the large white chunk of metal in the middle of the road. Lying on its side, the wheels of the taxi still turned, like an insect on its back struggling to right itself.

Tanya knew where she was going. She went straight to the front of the taxi and peered inside. There he was, in a human heap. He was a mess, but he was alive. He was groaning and trying to move, trying to wipe his bloody face. He was alive. How could he be alive? Why the fuck was HE alive?

As though she was channeling the world's anger, Tanya began to scream. The demonic scream started in her ankles and poured out of her mouth, over the human mess on the floor.

'You killed her! You fucking crazy bastard, you killed her and now she is dead, you stupid fucker!'

More screaming. More words. Her spittle frothed on her chin.

No one could ever tell her how long she had screamed for. All Tanya remembered was that eventually a strong grip firmly lifted her from the ground, and carefully moved her away from the taxi.

Tanya found herself in the ambulance. Kate and Liz were already there. The sound didn't come out of her mouth anymore.

Kate and Liz were staring at the ambulance walls. Liz was gulping in air and sobbing. Kate just stared.

Tanya's whole body started to shake. She turned her head away from Liz and Kate and looked outside the van; a woman, in lingerie, stood speaking to policemen and paramedics. She was telling them something, her red hair glistening in the early morning sun. Tanya couldn't hear what they were saying. All the sound was gone; it was as though her ears had shut her out. She turned back to Liz and Kate, grabbing Liz's hand and dragging her to Kate, using all the force of her small body to draw them both into a desperate embrace. The three women imploded into one another. Their sobs racked their rib cages and as they wept, their tears and snot mixed into each other's hair and faces. No one outside disturbed them. The doors of the ambulance were quietly shut, and the women were left to their pain.

James

The sun shone a steady beam across James's face, forcing his eyes open. He stretched his body across the bed. Claire had said she was going for a run and as usual, as quiet as a mouse, she had gone without waking him.

He slowly began to realise that the sun seemed brighter than usual and wondered what the time was. He rolled over, stretching towards his bedside table, thumping his hand clumsily over the pile of books, and eventually finding his mobile phone. It was really late, 7:30am.

Where the hell was Claire? She usually woke him up when she got back. When the girls ran at the weekend, they'd go for a coffee and dawdle back, but it was definitely not the weekend. James knew this because he had stayed up late the night before, working on a presentation for today's meeting. The feeling of dread made his stomach turn. The image of his boss, with that pained expression she used to show her displeasure, came into his mind. His skin crawled.

He swung his legs out of bed, feet planted on the floor. With elbows on his knees, he hunched over his mobile phone. There were no messages on his phone, and as he got to his feet he heard a knock on the door. That was what had probably happened; Claire had forgotten her keys and now couldn't get back in. He hoped she hadn't been knocking for ages while he'd been in dreamland.

'Hang on Claire, I'm coming,' called James across the apartment. Making his way to the door, he unlatched it, before opening the door and standing back. He caught his breath; it wasn't Claire, it was Kate. Her hair was a mess around her face; she was pale with sad, red eyes and still in her running clothes.

'Kate, are you ok? Where is Claire?' asked James, taken aback and unsure what to do next.

'Can I come in?' asked Kate, her voice raspy.

James felt unsteady and stepped back awkwardly, letting Kate in. She followed him and closed the door behind her, leaning against it for support. The silence hung in the air as Kate was forced to tell James the worst news of his life.

'James,' she paused, breathing audibly for courage, 'James, Claire was killed earlier. A taxi drove into her and she didn't survive. She died on the road.' Kate managed to expel the words and then brought her hands to her face and sobbed into her palms. She couldn't look at James; she just couldn't look at what she had done to him.

James stumbled back and dropped onto the couch. He tried to push himself up again, but he couldn't get up. His legs couldn't hold him.

'Claire's dead?' he whispered and looked at Kate. She sobbed uncontrollably.

'Kate!' he shouted at her, trying to be heard above her sobs. 'Are you saying Claire is dead?'

He needed her to answer; why was she sobbing like that?

Kate pulled her hands away from her face and dug her fingers into her chest. She stared at James,

'Yes, she is dead,' she answered, as she walked to James and sat next to him. 'I'm sorry James,' she said, her tear-soaked face close to his, 'it was an accident.'

She hugged him and held him tightly. James's mind ceased to ask questions, and he began to cry as his body took over.

James drove Kate to Liz's house where the other girls were waiting. His body moved the steering wheel and changed gears, but he felt completely disconnected. Liz's place was in Sun Valley, a southern peninsula suburb, originally built by the apartheid government as a white residential township in the 1960s for the 'poor whites'. Today, Sun Valley was a cluttered array of houses made up of free-standing and semi-detached homes, surrounding a primary school, and a large bland park with a few trees for decoration.

Liz still lived with her parents in one of the free-standing homes. They had built a flat for Liz above their garage and converted the garage into physiotherapy rooms below, for which Liz paid a fair rental every month. Far less than she would have to pay if she were renting from a stranger, but still enough to know she wasn't getting a free ride. The building was functional and there was nothing aesthetically pleasing about it: white walls, red tiled roof, burglar bars on the windows.

Functional. Like Liz's life.

She was completely unconcerned that she actually lived with her parents at 34 years of age, ate in their kitchen for every meal, and was well on her way to becoming a spinster.

Like Claire, Liz was an only child and had a close relationship with her parents, especially her mother. James had overheard the girls discuss how worried they were that Liz would never find a man able to deal with the interfering Mrs Gail Patterson. All previous boyfriends had managed up to a point, but something always seemed to become insufferable as the relationship progressed. A too big nose, a too small willy, a poor vocabulary, bad taste in shoes. You could pick any random problem, and Liz would use it to get rid of some suitor who stole her attention from her mother.

As James pulled into the drive, Raymond, Liz's father came out of the main house and pressed a remote in his hand to open the gate. James had met Raymond a few times, when he'd wave from the car while he waited for Liz to come down, or when he dropped her off. Raymond seemed to hold the fort of his home from his front garden. James couldn't understand what Raymond did in the front garden.

For all the attention it received, the garden was underwhelming, with its small patch of grass and brown brick path that led from the driveway to the front door. Grey concrete pots were filled with drab little orange and yellow flowers, alongside a one-metre-deep bed of agapanthus and other hardy indigenous plants. James wasn't sure the garden actually required all the attention it received from Raymond Patterson. He guessed that Raymond liked to keep his finger on the pulse of his sleepy suburb from the front garden, and spent most of his time there peering over the vibracrete wall.

James drove in once the gate had opened and Raymond came over. He avoided eye contact with Raymond as he climbed out.

'Come in James,' said Raymond, clearing his throat and showing James the door. 'Kate, come in darling,' said Raymond as he took in the state of Kate. 'Can I make you some tea or coffee? Rooibos?' Raymond asked the two numb adults who walked into his home.

'Thanks Raymond, coffee would be good,' stated James. He walked past Raymond into the dark house.

James blinked to adjust his eyes. Kate walked in behind him and went straight to the couch. She crawled under a crochet blanket, hugging her knees, her hair loose and hanging around her face. James had always thought Kate was pretty: her big brown eyes and thick hair, and full red lips. She was carelessly easy on the eye, and he could never understand why she couldn't hold down a relationship. Claire always used to say that Kate was still growing up and finding her feet with men.

James had overheard a few conversations that indicated Kate knew plenty about men, and little about relationships.

Kate's big eyes lifted from under her wet eyelashes and looked at James. James's legs stopped moving. He was no longer in control of his body; all he could do was stare at Kate. It was as though all the pure pain she was experiencing met his own. He managed to heave his frame forward once more and slumped on the couch, hugging Kate and her bended knees into him, their sobs making the couch rock. Raymond stood at a distance and watched. He turned and went into the kitchen to make coffee, his old heart heavy.

When they could cry no more, James moved back from Kate. They each wiped at their faces, trying to smear away their tears, snivelling as Raymond returned with coffee.

'Milk and sugar? Kate?' he asked.

'Just black, thanks Uncle Ray,' mumbled Kate. She struggled to push her hair behind her ears as Raymond handed her the cup.

Shakily she reached for it and took a tentative sip. The thin porcelain was decorated with botanical flowers. Gross, she thought to herself, as she tasted instant coffee. In an attempt to hide her distaste she faked a small smile at Raymond. He smiled back.

'Milk and two sugars for me please Raymond,' said James.

Being in the advertising industry, James consumed many cups of coffee a day, and often skipped meals due to deadlines. He believed that the sugar in his coffee kept him going until he could get to a meal. Claire would always try and just put one spoon in his cup, but he always knew, and when she wasn't looking, he would slip another one in his coffee. It was their little game. Or at least, it had been their little game.

'Thanks Raymond,' said James holding the dainty floral cup, so out of place in his large hands. He sank back into the old couch next to Kate. They both stared into the space in front of them, occasionally sipping their coffee.

'Well, I'll just go and check how Liz is doing. Perhaps she'll be able to come through,' said Raymond as he stood up.

'Gail is with her, but I am sure she'll want to see you James,' said Raymond, as he left the two bodies on the couch.

Kate and James were quiet. They just sat. Like two spinning whirly gigs standing next to each other in the breeze, their thoughts spun round and round in their heads.

Kate kept asking herself how this had happened. They had been on a morning run, like so many times before. What had they done differently to deserve this?

James kept trying to remember every detail of the previous evening with Claire. 'What had she said before they went to bed? What was she wearing yesterday? How had she smelt?

Their internal monologues were interrupted by the doorbell, and Raymond came down the passage.

'I'll get that.'

Grabbing the remote, he opened the door and walked outside. They could hear muffled voices, car doors and then a car leaving. Raymond came back in with Tanya.

'Tristan has brought Tanya to be with us,' explained Raymond. James stood up to greet her and she launched herself into him and sunk her face into his lower rib cage, James's 6-foot frame overshadowing her.

Awkwardly, James put his arms around the small crying woman. Although he and Tanya had a good rapport, she was always cool and unaffectionate, and he usually only got a well-placed peck on the cheek and a sweet 'Hullo Jamesie' whenever they met.

James hugged Tanya closer, letting her weep into his shirt. Eventually she managed to contain herself and pull back. She let James go and went over to Kate on the couch. She sat close to Kate and leant her head on Kate's shoulder.

'Kate, I just can't believe what's happened. I have so many questions. I don't even know how I got home. I just remember being in the back of the van, and then it's all hazy.'

Kate opened her arm and hugged Tanya's shoulders. She placed her chin gently on Tanya's head.

'I know Tan, it's the same for me too. It's all so weird, like it's not real, but it is so very real because it hurts so much.'

Kate looked up at James, who was standing on the other side of the room, looking at them - a wet patch on his shirt where Tanya had cried her eyes dry.

He slumped into an armchair.

'Claire's parents… has anyone told her parents?' asked James, surprised by his ability to think beyond his own grief.

'The police called them. I gave them their number after we gave our statements,' said Kate, her words strained.

'I followed up with them too,' explained Raymond. 'I had their details. Got hold of Mrs Southbridge. Probably the worst call I have ever made. She said she would book a flight as soon as possible,' Raymond informed them. 'They were extremely shocked, obviously. I should hear from them later and will help sort their details for the trip here. They just got back from Spain, and were just walking into their home,' he said shaking his head.

James felt the usual dread rise when he was to meet the Southbridges. They were nice enough to him, but he could tell they felt he was a halfway stop for Claire to something better - someone smarter, richer, fancier, with better credentials and a better job (in banking preferably).

James's government school education at Wynberg Boys High School didn't quite cut it, and his Account Manager role in an advertising agency was very unimpressive. Mr Southbridge had, on more than one occasion, asked James why, as a Business Science graduate from UCT, he'd gone into the 'ad game'. James had been taken off guard, because it was then that he realised his job wasn't good enough for the Southbridges. He had mumbled something about loving seeing clever adverts in magazines and how he was inspired by the Mad Men series.

He could recall with clarity the blank, disdainful look on Mr Southbridge's face. A look that said everything about what he thought of James's career choice. In an attempt to lighten the cold silence, he remembered how Claire had appeared at her father's side with a full glass of whiskey that James couldn't afford, but had bought for Mr Southbridge nonetheless, smiled her magic smile and said,

'Oh daddy, stop harassing poor James. He loves what he does and he is going to own his own agency one day, it just takes time that's all. It's different from your business. Now let me tell you about the Hepworth's and the scandal there…' and in her way, Claire had diffused the situation, made everything understandable, made James seem like a hero, and distracted her father with her knowledge of some other family's scandal.

How on earth was James going to face the Southbridges without Claire by his side? How was he going to face tomorrow?

His mobile rang, interrupting his grief. He rummaged through his pocket until he found his phone. It was work; he hit the red button and hung up. Kate hadn't even noticed.

His phone started to ring again. Work, again. He walked outside into Raymond's garden to answer the call.

'James, it's Abby, where are you? The boss is starting to froth. We have to go over the presentation before the client arrives.'

James breathed in deeply, drawing on his reserve,

'I'm at a friend. Claire's dead. She was killed this morning in an accident. I can't come in. I mailed the presentation through last night. Make it happen Abby, please, I just can't do this, I'm a mess. I'm sorry…bye.'

He hung up and turned his phone on silent.

He walked back inside wondering where Liz was, and asked Raymond.

'They gave Liz some pills, she is asleep,' Raymond responded.

'Ok,' he said, and turned away to pull his phone out again, by force of habit. Scrolling down the screen he saw over ten messages; Abby from work was the first one: 'Sorry James. I'll let the boss know. Call when you can. A'

The rest were other work-related messages, some work emails, and a few missed calls.

He switched the screen off and looked straight ahead of him, it didn't mean anything anymore.

James couldn't recall how he'd got himself to the Salt River Mortuary. All he knew was that he eventually found himself in a cool odourless place that made him shiver deep in his bones.

The woman at reception had directed him to a passage and told him to wait outside door 5E.

He stood in the hallway for some time, before a few people, nurses and doctors bustled past ignoring him. Eventually a small nurse in a lab coat opened the door. She peered at him, and in a gentle voice asked,

'Who are you here to see?'

For a split second James forgot why he was there. It had been 48 hours since Claire had died. He still wasn't sure this was all true.

'To see?' he stuttered.

'Yes Mister, the deceased's name Mister, what's the name?' she asked.

James blinked hard. He stared at the nurse's earnest face.

'Claire, Claire Southbridge. They told me to come today, because the autopsy would be finished and she needed to be officially identified' he stated.

'Are you family?' asked the nurse checking her clipboard.

'I'm her… her boyfriend, my name is James Simmonds. When I phoned, they said that friends are also allowed to identify people… I mean bodies. 'James mumbled, twisting his hands and wringing his fingers, feeling incapable of finding the right words.

'That's correct,' said the nurse as she averted her gaze to the clipboard once again. She looked down the passage, and sucked in her breath.

'Ok, you can come with me,' she told James, as she opened a swing door into a small room, with a glass window onto another small room.

'Please wait here,' she told James as she disappeared through a different door. He waited for a few minutes, pacing across the room, not understanding what would happen.

The nurse reappeared through the door as a trolley with a body was wheeled into the room on the other side of the glass window. She looked down at her clipboard.

'Mr Simmonds, we will lift the sheet off the body and then you will be required to tell me if this is Claire Southbridge. Do you understand?' she asked gently, peering at James. 'I realise this is difficult, but I am required to follow this procedure.' She continued.

James looked at her, focusing his attention away from the window.

'I understand.'

The nurse nodded to the man next to the trolley, as he lifted the sheet.

'You can look now Mr Simmonds,' she suggested.

James slowly turned and looked through the glass.

Her blonde hair lay lifeless around her, speckled with black flecks. He stared at her for what felt like an eternity, wishing her eyes would open. He felt unable to believe that the one person in the world, who exuded so much life, could have none of it left in her body. His hands came to the glass and he leaned his face into the cold divider.

'Claire,' he whispered through the glass. Slowly he turned his eyes away from her and looked at the nurse. 'It's Claire Southbridge,' he confirmed, his chest sucking in deep gulps of air.

He turned back to look through the glass, 'My Claire, where have you gone? How could this happen?' he pined. Eventually he could take it no more, and was desperate to touch her, just one more time. He turned to the nurse, 'please, please can I go and hold her,' he begged.

'I'm sorry Mr Simmonds; you will have to wait until she is at the funeral home. We cannot allow you to touch her here,' said the nurse. She spoke kindly, her face sympathetic.

He digested the information and returned to the glass to stare at Claire. Tiny little cuts covered her beautiful face. He felt frozen, unable to take his eyes off her.

She was still exquisite; not even this could ruin her. 'You are my goddess Claire. Aphrodite in human form,' he used tell her, with a cheesy grin across his face. 'Oh please Jamesie, what rubbish!' she would retort, rolling her eyes and flicking her hair like a high school girl.

How had this happened to Claire, of all people? How had this happened to him? He had wanted to marry Claire; he just wanted to wait until he was made Account Director. His salary would then take a significant jump, and he wanted to ask her when he had more to offer.

How foolish he had been. Claire could have been his wife. They could have moved somewhere better and maybe lived in a place without South African taxis. But they hadn't, because he had been waiting for more.

Now she was gone.

James's earlier resolve left him. Seeing Claire like that, with her eyes closed, and her beautiful face cut. He slumped against the wall and slid down to the cold floor. Time stood still until he felt a hand on his shoulder.

'Mr Simmonds??' asked the nurse gently, patiently.

James looked up at her, clearing his throat, 'can I go now?' he asked, his duty complete.

She nodded her head, and looked at him sadly. As she turned away and walked back towards the door James called after her,

'Nurse?'

'Yes?' she said turning to face him.

'You'll look after her?' he asked, his face pale and blotchy, with eyes red and desperate for confirmation.

'Yes we'll take good care of her, I promise. She goes to the funeral home tomorrow. You can visit her there.' She smiled softly at him, before leaving the room.

James stared after her, until he eventually shook his head and pushed himself up. He had to leave her here, and his heart ached.

Pain and Guilt

Stage 2

Shock wears off and is replaced with suffering of excruciating pain. It's important to experience the pain fully and not numb it artificially

Chapter 2

Tshepo

Despite Tshepo's prayers to die, he didn't; he just got better. The wound at the end of his stump stopped seeping, and over five weeks he watched in amazement as his body healed itself.

Dr Yusuf visited regularly enough to check on him. His bandages were changed, and he was moved to various wards within False Bay Hospital, before ending up in a large general ward. People came and went, nurses changed shifts, the arms of the clock on the wall moved around, and he just lay there.

Once in the large general ward, the police officer returned, and came to handcuff him to the steel bed. On seeing Tshepo's one-legged situation, he'd looked at Tshepo pityingly and asked the nurse, 'sisi, can this one walk like this?'

The nurse flared her nostrils in distaste at the policeman; clearly he lacked any medical understanding.

'Haaibo, what do you think? This one, he hasn't gone anywhere for five weeks. He sits there and stares at what was his leg. Chain him to the bed if you think it will make a difference, but it will just make our lives harder. He doesn't even go to the toilet by himself yet,' she said, clicking her tongue disapprovingly.

It was true. He hadn't left his bed, unless he was being wheeled to yet another ward. If he needed to use the toilet, he had to wait for a nurse to haul him out of bed, and help him to the bathroom. Then he had to sit on the toilet like a girl to pee. He often wondered if he'd ever stand again.

The physiotherapist, Jenny, came every second day to do exercises with his leg. She was gentle and sweet, but had blonde hair that reminded him of the one he had killed. He felt nauseous every time Jenny came, and he looked away from her while she lifted his leg and moved it from side to side.

'Hullo Tshepo, how are you today?' she'd ask cheerfully every time. In order to not be rude, he'd look down at his chest and respond, 'fine Jenny' and leave it at that, until it was time to say 'bye Jenny', and then he could look up again. The nausea would lift a little, but it didn't last very long. He would either find himself staring at the stump, or questioning why the one he had killed was running on the road that rainy morning. Had his ancestors decided to teach him a lesson? What could this lesson be? He had a good job; he earned his keep and provided money for his mother in the Eastern Cape. The money he sent helped his mother feed his sister's children who lived with her. What had he done that deserved this stump of a leg, and the death of a woman on his conscience?

The guilt of her death washed over him regularly. He wanted to know what her name was, so he could stop calling her the dead woman. Did she have children? Were they now orphans? Was there a husband? Would the husband come and kill him in the night to take revenge? He had to know more about her to stop the questions going round and round in his head. Who was the woman he'd killed?

The doctor who asked lots of questions, and wrote down everything he said, came to visit him every week. She was an Indian woman called Dr Naidoo, skinny and frail-looking with slightly stooped shoulders, and big brown eyes that searched his face when she asked him questions. She didn't wear her hair covered. Instead her long dark hair was plaited down her back, sometimes swinging over her shoulder to rest on her flat, skinny chest.

Once her questions and writing were done, she would go and speak to the nurse, write in his file and leave. He always felt empty after she left, with nothing inside but words and sadness. She was the only one who ever asked how he felt about killing the runner. No one else asked him; they just looked at him pityingly. He had made a terrible mistake by going too fast, and maybe he would have to pay for it by going to jail; but what did they know, these stupid sick people and nurses that gossiped all the time'

He only felt better when he swallowed the pills Dr Naidoo gave him. They made him sleepy. He loved to succumb to the drowsiness and sleep, to avoid the looks from everyone around him. He was convinced they were all judging him. Every new patient who came in was told by another about Tshepo and what he had done, craning their necks and taking turns to stare at him. The looks on their faces going from curiosity to shock, followed by head shaking and tongue clicking, indicating they knew that he was in big trouble. The taxi driver who killed the runner in Fish Hoek; that was him. Forever.

He had some visitors. The Boss had sent his Nigerian neck-breaker. He remembered how, after being mostly unconscious in the hospital for three or four days back in Fish Hoek, he'd woken to find Emmanuel standing above him. The 6.5-foot man was terrifying, especially as Tshepo was lying down. As his eyes widened to fill his face, Tshepo believed that the Boss had sent Emmanuel to finish him off properly, because he'd destroyed the taxi.

Tshepo's words left him as he stared up at Emmanuel's dark grim face staring back at him, a demon sent to determine his fate. As he started to wriggle, he began to search frantically for a nurse, but they'd all disappeared. With only two patients in the ward with him, both asleep, he'd convinced himself this was it: he was about to be killed. Emmanuel laid his enormous hand onto Tshepo's chest to stop him wriggling, not quite crushing his lungs, but definitely holding him firmly.

'Relax Tshepo, the Boss sent me to check it is you, and that you are indeed now a cripple, as they say,' he said in his deep Nigerian accent, his face close to Tshepo's, who was now nodding frantically.

'You really fucked up my friend. Boss was pissed when he heard you fucked his taxi. It was old, but it could still work. Now Boss has to buy a new one. You know he doesn't like that,' he explained.

Tshepo's eyes widened, his breathing shallow under the pressure of the big Nigerian hand.

'But, seeing as you killed that runner, you is going to the slammer. So Boss says you will pay when you come out. He sent me to let you know, he is waiting for when you is coming out. You is owing the Boss, see?' he asked Tshepo, as he lifted his hand from his chest. Tshepo nodded frantically. Emmanuel smiled. 'Good my brother,' he said and walked away, straightening his collar shirt.

Tshepo sucked in air and pushed himself up, looking around to see if anyone else had seen the interaction. No one was there. Relieved, he collapsed back into his pillow. Emmanuel had just confirmed Tshepo's fears: the Boss owned him, and he would call on Tshepo to do whatever dirty work was required, for possibly the rest of his life or until he died of an unnatural cause. In prison, out of prison, it actually wouldn't matter. He would never be a free man again.

Boetie, Tshepo's friend and fellow taxi driver, had also come to visit him. The men had made friends at the shebeen they went to, after work or on weekends. Tshepo had been sitting around the open fire at the back of the shebeen, enjoying his zamaleker[4] quartz, listening to the ramblings of the other men around the fire, when Boetie had squeezed in next to him.

'Hey, I've seen you at the Boss's place. You the new driver hey. You wanna know what happened to the last guy?' said Boetie, his eyes lighting up at the thought of sharing some gossip.

'Yaa, you're Boetie ne? So tell me what happened,' he said nonchalantly.

This allowed Boetie the opportunity to sit tall, and look around to make sure the others around the fire weren't involved in any of Boss's businesses. Then he crouched close to Tshepo and whispered, his hot breath against Tshepo's face.

'This guy, his name was Jacob, was a real smart mfana[5]. Thought he could trick Boss, tried to steal petrol money and taxi money, but Boss hears things, because turns out Jacob liked to fuck with the same nyukazi[6] that Emmanuel fucks.'

At this point, Boetie sat back, raised his eyebrows in mock shock and fear, took a breath and continued.

'Turns out the nyukazi is a good listener, especially for Emmanuel, and for a few extra Randelas she tells him that Jacob pays for her using his stolen Boss money. Couldn't keep it to himself. Stupid hey. So Jacob ends with a bullet in his face. BOOM! Just like that. Boss and Emmanuel tell the Abo Gata[7] it's a taxi war. Then they tell us taxi drivers it's a warning. You steal, you pay with your life,' and with that he thumped his hands on his legs, and leaned back against the fence, away from Tshepo's frozen face.

At first Tshepo wanted to be angry with Boetie for telling him the story and trying to scare him like that; then he realised he was grateful. The thought of stealing a few five Rands here and there had crossed his mind, but he hadn't figured out a plan yet. He wanted to understand the whole system first. Now that he knew what would happen if he got caught, he wasn't going to touch a cent. As the new guy, he had to be squeaky clean. He had decided there and then to harness Boetie's enthusiastic friendship.

---

4   Black label beer

5   guy

6   prostitute

7   police

Boetie had told him that he had been with the Boss for five years, nearly the longest anyone had survived as a taxi driver. Boetie knew how things worked and how to keep a low profile. Tshepo decided to follow his lead, keep the boss happy and stay out of Emmanuel's way. It had worked well, and he was hoping that he would soon be getting a better taxi, but he had stuffed it all up with the accident. Now all he had was a life sentence as the Boss's puppet.

When Boetie had visited, he had tried to keep it light and had cracked a few jokes. But eventually he'd sat down on Tshepo's bed, hung his head and said, 'yoh Tshepo, this is bad umhlobo wami[8]. You killed that runner woman, and the Boss owns you now. Eish my brother, maybe prison will be a good place for you to be, except if they send you to the prison with the gangsters. Then you are more fucked than now. Yoh, this is bad my friend. Wrong place, wrong time my friend.' It was the truth. Boetie said it like it was. Tshepo's life was a mess.

Tshepo's strangest visitor arrived a week before he was to be discharged; Jenny came in with another white lady. She seemed nervous and kept looking to see if the nurses were looking at her. This was unlikely, given that they spent most of their time shouting loudly to each other across the ward, while they performed their duties.

'Liz, this is Tshepo, Tshepo Dlamini. He… he is the taxi driver you wanted to meet,' Jenny said, as her eyes continued to dart around the room nervously.

Tshepo frowned at Liz and pushed his body up higher in his bed. He looked at her carefully. She was an average sort of height, brown hair that hung straight on either side of her face, with a fringe that framed her face. She had watery hazel eyes and a small nose and a small slit of a light pink mouth. Rather unimpressive, and pale. She stared back at him, as though imprinting his face to her memory. She scanned him from head to stump, sucking in her breath at the sight of the stump, and then returning back to his face.

'You are the taxi driver?' she asked.

'Yes, who are you?' asked Tshepo in an attempt to derail her. He could see she was working herself up to something, her breathing was short and fast.

'I am Liz and you, you killed my friend Claire,' her face started to become very pink.

Claire. So that was her name.

---

8   my friend

The girl whose life he had stolen. She was called Claire. Now he knew. Stupidly he spoke her name,

'Claire?' he repeated, testing it out on his tongue.

'Yes, Claire. I was there you know, right next to her. But you missed me somehow. You just took her, and you left me and my two friends,' said Liz, whose fast angry breathing was being overtaken by silent tears running down her cheeks. She wiped at her cheeks furiously, as the pain in her chest squeezed on her heart.

She'd waited this long to come and see him, because she knew she had to be stronger to face him. Her physio network revealed the news that the taxi driver had lost his leg and ended up at False Bay Hospital weeks ago. She'd known that facing him would be hard, but she couldn't believe how hard. She'd hated him for so long, and now here he was: this small man, with only one good leg, about to go to prison.

She felt desperately sad…for him, for herself.

How could she, how could she feel pity for this murderer? What was wrong with her? He had killed Claire, and here she was feeling sorry for him. She looked away and faced Jenny.

'I think it's time to go Liz, maybe this wasn't a good idea. Come, let's just go and you can come back another day. Ok?' said Jenny reassuringly, as though talking to a child. Liz nodded and was led away, leaving Tshepo staring into space, ruminating on a name.

The woman runner's name; finally, he knew it. He had killed a Claire.

Maureen

'Maureen, is that right, is that how you say your name?' asked the psychologist, a non-descript white blonde with cool blue eyes. Maureen nodded. 'The form you have filled in says that you are here to deal with trauma, post an accident you witnessed, is that correct?' she asked.

Maureen hesitated. 'Yes. I think so Dr Venter,' mumbled Maureen unconvincingly.

'Just call me Alice,' she said, smiling warmly.

'Why don't you tell me what happened and then we can take it from there, shall we?' asked Dr Alice Venter, a clinical psychologist.

Maureen settled back into her chair and described how she had seen a taxi come speeding past her home and knock over one of four women who had been running. She explained how she had called emergency services, and had met the paramedics on arrival and told them all about the accident. She said she hadn't really seen the dead woman's body, so that wasn't haunting her.

'You seem to be relatively calm, despite the tragedy of the situation Maureen. Tell me why you describe yourself as traumatised?' Alice asked, tilting her head to one side. Maureen squirmed in her seat, her body tensing before she continued.

'My husband, Chris, said I had to come and see you. He says I'm acting all funny since the accident. But I don't know how he even knows that. He's hardly been home since he came back from the rig. Anyway, he wasn't even there when the accident happened; he only came home after the paramedics had left. He had been out the whole night, doing whatever it is that he does with his stupid friends,' said Maureen, working herself up, so that she had to pause and catch her breath before continuing.

'You know when he walked in after the accident?' she asked Alice rhetorically, 'the next morning! He was stumbling around in the kitchen, so I went downstairs and asked him where he had been, and he just looked at me and said "none of your business wifie",' and then pushed past me and went to bed. Just like that. Only when the cops came later that day to confirm my statement, did he wake up and hear what had happened. He first thought he was in trouble. Guess that says something about whatever he was up to.' She looked down at her pencil skirt, embarrassed that she had just told a complete stranger about her husband's mysterious behaviour.

'Yet, your husband said that you needed to come for counselling. Why has he asked you to come to see me?' probed Alice, her eyes curious and voice calm and reassuring, to dampen Maureen's anger.

Maureen looked up at Alice, her cheeks warm and flushed.

'He says I'm like all spacey and far away. That I'm not speaking to him and that, excuse my language, the sex sucks. Ya, that's what he says, when he is around. But out of the three weeks he's been back, he's only been home five nights.'

The anger overwhelmed her again and she hissed: 'the other nights he just goes out with those friends. Comes home at crazy times in the morning, or not at all.' She breathed in deeply and launched into a rapid explanation, 'you see he works offshore, so when he is here, I really want to see him. But he just goes out without me all the time. And now, he goes back to the rig next week.' She paused and looked at Alice, her breathing calming.

'It's not this bad usually, but over this past year he has been much worse. It's like they mean more to him than I do. I miss him so much, and then he arrives and just chooses them over me,' said Maureen as she hung her head, ashamed and defeated.

Alice had seen this all before: women who married wealthy men - men who offered completely new lives, homes, cars and friends. Maureen had bought into a lifestyle and was now waking up to the real cost.

'I'm so sorry,' snuffled Maureen, as Alice handed her a tissue.

Alice waited before gently prying further into Maureen's concerns regarding Chris and his escapades. As she asked questions, Maureen's bottled up emotions were revealed, many of which she probably didn't realise she'd been harbouring. The poor woman dipped in and out of bouts of crying for the majority of the session.

'It's ok Maureen, this is why you are here. Take the tissues,' she said, passing her the box. 'Let's make another appointment for next week as we are nearly out of time,' she said, glancing at the clock on the wall.

'It's ok, thanks doctor, I mean Alice. We can carry on next week. I would like to see you again. I don't really have many friends, and it would probably be good to speak to someone. Like you I mean. Sometimes I speak to myself, and I'm starting to think that it may mean I'm a little bit mal,' she said, looking at Alice. Alice's expression confused Maureen, so she continued, 'mal, you know, the Afrikaans word for crazy?'

'I don't think you're crazy Maureen. I do think that you could benefit from expressing more of your emotions, and understanding how and why you are feeling the way you do. I'm really glad you have come to see me. I think I can help you. See you next week my dear,' she said, ushering Maureen out of her pale rhino board office and into the reception area.

Maureen found herself in front of the receptionist, her hands clutching a handful of used tissues, a little bleary eyed. The receptionist seemed unfazed by Maureen's state, and swiped her credit card before booking her appointment for the following week, without a second look. 'Thank you Mrs Klaasen, see you next week,' said the receptionist as Maureen clip, clopped out.

Maureen had decided to come to a psychologist on the other side of the mountain, a 30-minute drive from home. She couldn't face bumping into a familiar face at an appointment. She didn't really have any friends, but she was a part of a book club, and knew many of the housewives at the gym. In a small town like Fish Hoek there would be no way of going to a psychologist without someone knowing. In the suburb of Bergvliet, she was completely unknown. This made her feel secure in the knowledge that no one would judge her. Her mother had always scorned any of her friends who went to see a psychologist.

'It's so pathetic, this new-age rubbish of having to get someone else to solve your problems for you. I mean really, in our day we just bloody got on with it. There wasn't any time to feel all sorry for yourself. It's all just modern day hocus pocus I tell you Maureenie. Thank goodness you are solid like me,' her mother had said.

What would her mother say now if she knew she was visiting a psychologist? She knew her mother meant well and she adored her, but how could she explain Chris's behaviour, or the need to speak to someone who really listened, without all the preconceived judgement. She needed someone who would be able to help her understand what was going wrong with her life. Some days she felt like she was watching her life unravel, ever so slowly.

When Chris had told her to see a shrink she became angry, and had shouted back at him to go and see one himself. He'd actually stopped in his tracks and slowly turned around to look at her. His ice-cold glare had frozen her heart, and for a split second she thought she had gone too far and that he was going to hurt her.

Then almost instantly, his face had changed and he started to laugh at her - a loud, sarcastic laugh. When he stopped laughing he looked at her squarely and said: 'Me? You want me go to a shrink. I fokken live on a rig, baby girl. I know my head inside out. There is nowhere else to go. You're the one who's got too much time and fok all to do. That accident you say you saw has messed with your pretty head. Deal with it and go see a shrink. I only have one more week, and I want to leave knowing you're sorted. Besides, I'll need one decent screw before I leave. Can't handle the rubbish you're dealing up in the bedroom lately.'

He looked down at her, his lips taut. Then he turned and disappeared into the garage, leaving her staring at his back.

She couldn't believe that he'd realised she wasn't invested in their love making. She'd thought that she could fake it, like they did in the movies, but she obviously wasn't a very good actress. She just didn't feel anything. She couldn't care if they did or didn't have sex. It was as though there was something missing between them. The spark that he usually ignited in her, just by looking at her, was gone. She'd tried her best to pretend she was keen, but she obviously hadn't perfected the art. She still hadn't pulled out the lingerie she'd worn when she'd seen the accident. It was almost as if those clothes represented something bad; that by wearing them again she might see someone else get killed. Instead, she'd shoved the lingerie into the bottom of her other ski boot.

She shook her head, started the car and drove home from Alice in a daze.

As she pulled into the garage at home, she realised she couldn't even remember which route she had taken. She closed the garage door behind her, as she parked her small and compact gold Mini in the oversized garage. When they renovated the house, Chris had insisted on a large garage for his car and motorbike. Chris's car and motorbike were home. This meant very little as he had taken to using Uber to get to wherever he was going. She secretly hoped he wasn't home. Her emotions felt raw after her hour with Alice, and she wanted to go and lie down and sleep the feeling of confusion away.

Maureen climbed out of her car, eyes adjusting to the dark garage. As she closed the car door and turned around, he was there. She jumped back with fright, bashing her back into her car. 'Chris, oh my god, you frightened me to death, what's the matter? I'm on my way inside,' she said, her voice shaking.

'I couldn't wait another second,' he said, pushing her up against the car. 'What did the shrink say? She say you gonna get better hey?' he said, peering into her eyes.

Confused and taken aback, Maureen answered. 'Yes, yes she says I am going to be fine. She says I'm not so bad, just a few more sessions. Are you ok? What's wrong?'

'I realised why my luck's been down. It's you, you're my lucky charm, and I haven't had enough of you. Been spending too much time with the guys, strategising how we gonna win big. Not enough time making my own luck,' he said, pushing her harder against the car. She could feel his hard member digging into her pelvis. He took her handbag off her arm and dropped it the floor, spilling its contents across the garage floor. He put his fingers in her hair, firmly drawing her head back towards the roof of the small car. He started to kiss her neck as he spoke. 'It's you baby, you're the reason I never lose. Don't know why I forgot. Since I've met you, my luck never runs out.'

His hands moved over her breasts and caressed her body, snaking round to the back of her pencil skirt, pulling the zip down and letting her skirt fall. Maureen was frozen. It was as though his words didn't make sense. What was he saying? Why did he call her a lucky charm? What was he losing at? She didn't understand at all. She felt her heart beat faster in her rib cage as he leaned into her. He was pulling her hair and it hurt, straining her neck backwards. What was he doing?

He was speaking again. 'Loosen up baby, we gonna fuck right here. Remember how we used to do it everywhere we could? I know you love it like I do. Maybe you're just bored with the bedroom stuff. Time to spice things up. Take things outside.' He let her hair go and, with both hands, drew her panties down. His rough hands felt like sandpaper over her smooth thighs.

Taking a step back, he pulled his shirt over his head and threw it across the garage. He stood there, letting her admire his chest. Her body felt frozen. He was going to screw her here in the garage. Is that what he was saying?

He unzipped his jeans and let them fall to the floor. He never wore underwear, so his erection stood proud in front of him. He rubbed his hands over his nuts and took a step towards her, undoing the buttons of her shirt and exposing those perfect breasts held neatly in a lace bra. He drew the shirt down and let it fall off her arms. Expertly he unclipped the bra and drew it off her slim shoulders.

'That's what I'm talking about baby. You and me, here. Fucking like we used to.'

He smiled at her. Then he was on her, starting to kiss her almost frantically. Her body responded while her mind switched off. As he crushed into her, taking her whole being into him, she felt her body feed into his need. He was inside her, pushing hard into her. As he lifted her off her feet, she wrapped her legs around his body, hearing her voice moan as he thrust into her. Her mind was blank. He pushed and pushed, her spine bruising as it bumped over and over against the car. Then it was finished. The thrill of taking his wife in the garage had got the better of Chris, and he had come quickly, slumping over Maureen, holding her between his body and the car. Her legs now hung limp on either side of him, his body weight holding her off the floor.

'Yes baby, that's what I'm talking about. I knew this would work. Man I love fucking you,' he said, breathing heavily.

He drew himself out of Maureen, letting her slide back to the floor. He pulled her face to his and kissed her again. 'Thanks baby,' he said, holding her small face between his large hands. 'I'm gonna have a shower and then head out. You look shattered, think you should have a lie down hey.'

She nodded in agreement, slowly and without understanding. Her legs felt strange and she fumbled for her clothes and handbag, holding them in a mess close to her chest. She tried to collect the lipsticks that had rolled out of her bag, but things kept falling out of her hands. She gave up, and gripping what she had tightly, walked to the downstairs bathroom. Hearing the upstairs shower running, she closed the door behind her with one hand, still clutching her bag and clothes. Failing to lock the door with one hand, she dropped the clothes and pulled at the handle with both hands to lock the bathroom door securely. Walking backwards away from the door, she made her way to the toilet and wiped herself clean. Then, still in a haze, she walked to the shower and turned it on. Stepping back she sank to the floor. Her head hung off her neck and her legs crumpled below her. She breathed, and blinked her eyes slowly.

The door banged, jolting Maureen out of her daze. She stiffened and starred at the bolted door. 'Cheers baby, see you later. Was great, thanks,' he shouted through the door, his footsteps fading as he walked away. Maureen sighed with relief and began to cry. Not because she was married to a man who raped her in his garage, or because she now knew that he spent all his time and money in gambling dens, but because she had seen a girl alive, running on a road, and then she had become a body on the tar. For the first time since the accident, Maureen cried for the beautiful girl she'd seen being killed by a taxi. The guilt of her hatred, towards the runners that morning, enveloped her. At least I am alive she told herself, over and over again.

Awesome Foursome

Claire's funeral somehow managed to be exactly like Claire: beautiful and effortless. Friends spoke kind, careful words and the large church hall was filled with over 300 people including community members, old school friends and family. The school in Masi, that Claire had worked in as a speech therapist, brought the children to the funeral and they sang a beautiful hymn. It was an almost surreal experience of pain, and a celebration of her life and her special connections with so many people.

Claire's father spoke, as did Tanya. Liz and Kate turned down the opportunity to speak. Close family and friends occupied the front row and tears ran down their cheeks as those brave enough to speak, told of Claire's life as though it were a fairytale. James sat next to Kate. There were no more tears left in him; they'd stopped the day before and left behind a hollow feeling. James felt numb.

Tanya had always been an excellent speaker, and although her eyes glistened with tears, she never faltered in her stories of the girls' lives growing up in Fish Hoek. The memories, serving as relics of another time, were spoken in Tanya's words, and shared in an effort to describe Claire and what she'd meant to them.

'We will miss you Clairey, more than you could ever know,' she said, finishing her speech. Tanya returned to her seat next to James. She smiled at him bravely as she sat; he squeezed her hand reassuringly.

'Well done Tan. That was a great speech. Thank you. Claire would have loved it,' he said, looking down at her. She was so little next to James, yet such a strong personality, and it was only when she sat next to him quietly that he realised how tiny she was.

Claire's father, Mr Southbridge, now stood at the front of the church. A tall and strong man, still with a full mop of grey hair, he spoke with clinical accuracy and conviction.

Unconsciously Kate moved closer to James. Her eyes were fixed on Mr Southbridge's face. As his voice droned on, she was transported back in time. The girls had known Claire's parents for most of their lives, yet they felt they hardly knew them at all. Claire had lived in a house on the mountain, while the other girls had lived in the valley - a geographic, and by inference, financial split. The houses on the mountain were, more often than not, owned by wealthier families or retired people from Johannesburg. The exquisite views across False Bay from the mountainside commanded higher property prices than those in the valley, which could have views of the mountains or their neighbours' walls.

Claire had always shrugged off her parents' wealth, preferring to spend time at either Kate or Tanya's house. Claire would often use the excuse: 'Mom isn't home, you know how busy she is doing her charity work, can I come over to you to study?' Only when the girls had gotten drunk on Claire's 16th, had they understood more about Claire's family.

Claire's 16th was a rather formal tea at the Southbridges home, with her parents and their friends. Kate had organised a sleepover at her house for Claire, so that the girls could celebrate together after the tea. Liz's mom, Gail Patterson, had volunteered to collect the three girls and drop them off at Kate's house. As a housewife, she relished the opportunity to collect and deliver children from point A to B. It gave her purpose, and ensured she knew what was happening in her daughter's life.

Kate lived in a ramshackle house at the bottom of Fish Hoek, where a light-brown, one-metre-high brick wall enclosed the front of the property. Her mother, Zelda, was a single mom who spent most of her time at her latest boyfriend's home. A free spirit, in search of herself, Zelda found it difficult to parent Kate as she became older and more headstrong. Besides, according to her, Kate was more than capable of looking after herself for a night from the age of 12. Luckily for Kate, Zelda rented her back room to a kind Zimbabwean woman who worked in the hospital as a cleaner. Kate would end up spending the night in Mama Jean's room when her mother decided she wasn't coming home for the night. Mama Jean would allow Kate to curl up next to her, and fall asleep to the sound of late night TV soap operas, the smells of coconut butter and pap filling the small room.

Kate knew that Gail suspected Zelda wasn't the best role model, and often prevented Liz from visiting her house. Claire's 16th however was a special occasion, pushing Gail to give in to the girls' idea of a sleepover celebration. As she dropped the girls at Kate's, Gail - an older version of Liz with greying temples - peered past Kate.

'Hi Kate, how are you darling?' asked Gail, craning her neck to see into the house.

'I'm fine Mrs Patterson, so excited to have my besties sleeping over for Claire's birthday. Thanks so much for bringing everyone. We will be really good I promise. Just girlie stuff you know,' said Kate, using all her charms of persuasion on Mrs Patterson. 'Is mom home dear?' asked Gail, craning her neck further out of the car to try and spot Zelda.

'Yup, she will be here the whole time. She's just out the back hanging washing. Mama Jean's also here, so we're sorted,' said Kate matter-of-factly. Kate had a talent for spinning white lies.

'Ok dear, that's great. Let mom know I say hi. Bye,' said Gail as she slowly pulled away, staring into her rear view mirror at a slightly-too-sure-of-herself

Kate, smiling and waving her off.

The evening had been silly, exploratory and had bonded the girls to each other, even more so than before. Claire had managed to steal a bottle of champagne from her boring sweet 16th tea with her parents and their friends. Tanya's parents never drank, so she had only managed to bring a bottle of really old wine that her father had received as a gift from a work colleague years back. Liz had come empty handed, too petrified of being caught out and convinced her father counted the millilitres of alcohol per bottle in their drinks cabinet. She had however, managed to convince her mom to bake a chocolate cake. Slathered in sweet chocolate icing, and topped with marshmallows, it was the perfect accompaniment to Claire's champagne. Kate had a fridge with a few beers, crisps and a bottle of vodka she'd managed to nick from one of her mother's parties. They piled their loot on the melamine kitchen table and squealed excitedly.

'Let's start with the champagne,' Kate decided, pouring equal portions into an unmatched assortment of mugs. Claire cut the cake in four and they all went and sat outside on a blanket in the garden. Mama Jean was working night shift, and Zelda was away. 'So where is your mom Kate?' asked Liz, who knew that Kate had lied to her mom. 'At some spiritual retreat thing. Dwain, mom's new guy, is all into like connecting with his deeper inner guru,' said Kate in a deep voice, sitting cross-legged like a Buddah. 'Sheewah man,' she said making peace signs with her hands. The others giggled at Kate's antics.

'You're so lucky. I wish my mother would go away for just an afternoon, never mind a whole weekend,' said Liz, taking a glug of her champagne and making a face.

'Urgh Claire, this stuff sucks, why do your parents like it so much?'

Claire's eyes widened at Liz. She'd been sipping champagne from her mother's glass since she was at primary school.

'Liz, it's French champagne. You don't get better than this,' burst out Claire before rolling onto her side, unabashedly laughing at Liz. The others couldn't help themselves and soon they were all laughing. The rest of the evening passed in the same manner. Drinking, eating junk food and teasing each other.

Kate switched the fairy lights on in the small backyard. Overgrown and hidden, the yard took on a magical glow with the twinkling lights. A light breeze lifted the leaves and lights, shadows dancing playfully around the girls. Rodriguez's song, 'I wonder' played loudly and Kate swayed in the soft breeze. Falling into the damp grass near midnight, pleasantly drunk, Claire said too loudly, 'I love you guys, you are my BEST. Now THIS is a birthday party!' The girls had all piled around Claire, heads on laps and stomachs.

'Why didn't your folks throw a proper bash for you Claire? I mean, you have the house and the bucks, right?' asked Tanya, unable to keep her curiosity to herself.

'Ha, you must be joking Tan. My mom doesn't do kids or events that she isn't in perfect control of. Besides, she is so self-involved, how on earth would she know what I want?' asked Claire, sitting up. She crossed her arms and continued, 'And then my Dad, well he's always at work and doesn't like too many people at the house anyway. Basically they used tonight as an excuse to invite some guy my Dad is doing business with, so he can talk work and show off his big house on the hill. Seriously, there was like only one woman who even asked me what I want to do with my life. The rest were all like 'Happy birthday Claire. Sweet 16 and never been kissed! All the best darling, here is a gift. Now tell me, where is Mama?' said Claire, in her best mock Queen's English.

Tanya's eyes were wide with surprise as she listened to Claire's tirade. 'Seriously guys, I don't even know why my parents had me. They are nice and all, but I'm just another thing they own,' said Claire with a deep sigh. Her eyes welled up with tears and her chin slumped to her chest.

Liz scrambled to Claire's side, scowling at Tanya. 'Claire-bear, that's not true, they really love you. My mom says so all the time. Mom will be like "Mrs Southbridge is such a wonderful mum, look how she always helps at the school, darling isn't she",' said Liz impersonating her mother. Claire's face burst into laughter, her tears forgotten.

Kate attention was brought back to the muggy, hot church as Mr Southbridge paused in his speech. She shifted uncomfortably on the hard chair and looked up at him. He peered through his glasses at the paper shaking in his hands, and continued.

'Claire was always passionate about Africa. When we moved back to England ten years ago, we asked her to come with us. As a speech and hearing therapist, she would have done very well in London. But Claire said she wanted to stay here. She was going to work with the children at the Masi school, who have sung for us here today. A mind and will of her own our Claire, that's for sure,' said Mr Southbridge, his shoulders starting to sag under the weight of his words. 'It's an uncertain world, and you can never be sure of what will happen next. We definitely never thought this would happen to Claire. We ask that each and every one of you live your lives to the full, and take care of yourselves. God Bless,' he said and walked off the stage, slightly stooped and not the same imposing man Kate remembered him being.

After the service, the large church foyer was filled with food and people talking in hushed voices; some clutching tissues, others bustling trays of eats from one table to another. Men stood and stared at the tea, coffee and juices on offer, with faces revealing their real desire for a beer.

The Southbridges had catered enough for a small army, and they now stood on the periphery, nodding, hugging, and shaking hands as people filed past them.

James, Tanya, Kate and Liz immersed themselves in old friends. Catching up on tales of newlyweds and children, Tanya heard herself say, 'wow 7 and 9 already, can't believe they are that big,' as she nodded her head enthusiastically at an old school friend's recount of her child's antics. The woman continued on the virtues of motherhood, as Tanya tuned out to watch Tristan in the distance, speaking to a pretty strawberry blonde. She recognised her from school, a year or two below, but couldn't remember her name. He touched her arm and then her shoulders, then he lead her outside. She seemed upset. Maybe he was trying to make her feel better by taking her outside, she told herself.

'Hilarious hey, kids I tell you. And you Tan, have you got any kids?' came the voice of the woman Tanya was facing. Tanya focused and applied herself.

'No, no, not yet. You never know though. Maybe later. I'm still focusing on my career,' she stumbled, a well-versed response. What was wrong with these Fish Hoek people? Why did you have to be married off with kids at 25? So pathetic and small-minded, thought Tanya.

'Well, don't wait too long, we're not getting any younger AND kids are hectic, you'll need all your youth. Well, whatever's left, ha ha,' she said as she turned and walked away, leaving Tanya standing there with her mouth hanging open.

Kate appeared at Tanya's side, 'I see that bitch had her say with you too. I was hoping you would be more on it than me. Did she give you the "have your babies now" speech?' asked Kate raising her eyebrows. Tanya nodded, closing her mouth.

'She's a real charmer that one. Clearly her kids haven't done anything for her personality or the size of her arse!' said Kate with a naughty grin. Tanya cooled a little and smiled at Kate's mean joke.

'Thanks Katie. Seriously, where does she get off? And saying it now. Really, there are days when I just want to leave Fish Hoek and never come back. People like her kill me,' said Tanya in exasperation.

'I hear you Tan. Come to Kommetjie, just beach bums out there. Fewer of these holier-than-thou types,' said Kate in jest.

'I'll pass, thanks Kate. Maybe time to make that move to Town. Will try with Trist again to see if I can convince him,' said Tanya, staring out the door towards where Tristan had gone.

Kate followed Tanya's gaze as Tristan and the pretty strawberry blonde came back in. Kate's eyes widened. Tristan was an ok guy - good looking in a built, crew-cut kind of way. His broad chest and hard biceps were appealing, but she hated the way he treated Tanya. He was dismissive of her, despite her being one hundred times smarter than him. Kate wasn't averse to sea-smelling surfers or their rank cars, but the smell of car fumes and petrol that hung over Tristan, the grease monkey, made her nostrils curl. Tan never complained, always talking Tristan up and saying he was going to own the garage one day, but Kate had her doubts.

Tristan had his hand on the blonde's lower back, guiding her back into the room. He spotted Tanya looking at him and gave her a nod, as if to say 'all good here'. He gave the blonde a hug and came over to Kate and Tanya. 'Who is that, babes?' asked Tanya in her sweet girlfriend voice. 'Old school friend. Turns out she was a mate of Claire's. She lives in Blouberg now. Haven't seen her in ages. She was pretty cut up hey. You girls ok? I'm starving, gonna grab some grub. Want anything?' he said, quickly and expertly shifting the focus. Tanya and Kate shook their heads in unison, and Tristan headed towards the food table.

Kate gave Tanya a hug. 'Just going to go and find my mom before she grabs herself a pensioner,' she nodded, leaving Tanya before she said something. Kate knew who the blonde was and recognised her from school. Kate had seen her at a few school parties that Tanya hadn't been allowed to go to. Tanya hadn't seen Tristan at those parties. Already out of school, he would join in the school parties, despite being much older. Kate remembered how she'd walked into a bedroom at a house party, a little drunk and looking for a toilet, and had turned the light on Tristan's arse working on that very strawberry blonde. Now here she was at Claire's funeral. How interesting, thought Kate, as she eventually spotted her mother.

Kate needed to go. The girls, some close friends and James were coming to her garden cottage in Kommetjie for some drinks. She saw James and walked herself and her mother towards him.

He was speaking to the Southbridges. 'I don't know what to say, I'm so thankful. Are you sure?' he was saying to them. Kate came up behind and interrupted loudly, ensuring she didn't overhear anything she wasn't supposed to.

'Hi Mr and Mrs Southbridge, I'm going to take mom home and then head to Kommetjie. Some friends are coming over. Not sure if you would like to come too?' asked Kate, knowing what their response would be.

'No, no thank you Kate dear. We're going to go back to the hotel. We are leaving in a few days, once we've sorted out a few things. Please come and see us. You know where we are staying?' said Mrs Southbridge, placing her cool, thin hand on Kate's forearm.

'Sure, yes, thanks, yes, I'll pop in' said Kate, knowing that she wouldn't visit the Southbridges in their boutique hotel in Noordhoek. She turned to James, 'we'll see you at my place later then James?' asked Kate.

'Ya sure, see you there Kate. Bye Zelda,' waved James, as Kate led her mom out. Zelda had hugged the Southbridges enthusiastically earlier, and received a stony pat in return.

'God they are awful, where on earth did Claire come from?' grumbled Zelda, pushing her wild mop of hair behind her ears. Kate started the car. 'Oh mom. Just leave it. They've always been like that. Besides, you're the one who always said to Claire that she was magical. Guess she came from a magical place,' said Kate as she drove towards her mother's home, alone inside her head. Thoughts of Tristan and the strawberry blonde, James and the Southbridges, and Claire made her head spin and she felt giddy.

James

James drove slowly away from the church. He needed to clear his head before he reached Kate's place; choosing the Cape Point route that looped back to Kommetjie, via Simon's Town and Scarborough, seemed the best way to unclutter his thoughts. The slow meander along the coastal road allowed him to unpack Claire's funeral. He tried to remember all the wonderful things everyone had said about Claire, but he just couldn't. It was as if the words didn't stick. There was only one sentence that stood out for him that Tanya had said: 'Claire had a magical sparkle in her eyes and in her step...' It was true, she had sparkled for him. He had always thought it was just his infatuation with her. He could never tell his friends that she sparkled, they would have ripped him off. The word 'sparkle' wasn't exactly manly or up there with great tits and arse.

He remembered the first time he saw her; he was at the Fish Hoek Lifesaving club. A fellow surfer had insisted he come to the club for a drink on a Friday, believing that James would definitely meet a 'chick' there. After an hour and a half of insane Cape Town traffic, from the centre of town to Fish Hoek, he had arrived annoyed, sweaty and in his work gear. He stood in the car park outside the club, pulled his square-toed leather shoes and socks off, chucked them in the back of the car, and then rolled up his work jeans a rung or two, before strolling in looking as Cape Town-casual as he could. The club was a large square, grey concrete block; the lookout tower rose above the club and over the bay. The open quad inside the square enabled the various flotation and paddling craft to be manoeuvred from inside the club to the beach. A small club house was on the left and included a small bar, with a few benches and tables outside. This was definitely a far cry from the trendy restaurants and bars James usually hung out in.

As he walked in, he managed to spot his friend and sidled over. 'Hey hey, howzit Jamo,' said Mikey, slapping James on the back in greeting. 'You look like you need a beer dude. Haven't even lost the work kit hey. Glad the shoes got left behind. Come let's get that beer,' continued Mikey.

James was a little mortified by Mikey's public announcement. He already felt like he stood out. Everyone around him was dressed in either a wetsuit, a costume, a combination thereof or shorts and t-shirts. He followed Mikey through throngs of wet children, teenagers and adults of various shapes and sizes. Mikey quickly organised the beers, indicating to James to follow him outside to the benches and tables. There wasn't any space to sit, so the two of them leant against the wooden pillar and spoke about what the swell had been doing, the wind and the best places to surf when the wind died, which luckily wasn't often in Cape Town.

A young, curly-haired surfer accidentally bumped past Mikey and James. He looked up to apologise and recognised Mikey. Cradling three beers he introduced himself to James. 'Hey, why don't you guys come and join us,' said the surfer as he pointed to one of the tables where two girls were sitting. 'Sure,' said Mikey as he shrugged and gave James a knowing look. James couldn't help smiling at Mikey. Mikey was a pretty average looking guy, average height with brown hair and eyes, a nose that had probably had a little too much action in high school rugby, and a great sense of humour. James had watched Mikey charm the coolest of ladies with expert care. He just had it.

After completing the laborious process of squeezing his legs under a bench with three other people at the same time, James sat down and locked eyes with the girl opposite him. He blinked slowly and managed to keep it cool.

'Hey, I'm James,' he said.

Claire looked back at him and smiled, telling him her name. He couldn't remember if Kate had introduced herself or not. She may have. He was unable to take his eyes off Claire. Not that he didn't noticed Kate's low top and easy smile.

He slugged his beer, desperately seeking some courage and eventually started speaking to Claire. She had enchanted him from that instant. She spoke about her speech and therapy work in the schools in Masi, and how she'd grown up in Fish Hoek. She was at the Lifesaving club, because Kate was seeing the curly-haired surfer and had dragged her there. Claire loved the outdoors and the sea, but was not lifesaving material. The beers flowed with the conversation.

The Lifesaving club eventually closed and the group grabbed pizzas and went to Kate's mom's place. At the end of the evening James, now a little drunk, had asked for Claire's number. Slightly drunk herself, Claire had leaned into him and said 'I never kiss and tell'. When he drew back to look at what she meant, she took his face in her hands and kissed him so gently and sweetly that he stopped breathing. She let him go and Mikey swung past to grab James by the arm and drag him to the car. Claire waved at him as he craned his neck back to see her.

It had taken James over a week to get hold of Claire's number. Mikey took his time in getting hold of the surfer, who in turn was slow in getting Claire's number from Kate. Once he had the number in his hands, James let it stew for a day, not quite sure what he was waiting for. Then he called her on her mobile. Once he had explained who he was, she had laughed out loud. 'Well hello there, took you long enough to get hold of me. I was starting to think you may have given up. So, where are we going?' she had confidently demanded. That sealed it and they had been James and Claire ever since.

He still couldn't completely understand what she had seen in him. He thought of himself as a pretty regular guy, a bit taller than most, dark hair, blue eyes. Not exactly Brad Pitt. Claire always told him he was 'delicious' and everyone else thought so too. It was going to be weird not being James and Claire anymore. He was going to be 'Just James'. Maybe even 'Poor James'. The pitiful looks had been getting to him. At first he hadn't noticed them, but now he saw how people's faces melted when they saw him. They also said 'shame' a lot. He detested that word!

The past week at work he'd received some really kind and thoughtful emails and arm rubs, as people said how sorry they were and how wonderful Claire had seemed. It faded pretty fast, and the work came thundering back in after a few days. His boss had looked down at him as she stood over his desk, her angular bob framing her cool sharp face. 'Sorry to hear about Claire, James. Hope you will be ok. Nothing like getting back into it hey, to feel better? Will you be joining us at the 12:30 meeting? New pitch and I think you should work on it,' she said coolly. James nodded, dumbstruck.

Abby, who was sitting nearby, overheard the conversation and once the Vampire Queen (as they fondly referred to her) was out of earshot, came over. 'Shit James, not sure what to say here. She is just like so bad. Do you think she really is a vampire? I mean she must be, to say shit like that?' Abby's young fresh face had gasped. James fell back into his chair and started to laugh. They had laughed so hard that other people in the office started to stare.

His boss had been right, the work had been a good distraction. Kate had also checked in on him. He enjoyed her company and felt comfortable with Kate. Her easy-going attitude always made a slow smile cross his face. It was easy to talk to her, the words flowed easily. She had popped in to the apartment and dropped off some of her delicious deli food, her own red eyes revealing her struggle with Claire's passing. They had hugged when she left and her citrus-scented shampoo had hung onto his shirt for ages after. He smelt his shirt now. It smelt of nothing.

He rounded Cape Point and was heading towards Scarborough. He opened the window. The smell of fresh fynbos mixed with sea filled his car. He sucked it in as his mind turned to the conversation with the Southbridges. After the ceremony, and when most people had eaten their fill and were leaving, he'd gone to say goodbye to them. Mr Southbridge said, 'James, we must just finalise the details of Claire's will,' as though James had known such a thing existed. The surprise showed on his face. Claire had a will?

Mrs Southbridge softened when she saw his shock, and reached out to him and said, 'she got the will about a year ago James. She drew it up after the riots in Masi. She didn't want you to know she was feeling unsafe, she knew you wouldn't allow her to go back.' She smiled knowingly at him.

'Claire was always prepared for everything, wasn't she? She only told me about it, and we had it stored at the bank,' explained Mrs Southbridge.

James found himself looking at the floor.

'She has left you everything except her life insurance package. That goes to the Masi school. But her car, the other half of the apartment, all her furniture... That's yours... And the cat! She specifically mentioned the cat in her will. You have to look after the cat,' reiterated Mrs Southbridge.

James looked up at her and, for the first time since he had known Claire, he saw her in her mother's eyes. He stammered something about the cat and some form of thanks, then quickly retreated when Kate came to say goodbye.

When had Claire managed to get the will done? He wished she'd told him. He knew she was distressed and upset about the riots that had happened in Masi. She was worried sick about the children and if they were safe, but he hadn't realised that she had felt threatened herself. Claire always underplayed her work, and the threat she may have faced working in a volatile township.

Masiphumelele was a relatively peaceful area, but there had been chaos when its residents had become angered by poor policing services. After a child had been killed, residents had taken matters into their own hands and killed the perpetrator. Days of riots and fires had ensued, and no one could get in, out or through the township.

Claire had managed to stay in touch with the teachers at the school, and had spent most days rallying friends to pull supplies together, which she then took to churches for distribution to the community. When the situation had settled to a gentle simmer, she'd been one of the first non-residents to go back into Masi. He remembered how she had underplayed her first day back at school. He had found it odd, but just assumed that it had been because there had been so much devastation. Maybe it was then that she had felt unsafe? He would never know. His heart felt heavy.

James's Landie pulled into the pavement outside Kate's cottage. She had a thin little panhandle entrance, straight into a garage down the side of the larger main house. A golden shower creeper lined both sides of the drive, making the driveway seem smaller, yet warm and welcoming with bright green leaves and orange flowers. He spotted Tristan and Liz's cars. They had all come straight here. He didn't recognise the other cars, but assumed there'd be a few familiar faces that he sort of knew. In a small community it felt like everyone had been to school together, kissed each other or their brother, and there was always a really long story describing their life trajectory, if you chose to ask. Even though he had lived here for four years, James still felt like an outsider, especially when the girls got together with old school friends.

Shoving his hands into the pockets of his formal pants, James stretched his chest open, breathed deeply, and walked in.

Kate's small garden was neat. Mostly grass with bushes along the wall. A lonely Milkwood tree stood away from the wall near the centre of the garden. Her couch, rug and some pillows were scattered on the grass; She must have emptied her lounge out into the garden. There were people milling about, clutching drinks close to their chests. Some were laughing, others seemed really sad and rubbed at their eyes. Two children ran past him, and he had no idea who they belonged to. He stood for a moment looking at everyone and wondering where to take himself. Kate's face appeared out from a group, paler than usual but with a warm, brave smile.

'James, there you are. I was worried you weren't going to come. Are you ok?' she said as she walked towards him. A few people looked at him, before returning to their conversations. He was relieved that no one else approached him.

'Hey Kate, ya, I'm fine. I came via Cape Point. Needed the drive. Everything ok here, you need any help?' asked James, noticing all the drinks and snacks lining the tables.

'All good James. Tan and Liz are on it, and the deli helped out too. Here, come have a drink, what can I get you?' asked Kate as she walked James to the drinks table.

Kate had told a few close friends that she was going to hold a mini-wake at her place after the funeral. She knew she would need a few stiff drinks and friends after the funeral.

'A Jamesons is great Kate, just ice please,' said James as Kate expertly poured him a double tot and threw in a few blocks of ice. James sipped the whiskey, savouring the warm feeling as the liquid slipped down his throat.

He felt Kate staring at him. 'That hitting the spot?' she said with a raised eyebrow. 'Yup,' he said, raising his glass to Kate in a mock salute.

'Great, I'm just going to fill up other glasses and will catch up with you in a bit. Was a rough morning,' stated Kate, before she walked towards a group of friends.

James spent the rest of the afternoon moving between groups of people. Mostly nodding and sipping his whiskey, which Kate magically seemed to know when to fill, and occasionally telling people what work he did. He was amazed how people just seemed to babble at you. Neil, one of Claire's adoring friends, was an insurance salesman; he spoke at James for what felt like the whole afternoon, about the issues facing the insurance market now that brokers were required to write all sorts of tests. At one point, James felt as though he was standing next to himself: watching Neil from the side babbling away at him, occasionally pushing his specs back up his nose, building up a little white ball of foam in the corner of his mouth, to match the speed of his chatter.

Eventually Tristan had appeared and interrupted Neil. 'Hey Neil, can I chat to Jamo here about something. No offence bru, but private you know,' said Tristan, herding James out of Neil's reach. Left behind, Neil looked slightly put out and turned his head left and right until he spied another victim.

'Fuck dude, that oke has been at you for ages. I couldn't take your sad face anymore, had to save you. You ok bru? Wanna get a refill?' said Tristan as he looked at James's empty glass. James shook his head, and as he did so, he realised he'd had one too many Jamesons. He couldn't remember eating anything that day. His feet did a double step. Tristan steadied him and led him to a chair under the Milkwood tree. Tanya and Liz joined them and quickly guessed at James's precarious state. 'I'll go grab some food from the kitchen and a cup of tea. He looks bad,' he heard Liz say.

James was leaning his elbows on his knees to try and steady himself. He felt deaf and the ground seemed to move too much. He could see different toes and shoes. He lifted his head, 'Fuck guys, I'm drunk,' he said as the whole garden spun around him. He felt the saliva start to ooze between his cheeks and gums. He managed to push himself off the chair and get behind the back wall of the cottage, before his stomach heaved its contents. Eventually he was dry heaving, his body tormented. Tristan lifted James up and walked him back to the front garden where Liz and Tanya were standing, holding tea and food. Kate was in the distance, shunting the last few visitors out the gate.

The sun had dropped out of the sky and the garden was dark. Kate shut the garden gates and went inside. The garden lights came on and Kate reappeared. James tried to get up, mumbling and stumbling, saying he was going home. Tristan took him firmly by the arm and deposited James on the carpet on the grass. James sat, legs stretched out in front of him, with his head hanging limp, staring at his knees.

'Here Jamesie,' said Liz. 'This will help. It's sweet tea,' she said, as she touched him gently on the shoulder to get his attention. He looked at her, then took the cup and slurped it. Liz sat next to him and rubbed his arm. Kate, Tanya and Tristan sat down on the carpet too. They formed a sloppy circle of sad friends.

Managing to keep the tea down, James mumbled 'sorry guys'. Kate smiled, 'no worries James, at least you weren't pissing against my back wall. Like Dino, who I caught having a slash against my freaking wall earlier. Can you believe it!' said Kate horrified.

'You serious Kate?' asked Tanya, putting her hand over her mouth.

'I'm sure it's because he was desperate Kate, one bathroom and all these people, you know,' said Liz as she tried to find a reason why someone would pee against the host's house wall.

'He's just a pig Liz, we both know it. Men,' said Kate flatly.

They all sat quietly for moment. The garden seemed to sigh in relief. There were glasses in odd places across the garden. Perched in branches, on top of the perimeter wall - scattered remnants of the afternoon.

'One last drink everyone?' said Kate as she stood up and headed to the drinks table. 'Ya ok Kate, then we heading,' said Tristan matter-of-factly. Kate poured the drinks, then disappeared inside. The sound of Rodriguez's 'I wonder' came floating into the garden, his distinct voice filling the garden with memories of Claire. James was nibbling on a piece of carrot cake, the sweet icing working its magic in his bloodstream.

'Claire loved Rodriguez,' he stated. Looking up, Kate floated down the stairs, grabbed the drinks she had poured and came to the carpet, handing out drinks to everyone, except James. 'Sorry James, think you should stick to your tea,' she said, tilting her head sideways and smiling at him kindly. He nodded. He was finding words hard to put together, and was just managing to get through the tea.

The friends raised their glasses into the night. 'To Claire!' they said. 'To her gorgeousness in every way,' said Tanya, 'and to her kind caring heart,' said Liz, 'and to her amazing friendship,' said Tristan, 'and to her magical presence', said Kate. 'We are going to miss you Clairey.'

They sat in silence and drank in their pain and memories, swaying to the music, until their glasses were empty. Tristan bundled Tanya, Liz and James into his car and took them all home, leaving Kate alone in her garden. She stared into the garden waiting for Claire to appear, knowing she was there, somewhere.

The ringing doorbell raised Kate's head from her pillow, as the light streamed into her room. After cleaning up her home, she'd spent most of the night twisting and turning, getting up to sip water, feeling hot, then cold, then thirsty. The consistent drinking during the wake had added up to several drinks and it made her sleep fitful. Eventually the alcohol must have subsided, because she had slept well into the morning.

Luckily it was Sunday. Whoever was ringing the doorbell was persistent, and rude. She found her gate keys on the kitchen table and stumbled down the front steps towards the gate. 'Who is it?' she shouted from a distance. Although there weren't that many beggars in Kommetjie, there were enough, and she didn't have the strength to deal with the badgering up close. 'Hey Kate, it's me, James. My car keys are inside. You guys took them away from me last night. I just need to grab them and then I'll head. Sorry if I woke you?' he shouted through the split pole fence. She felt herself relax, 'don't stress, come in James,' said Kate, sliding the bolt open to let James in. She closed the gate behind him and turned around to look up at him.

Her ancient thin grey cotton nightie, with faded Garfield and the words *Love 2 sleep* printed on the front, barely concealed her full breasts in the mid-morning light. James's eyes widened and he quickly looked away. 'Hey,' he said. 'Sorry man Kate, you really were sleeping.'

Kate straightened up and folded her arms over her braless breasts.

'Come inside and let's look for the keys,' she said turning quickly and walking up the stairs. James followed, his eyes drifting to the back of her legs, traveling up towards her buttocks. Kate disappeared down the short passage to her room and shouted over her shoulder. 'I'm just going to change, have a look in the kitchen so long.' James stood in the middle of the lounge, blinking until his eyes grew accustomed to the cool light of the house.

He had expected to find the little kitchen littered with filthy glasses and plates, but it was spotless. Even the hired glasses from the bottle store were clean and stacked in their plastic red and yellow crates. He couldn't see the keys anywhere. He looked on top of the fridge, on the shelves, the window sill. Nothing. He guessed he would have to call Tristan to find out where he had put the keys.

Kate reappeared, her mass of hair pulled into a messy knot above her head, wearing shorts and a sloppy t-shirt. 'Sorry about that, I was half asleep when I answered the door,' she said, 'wasn't really expecting anyone,' she smiled, slightly embarrassed.

He couldn't help but find her unusually gorgeous - slightly put out, and not on her usual quick-witted, sarcastic form. She seemed almost a little vulnerable.

'No stress, I can't find the keys, so I'm going to have to call Tristan and find out what he did with them. How's your head feeling?' he asked with a grin.

'My head! You mean your head. You were the one watering my plants for me last night,' she jeered back at him.

James hung his head in embarrassment and covered his eyes. 'Urgh, that. I overdid it. I blame you for topping up my glass. But I think I got rid of most of it in your garden. So I think we are even.' He smiled, his cheeks going pink. 'I still don't feel great though, but I'm ok,' he said lifting his head and looking at her. She looked back at him, shifting her weight to her other leg uneasily, before quickly remembering why he was there.

'Your keys! Wait a minute, I do remember finding them. I think I hung them up when I was cleaning up. It's all a little blurry. Let me check the rack,' she said, as she turned and went to the hooks next to the door. 'Are they these ones?' she asked, holding up a set with a brown cat key ring. 'Yes, that's them. Claire and that cat, Arora has to be on everything. Thanks Kate,' he said, walking towards her to take the keys. 'I'll head out now,' he said slowly.

Kate stood in front of him. 'No, please don't, have you had breakfast? Or coffee? I'm going to make for myself so why don't you stay and I can make you some too,' she said, clutching the keys and taking them to the kitchen. James sighed. He actually didn't have anywhere to go and had been wondering what he was going to do with himself. His parents had invited him for Sunday lunch, but he had seen them at the funeral the day before. He just didn't think he could manage a blow-by-blow account of the funeral over a braai with his mother.

'Okay. I'll make coffee and you get the breakfast going,' he said with more enthusiasm. 'Great,' said Kate, as she got to work preparing scrambled eggs on toast. They bustled around the kitchen, mostly in silence. Kate had a shiny silver coffee machine for 'proper' coffee. James had worked in a coffee shop in university and took command of the machine. The waft of fresh coffee filled the kitchen.

James set Kate's cup near the stove where she was working on the eggs. She was throwing in some fresh herbs she had plucked from the pots on her window sill and was humming softly, mesmerised by her work. A few small tomatoes had been expertly chopped up and added with a dash of fresh cream. James sipped his coffee and looked out over the front garden. It looked so different today, as though yesterday's funeral gathering hadn't even happened. He was a million miles away when Kate announced breakfast was ready.

'Tadaaaa, scrambled eggs a-la Kate!' she said with her hands in the air. She grabbed her coffee and sat down opposite him. 'Mmm, good coffee James, I forgot you were Mr Barista,' she teased.

'Nice eggs Kate, and I bet this is your bread?' he asked, shoving a mouthful of food in.

'Yip, hate the stuff you buy in the stores. It's a bit of an ask to make it all the time, but it's so much better.' She said sitting straight, feeling chuffed with herself that he liked the bread. They wolfed down their breakfast and were looking at empty plates in minutes.

'That hit the spot Kate. Thanks,' said James, as he wiped the plate with his index finger and then sucked it. The past week had been take-outs or vending machine food at work. A home-cooked meal was just what he needed.

They chatted about his work. Kate was curious about what James did and always liked hearing about his bizarre boss and demanding clients. Kate told

James about the deli. It was her uncle's and she managed the shop now. She had been working there on and off as a student over the years. She loved chatting to her regulars and working on the menu. She did wish it was her own though. Her uncle pretty much left her to it, but her salary wasn't great, and she knew she could do much better if she worked for herself.

'Maybe one day I'll have my own place,' she mused as she washed up. 'Ya, you should Kate. You have the right kind of personality and you really love working with people,' said James, drying the dishes she handed him. When the dishes were all done and stacked, Kate opened the fridge, grabbed two beers and said to James, 'hair of the dog! Let's go sit outside.'

James couldn't resist the ice-cold beer thrust into his hand. He followed Kate down the stairs. She sat with her legs straight out in front of her drinking her beer, leaning on her free arm. She looked completely carefree. James sat next to her and they soaked up the spring sun as they sipped cool beers which bled water droplets into their hands. The awkwardness of earlier had evaporated and they chatted easily enough. Kate told James all about the old school friend that had told both her and Tanya to have children, because they weren't getting any younger.

'I mean, she is kind of right, but I'm not doing it on my own,' said Kate. 'Besides, I'm not even sure I want to have kids. I just think about my mom, and how I was this burden in her hippie life. I don't want a kid to grow up feeling like they aren't really wanted,' she stated.

James looked at Kate, reaching over and touching her hand. 'Kate, that is not what your mother thinks. She loves you and she loves having you in her life. You aren't a burden to anyone. Your mom just parents differently. That's all,' he said. He liked Zelda. She always spoke to him and made him laugh.

He lifted his hand off Kate's and shifted his weight back. 'Claire's parents, on the other hand, always gave me the impression that Claire was a sort of trophy, and less of a beloved child,' he said, his face sad. They sat in silence.

James eventually sighed and said 'ok Kate, one last beer and then I'm on my way.' He held up his empty bottle.

'On it!' said Kate jumping up.

James lay back on the grass. He closed his eyes and felt the sun on his face, breathing in the smell of the warm grass. He felt worn out. Where Claire had once filled his heart, there was just numbness. It felt as though his heart had turned to rubber and just squeezed and relaxed, squeezed and relaxed. It didn't feel anything anymore, it just pumped.

He opened his eyes and saw Kate was standing over him, looking down at him. The sun twinkled through the tendrils of her hair that had escaped from her bun. For a moment there was nothing else.

'Here's your beer,' said Kate, stretching her hand out in front of her. He sat up onto his elbows. 'Thanks,' he said and took the beer, turning onto his side. Leaning on one elbow, his long body facing Kate, he asked, 'Kate, can I ask you something?' He needed to find out if anybody else knew about Claire's will. 'Sure, I think…' said Kate hesitantly.

'Did you know Claire had a will?' asked James.

He had woken that morning, aching head and heart, trying to wrap his head around the fact that Claire hadn't told him about the will. Instead, she'd gone behind his back. It wasn't about the apartment or her stuff; he was hurt that she hadn't been able to confide in him.

'A will. No, not me. I mean, she wouldn't ask ME for that kind of advice. I could ask Tan, but Tan is pretty lousy with secrets, so probably not her either. Liz lives at home and is probably still on her parent's medical aid. So she wouldn't have a clue' said Kate. She was surprised that James had asked her this. She tilted her head to the side.

'Did you know about it, the will?' she asked

He was staring at the ground, pulling up bits of grass.

'No. No I didn't. The Southbridges told me yesterday at the funeral. Claire's life policy is going to the school, and she has left me the apartment, all the stuff and Arora, our cat,' said James matter-of-factly. 'I just don't know why she didn't tell me about it. We knew everything about each other. Or so I thought,' said James, pulling more viciously at the grass as he got worked up.

Kate looked down. She didn't know why Claire would do that. Claire was insanely open and honest with everyone, and she knew that James knew almost everything about Claire. It was weird, but she knew that Claire did everything for a reason. She wondered what the reason was this time.

'I'm sorry James. I just don't know. It's weird, but I'm sure Claire had a good reason. She always did. Maybe she just didn't want to freak you out or something. It's not a bad thing I guess. Everything is clear now. Sorted. Just like Claire always liked,' said Kate, a small gentle smile aimed at James as reassurance on her face.

James sighed. 'I guess. It's just hard you know. Anyway, sorry to drag you into it,' he said sitting up.

'I'm gonna go Kate. Thanks for the food and drinks, I'll just grab those keys,' he said, as he got up and went into the cottage. It took a few seconds for his eyes to adjust to the dark interior again. He picked up the keys and turned around to leave. Kate was standing in the doorway, leaning against the door frame, with the late afternoon light shining all around her. He walked towards her and stood in front of her. He stared into her face, taking her in, his breath coming quick and fast. Kate's breath picked up. She stood straight. James gently placed his hands on either side of her face. Drawing her in, he gently kissed her. She tasted of sweet beer.

She responded warmly, closing the air between them as she drew her body into his. The kiss made Kate's nipples harden and push against James's chest. She put her hands behind his head and held him close as she opened her mouth, and invited his tongue into hers. James eventually drew away. 'Kate, we shouldn't, this isn't right,' he whispered looking down at her full red lips, feeling his penis harden and push against his jeans towards her. 'I know,' said Kate as she kissed him again. Their kisses became more frantic as they began to pull at each other's clothes. James began to kiss her neck, reaching under her top, finding her breasts. She moaned softly. 'Don't leave me, I need you to stay with me, please,' she whispered into his ear. 'Oh god, I need you,' said James as he peeled her top over her head. He kissed her neck, sliding her bra straps off her arms and then unclipping the bra and letting it fall to the floor.

Kate began to pull James's t-shirt up and he reached behind to expertly pull it over his head with one arm. She pressed her body into his, her breasts full and hot against his bare chest. She kissed him hard and pulled away to draw him towards the bedroom. They pulled their remaining clothes off. Their bodies synchronised quickly in deep thrusts and groans, frantically groping and kissing each other as if perhaps the other may disappear. Eventually satiated, their bodies limp, James lay on top of Kate, breathing heavily. He eventually spoke into the cushion behind her, his body becoming rigid. 'What have we done,' he said quietly. Without looking at her, he pulled himself out of her, pushed himself up with his arms, and slid off the bed to stand over her.

'I'm sorry Kate, this shouldn't have happened. I don't know what came over me. I'll get my things and go,' he said. Without looking at her again, he began searching the floor for his clothes. He left the bedroom to collect his t-shirt.

Kate propped herself up, her heart rate slowing and body tingling from the ecstasy of the sex, while her mind tried to make sense of what he'd just said. She moved her legs to stand up, but she felt limp. She stared at the floor. He was back in the room, dressed, keys in hand. He sat down next to her, turning her face to look at him. 'I'm so sorry, it was a mistake. Please let's just leave it at that, it's been hectic, and it happened. It won't change anything, I promise. Ok? It will be like it never happened,' he told her, trying to make sense of what he had just done and said. The words left his mouth before his brain had time to think.

Kate nodded. She was my best friend. She hasn't been dead less than two weeks and I've slept with her boyfriend. What's wrong with me? thought Kate.

'I should go, I'll let myself out,' said James as he walked out. Kate watched him leave, the last rays of afternoon sun streaming through the passage, golden particles dancing in the light beam where he had been. Silent tears streamed down her face.

Anger and Bargaining

Stage 3

Frustration leads to anger. Uncontrolled, it can permanently damage relationships. May result in trying to negotiate with one's self (or a higher power) to attempt to change the loss that has occurred.

Chapter 3

Tshepo

Tshepo looked around his bleak, single cell. The hard concrete bench gave his wounds no comfort, and made him want to stand. But that would mean having to try and use the crutches properly, and he hadn't yet mastered the art. Once the leg wound had closed and his hip had healed, they'd brought him to the Simon's Town Court holding cells. He was lucky to get his own cell because he was a cripple. He never thought he'd be longing for that hospital bed again; but the pain of sitting on cold concrete made the pain from his recovering bed sores and aching hip so unbearable, that he wanted to cry out after a few hours.

Looking across at the drunks, thieves and hobos in the other shared cells, Tshepo felt grateful for the female officer who had been on duty when he'd arrived. She'd taken one look at him and put him in the single cell.

'Hai boetie, how does a one-legged man end up in here? I better put you on your own, otherwise the others will have fun with you,' she said, raising her eyebrows and gesturing towards the full cell. It became obvious to him that as a cripple, you were fair game for taunting. The anger towards his own disabled body made the bile rise in the back of his throat.

Tshepo couldn't sit any longer. He grabbed the government-issue crutches and heaved himself up on one leg. He'd been practising using them for a few days, struggling to get the rhythm of the movement, without tripping himself up and landing on his face. He hobbled from one corner of the cell to the next, moving slowly and carefully.

He'd been told by Jenny, the physiotherapist, that she'd apply for a prosthesis. It was a long complex process, and could take many months. Besides, the swelling on the wound wasn't completely gone, and the stump would need to be far more resilient before he could use a prosthesis. She'd also promised to get it to him, wherever he ended up. He shook his head and limped along. He was stuck in this place now, but who knew where he was going next; maybe his lawyer would show that it hadn't been his fault. Maybe the Claire had been running in the road and that meant it had been her fault and not his? Maybe this was all just a bad dream.

He flopped down on the concrete bench again, awkwardly untangling his arms from the crutches. He sank back along the cold wall and sighed. He could see the other inmates staring at him and looked down, not wanting to meet their eyes. He'd had enough of the looks of pity and disgust. He wanted to shout at them and tell them to look at something else, but he didn't have the energy. He felt drained.

The gruelling trip from the hospital to his cell had added a further knock to his confidence. The officers transporting him to Simon's Town were used to catching able-bodied men and women and throwing them in the back of the van. Any two-legged person would step up onto the back bumper, lean forward into the van and enter it, bringing the other foot through.

Tshepo was unable to haul himself up into the van, which meant one of the officers had to climb in first, then squat as he grabbed both of Tshepo's arms. The second officer had to stand behind him and push Tshepo's behind up and into the van. There was a split second when the officer in the van faltered, and Tshepo thought he was going to land face down on the man's belly, but somehow the officer righted himself in time to place Tshepo on the bench in the van. 'Heh heh heh, was a close one, neh,' laughed the pulling officer, as he climbed out the van and slammed the doors closed with an enthusiastic flourish.

The bumpy ride to the cell ensured that Tshepo knocked his head a few times, as he tried to stay upright. With only one leg to grip to the floor of the van, and precious little to hold onto, he struggled to balance as he was tossed around in every direction, bouncing on his bed sores. When they got to Simon's Town police station, the officers once again opened the doors of the police van and stood staring at Tshepo. Hands on hips, they contemplated how to extract Tshepo from the vehicle. 'Wena, sit on the floor, and we will pull you out,' said the pushing officer.

Seeing no other option himself, Tshepo had gently swung his behind around and crash landed onto the floor, back facing the open doors of the van. Large arms had grabbed him around the waist and dragged him out of the van till he could stand on one leg. The pushing officer dragged the crutches out and gave them to Tshepo. Once Tshepo regained his balance using the crutches, he was given a gentle nudge to walk into the holding area of the station.

As he curled up along the length of the bench, he closed his eyes to his new reality and tried to forget where he was.

'Mr Dlamini? Can you wake up please?' said a voice. Tshepo blinked and pushed himself up. It took him a few moments to remember where he was. The holding cell. He looked up at the voice to see a tall black man in a smart suit, wearing good Italian shoes. Rich kid, thought Tshepo. The man's accent betrayed him…must have gone to a private school, thought Tshepo his mouth frowning in distaste. He looked up at the man's face; a BMW-driving, BEE cheese boy thought Tshepo.

The man's cheekbones were sculpted and his jaw was sharp and perfectly symmetrical. His well-built chest muscles strained against his fitted shirt. His jacket hung open and he carried a leather satchel. Tshepo raised his eyebrows.

'Mr Dlamini? Can I speak to you? My name is Winston Buswayo and I am here to represent you, to be your lawyer,' he smiled a broad affirming smile at Tshepo. His eyes were wide and eager. He continued, 'my firm has appointed me as your lawyer,' explained Winston.

'I cannot pay you Mr Buswayo, I have no money. You will have to go,' said Tshepo. Was the Boss involved here? Had he got this fancy lawyer here to put him in jail forever? Whatever this was, he was not going to be saddled with some big lawyer debt. He'd seen the shows on TV, lawyers charging a fortune and making people bankrupt. He had enough problems, without extra debt to add to his troubles.

'You don't need to worry about the money Mr Dlamini, we are taking on your case probono – that means we will defend you for mahala[9],' said Winston, putting Tshepo's mind at rest.

'We heard about your case in the news, and would like to defend you, and see if we can get you a reduced sentence,' finished Winston. He sat next to Tshepo, nudging him to sit up. Tshepo stared at Winston, narrowing his eyes.

---

9   Free

'Why do you want to do this Mr Buswayo? I am a taxi driver, a nothing, maybe even a nuisance to people like you. And I have killed a woman, by mistake. I am a cripple and things don't look good for me. Tell me, why does your company want to help me?' asked Tshepo, the irony of his situation clear.

Winston smiled; he'd been waiting for this question. 'This is a good question Mr Dlamini, why indeed would we want to take your case?' said Winston, coming close to Tshepo's face, dropping his voice.

'You see Mr Dlamini, our firm prides itself on ensuring we are able to assist our clients, no matter the situations they find themselves in. You could say, we specialise in dealing with complex and sensitive cases that require expert legal knowledge,' explained Winston, sitting taller and rubbing his chin, before continuing.

'Your case is not complicated, but it is high profile. It blew up on social media and reignited issues around racial tension, safety and many other hot topics. If WE take on the case, probono, we will be seen as the firm that cares for the underdog, as well as our large corporate clients. By inference, the case ought to bring us more BEE business. Do you now see why we are taking your case?' asked Winston, his eyes glinting.

'Yes Mr Buswayo, I see you want to use me to get more business. A man with more options would tell you to voetsek[10], but I have no options anymore. This is your lucky day, you can be my lawyer,' said Tshepo, leaning back against the cold wall.

'Wonderful,' said Winston, 'we'll be in touch shortly. My associates will come by later and take down your version of the accident. I will liaise with the police with regards to any witnesses. I really do believe we can help you Mr Dlamini, I really do.'

Standing up and straightening his suit, Winston Buswayo took Tshepo's hand and pumped it strongly before exiting the cell in a puff of importance. Tshepo didn't move from his bench. The scent of Mr Buswayo's cologne hung in the air.

A day or two passed before Tshepo received a visit from the law firm. He learned they were called Waters, Shabalala and Associates, or WSA for short. The lawyers that came were younger than Winston, probably younger than Tshepo, but they had smart accents and smart clothes. They smelt clean and perfumed, and carried themselves in a way that made them different. He

---

10 go away/ leave

hadn't seen any other fancy lawyers coming in to meet with any of the other prisoners. He felt special.

The young lawyers asked him many questions about the morning of the accident. They even asked him what he was wearing. He couldn't remember and he'd never seen those clothes again. Tshepo also had to explain why he was trying to use a shortcut route that morning. He'd been going a little too fast, but the woman had appeared out of nowhere and then his taxi had just flipped onto its side, and he'd ended up with his leg squashed underneath.

They'd asked him what happened after the accident, and he told them about the screaming woman, and then how the paramedics had needed to use the jaws of life to get him out of the taxi. He told them it was fuzzy after that. He remembered the paramedics talking in the ambulance, but couldn't recall much more. All he knew was that he'd woken up in Victoria hospital to find his leg gone; there wasn't much to report after that.

They also asked him if he knew Claire before the accident.

Tshepo found this an odd question. How would he know her before the accident? What difference would that make anyway? She had found herself in front of his taxi, and that was how they had met.

When they were finished with their questions, they packed away their shiny laptops into their bags, called the officer, smiled reassuringly at Tshepo and left.

'Thank you Tshepo, this will help your case.' They then went on to explain that they'd only come back once more to ask him a few more questions, for clarification.

The next time he saw Winston Buswayo was on TV. Bolted to the opposite wall outside the cells, an old box-shaped TV, housed in its very own cage with poor image quality, blared out the news. It was mostly on SABC 1 or 2, allowing the key-carrying officer the opportunity to watch her favourite mid-morning soapies.

When Tshepo heard the voice, he instantly recognised Winston. There he was on the TV, in his crisp shirt and expensive looking jacket, talking about a case he was working on. Tshepo hadn't been following the news, but from the way Winston spoke, he seemed to know a lot and that his client was going to be free soon. This made Tshepo feel good. That smart and important man was his lawyer too.

Though he'd not seen Tshepo in a long time, Winston was indeed on the case. When he'd first read about the accident in the newspapers, and the resultant social media explosion, he'd seen the opportunity instantly. He'd managed to convince his partners that this was a great probono case. He knew that taxi drivers were under immense pressure to deliver, which resulted in reckless driving. He believed he could show that this had indeed been a case of reckless driving, rather than malicious intent to do harm. The social media onslaught had resulted in people calling for tighter regulations for taxi drivers.

The partners at the firm had been concerned that the case may draw the wrong kind of publicity. However, Winston had convinced them that this was an opportunity to showcase the firm's 'heart'; it would also debunk the myth that, as one of the largest firms in South Africa, they were not just a big business firm. The partners had eventually agreed, and Winston tracked Tshepo down.

He'd visited Tshepo in hospital, a week after the accident. Winston had spoken to the Medical Officer on duty and explained his reason for being there. The MO had been surprised that he was going to take on Tshepo's case, explaining that he would be in hospital for at least four to six weeks for a fractured hip and amputated leg. Winston had gone into the ward to see Tshepo and had found him fast asleep. He could see where the stump of Tshepo's leg ended, making him want to take the case even more. Without his leg, this taxi driver would never drive again. His life was going to be pretty miserable, and Winston could just imagine what prison for a one-legged man would mean.

Winston left Tshepo's bedside without speaking to him, but he knew the case was his. Winston's father had been a taxi boss and, despite his own occupation, he had believed that Winston should have the best education money could buy. Winston had gone to predominantly white, wealthy private boarding schools and studied law at UCT. He had never told anyone who his father was, leaving them instead to their assumptions.

That was why the case had stood out for him. He knew what went on in a taxi rank and in a taxi business.

As Winston left his office and headed towards the basement parking, he thought about the police report from the Dlamini case. He'd learned that, despite the early hour of the accident, there was a witness. Her report was in line with all other statements, however witnesses could be persuaded to revisit their statements. Winston wanted to see exactly where the witness had been standing when she'd seen the accident. Perhaps he could find some holes in her description of the event. There were always holes.

He climbed into his silver Audi A6, throwing his jacket and satchel onto the back seat. He was looking forward to the 45-minute drive to Fish Hoek from Cape Town's CBD. It would give him a chance to think about this case properly. Now that the Hanson case was wrapping up, he could focus his attention on the Dlamini case. 'Ok, Mrs Maureen Klaasen, let's see what you have to say,' he said to himself, as he put his foot on the accelerator and flew down the highway.

Maureen

'He's been gone two weeks now,' said Maureen to Alice, her psychologist. 'I was so glad when he left. He basically shagged me every day before he left, calling me his lucky charm, saying that his luck had turned and it was because of me. He isn't the man I married. It's like I'm some sort of lamp he rubs for luck. I'm not even a real person. It's just horrible, I don't know what to do!' said Maureen, desperation in her face.

Alice breathed deeply, allowing the weight of Maureen's words to fill the room. 'Maureen, I am truly sorry that this is happening to you. Can you try, and I know it's hard, but can you try and unpack how you are feeling?" asked Alice, searching Maureen's face for her first reaction.

'It makes me feel like shit Alice, that's how it makes me feel. I'm so angry with him. How could he do this to me? How could he treat me as his lucky toy when he is in town? I'm a human being with feelings. I hate him!' she shouted. Alice sat back at the outburst.

Maureen had been weepy but controlled up until now. They were making progress and Alice was eager to delve deeper.

'You are really angry Maureen, justifiably so. Now, what are your choices in this situation? Could you remove yourself perhaps?' asked Alice, guiding Maureen forward.

'Well Alice, let me tell you what I have already done. I got hold of the telephone number of one of the wives of Chris's mates, and I called her. We went for coffee and she told me what they do, these husbands of ours. They go to the casino and the race track and any other hole they can find to gamble in. They pass out in their cars in the parking lots of these dumps, then they come home when they can't draw any more money from the ATMs. It's disgusting,' she spat, looking around slightly wild-eyed, before continuing.

'I asked her how she found out, and she said her husband used to gamble and this is what they did. Her husband, who stopped for a while, has started again. It's really bad. She says she sometimes can't even pay the school fees. Thank god we don't have kids,' said Maureen, the horror on her face quickly changing to determination. 'I am going to tell him that it's either the gambling or me. I'm not sticking around to be used,' she said, sitting up straight and wiping her eyes with the back of her hand.

Alice paused, straightening her spine, her thin neck elongating 'This is great. How do you think Chris will respond to your ultimatum?' asked Alice.

Maureen's eyes widened. She hadn't thought that far ahead. She tried to picture Chris's face and she knew then it would be pointless to confront him.

'He will tell me to fuck off and get over myself,' she said, deflated, along with her resolve.

'Besides I don't have enough money yet and haven't worked for years,' said Maureen, the reality of her situation weighing in on her. 'It won't work Alice. I need to come up with another plan,' said Maureen flatly.

Alice gently chewed on her lower lip. 'Yes, perhaps this requires some more thought,' she said. 'Let's meet next week, and perhaps you can focus on envisioning what kind of life you could have without Chris, and what that could look like? Could you do that as some homework?' asked Alice, closing her notebook, indicating the session was over.

'Yes, yes I can Alice. I will do that. Thanks again, and I'll see you next week,' said Maureen as she lifted herself out of the chair and went to reception to pay. She seemed to have a bubble around her head. Everything seemed far away as she paid and walked out of the reception to her Mini. She climbed into her car, closed the door and sat staring at nothing. It all seemed so hopeless. She had nothing, she could go nowhere. She was trapped.

Her mobile beeped loudly, demanding her attention. She glanced at her phone. She had set a reminder about the lawyer's appointment. She had completely forgotten it was also today. She sucked in her breath, shook her head, trying to pop her brain bubble. She turned the keys in the ignition and drove home.

How was she ever going to leave Chris?

The doorbell rang.

'Hello?' she asked, as she picked up the receiver.

'Hi, is that Maureen Klaasen?' asked the voice on the other side of the intercom. 'Yes it is, how can I help you?' she asked tentatively. Although she was expecting the lawyer, she wanted to be certain that whoever she buzzed in, was in fact the Buswayo lawyer from WSA. 'It's Winston Buswayo, Mrs Klaasen, we set up a meeting to discuss the Dlamini case. My secretary contacted you,' came Winston's voice through the intercom.

'Of course, yes, come in Mr Buswayo, just pull the gate when it buzzes,' said Maureen, pressing the intercom button, listening to the familiar click of the gate as it opened. Placing the handset on the hook, she went to the front door and let Winston in. Maureen scanned Winston from head to toe. Tall, dark and handsome, she thought to herself. Slightly taken aback by his confident air, Maureen instinctively drew herself up.

Always in heels, due to her petite frame, she wore a fitted cream dress with a round neckline that revealed her beautiful bosom, but didn't give too much away. Her red high heels made her legs longer and matched the chunky red bracelet on her petite arm. Although the dress was a bit crumpled from sitting in Alice's chair, Maureen's perfectly constructed look took Winston's usually cool demeanor by surprise.

'Hello Mrs Klaasen, I'm Winston,' said Winston formally, extending his smooth hand towards her. 'Please, just call me Maureen,' she responded, taking his hand and shaking it in return.

'Why don't you come in,' she said, realising they were still in the doorway. 'Yes, thank you,' said Winston, still grappling with the stir the gorgeous little redhead was causing.

'Would you like a coffee? I have a Nespresso and can whip up a great cappuccino?' asked Maureen invitingly as she showed Winston to the lounge.

'That would be great, thank you,' said Winston, taking in the interior of the house. In comparison to the non-descript exterior, the inside was exquisite. The open plan layout led straight from the entrance to the view across False Bay. The glassy tiles opened the room up, while the sparse yet elegant furnishings created a calm space that made him want to slump into the couch and take his shoes off. He banished the thought.

'This is a lovely home Mrs, I mean Maureen,' said Winston, taking in every aspect of the lounge, view and stylish kitchen. 'Thanks Winston, we redid it about three years ago. I love restyling spaces. I used to work in corporate events and have an eye for staging a space, you know,' said Maureen, rattling away in an attempt to calm her nerves. She'd never in her life met such a gorgeous man.

'Where did you move from three years ago,' he asked Maureen. Her accent had a slight twang to it that he couldn't place, and curiosity was getting the better of him.

'From Joburg. I grew up in the East Rand, but lived in Sandton mostly once I started working,' she explained, as she came over to him with their coffees and sat opposite him in the lounge.

That explained the twang, Winston concluded, middle-class Joburg mixed with nouveau riche.

'I see,' he responded, before moving on to the reason for his visit.

'As you know, you are the only person who witnessed the accident in which Mr Dlamini, the taxi driver, collided with Miss Southbridge, the female runner. I would like to find out what you saw and if you could also show me where you viewed the accident from please?' asked Winston, carefully watching Maureen's face. He had conquered his initial surprise and was now fully engaged in unearthing anything he could, to help his client. Maureen put her cup down and sat back.

'The police did come and take a statement, and it was all in there. But I can show you where I was standing when I saw it happen. If that helps?' she responded.

'Yes please,' said Winston as they got up and he followed her up the stairs. The landing at the top opened up into a TV room lounge, and a study and two bedrooms peeled off from there. She took him into the large master bedroom, with a king size bed in the centre of the room. The entire bedroom looked as if it had been staged for a House and Leisure magazine article.

There were photos on the dresser: Maureen in a bridal gown, smiling as she was lifted up by a strong looking man with a shaven head. Winston hoped the man, assumedly the husband, wasn't going to come home now and find his gorgeous wife in the bedroom with a another man.

'Is that your husband Maureen?' asked Winston, as nonchalantly as possible.

'Yes, that's Chris. He's away at the moment. He works offshore, but he'll be back in a couple of weeks,' she said, sighing.

Winston couldn't gauge much from her response. 'I see. That must be quite tough for you, on your own for such long stretches,' said Winston, prying.

'Ya, its ok. I have my own life, and I'm a busy bee, so you know, you get used to it,' she responded.

'Tell me, was your husband here the morning you witnessed the accident?' asked Winston, reverting back to the reason he had come here.

She looked at the floor as she sucked in her breath.

'Yes, he was here, but he wasn't home.' She opened the doors to the balcony.

'He only came home later in the morning. He missed the entire thing,' she said, turning away from Winston and walking onto the balcony, framed by the view overlooking the entire False Bay.

'I see,' said Winston. He couldn't help but wonder what that meant, however he couldn't well ask where the husband had been. It bore no relevance to the case and so he had to let it slide. Maureen was now standing on the balcony, looking out across the bay. Winston followed her as she started to recount the morning of the accident.

'I woke up when the wind and rain stopped,' she said staring in front of her. 'I couldn't get back to sleep, so I decided to have a cigarette which I sometimes do, but not a lot, and I came outside here to smoke. The street light there shines across the road. I heard them, the four women. They were chatting as they were running, but I couldn't really hear what they were saying. They came past and were heading down the road. Then I heard that doef-doef sound the taxi music makes. I thought it was from the main road, just below, but it wasn't. This guy came down the hill like a bolt of lightning and took her out. The one with the long blonde hair. She flew up and over and landed over there,' said Maureen, pointing to the opposite side of the road.

'The taxi seemed to lose balance and fell on its side. It turned around a few times and then skidded all the way down the road. See there, you can see where it scratched into the tar,' she said pointing out the scrape marks on the tar road. Winston could see it all very clearly. Too clearly. Tshepo had definitely been going too fast; the hill down towards Maureen's house had added even more speed, making the vehicle's speed probably double the speed limit of the road.

There was however the street light. If the women had run past the street light, and were in a shadow, there was a possibility that Tshepo might not have seen them. At his speed, and with poor visibility, there could be something there to work with.

'Thank you Maureen, I appreciate you recounting this, I hope I haven't upset you?' asked Winston as he noticed Maureen's goose bumps on her arms, despite the warm weather. She held her arms crossed over her chest and shook her head.

'Can you tell me what you did after you witnessed the accident,' asked Winston gently. She continued to stare across the bay, holding her arms more tightly. 'I don't know, it was weird,' she started to explain. 'I went into robot mode. I must have dropped my smoke and run downstairs. I called Valley Medical Response and then went outside. Valley Medical Response were here in a few minutes because they are just down the road. I ran to the two girls standing next to the dead girl. The other one was screaming and shouting at the taxi driver. Then Valley Medical Response came and took over and bundled all the girls into the back of the hospital van. The dead girl was covered. I remember looking at her lying on the floor. The blanket wasn't long enough to cover her; she must have been tall. Her bright takkies stuck out the bottom and her hair was all around her head, sticking out from under the blanket. Anyway, I hadn't realised I was in my lingerie, so a paramedic gave me a blanket, asked me some questions and then sent me back home. That's it I guess,' finished Maureen, looking squarely at Winston.

'Yes, I think that's it. Is Valley Medical Response the local emergency service?' asked Winston.

'Yes, they're just on the main road. Actually, I have one of the guy's numbers. When I took the blanket back he gave me his number to call him if I ever needed anything. Very sweet and all,' she said as she walked back inside. 'I have it somewhere downstairs', she said as she left the room and headed down the stairs. Winston followed her with a final look at the beautiful bedroom. He could almost too easily picture Maureen naked on that enormous bed.

When he got downstairs, Maureen was taking out a business card from a drawer in the kitchen. 'Here you go,' she said, handing him the card. 'Karel Mostert,' said Winston reading the card. 'Thanks Maureen, I think I'll pop in there now, seeing as I'm on this side of Cape Town.'

'Oh, where do you live Winston?' asked Maureen, eager to engage Winston in conversation and keep him in her home for longer, even if just to look at him. 'I live in Vredehoek and work in town. It works for me. You don't get these sorts of views that side though. My apartment has a sea view, but yours is spectacular, almost 270 degrees I'd say,' said Winston, turning to look at the view again.

'Yes it is beautiful, thank you. So do you like being a lawyer?' she asked, immediately realising how silly her question sounded. Of course he liked being a lawyer, why else would he be one she thought to herself.

Winston smiled at the question, but answered kindly. 'I do. I always wanted to be a lawyer. No regrets here. And you, do you like…, what is it you said you did?' he fumbled. She averted her gaze and collected the coffee cups. 'I'm a housewife now but, as I said, I used to be in events. I loved it too. But you know, my husband said I should just relax and stuff. The work was hectic and he said I didn't need to stress myself out so much. But who knows, maybe it would be good to get back into it, you know, if the right thing came along again,' said Maureen, her eyes lighting up as she thought about going back to work.

'Well I'm sure it will, when the time is right of course. I better be going, thanks so much for the coffee and for taking the time to answer my questions. We really appreciate it,' said Winston, as he collected his keys and headed towards the front door.

'No problem Winston, just shout if there is anything else,' said Maureen as she followed him and opened the door.

'Winston', called Maureen, as he was stepping out the house.

'What will happen to your Mr Dlamini, the taxi driver? Is he going to go to jail because he killed that girl? I mean, he killed that girl by mistake,' she said, peering at Winston in the bright sunlight.

'I can't really talk about the case with you Maureen, you are a witness and you will need to come to court to testify. My client, Mr Dlamini, lost one leg as a result of the accident. Whether he goes to jail or not, the man is suffering and will bear this tragedy with him, forever,' said Winston staring into Maureen's eyes. He held her gaze until she looked down.

'I see, that's terrible. I'm sorry about that. Well, goodbye Winston, I suppose I will see you in court, if not before then,' she said looking at him again.

'Yes, see you then,' said Winston, as he turned and walked back to his car.

Winston stripped off his jacket and got into his car. He opened all the car windows to get rid of the heat and turned up the air conditioning. Sighing, he thought about the woman he had just met. He felt intensely attracted to her. As a man used to having anyone he liked, he found it irritating that she made him feel this out of control when he couldn't act on it. Winston had a regular stream of girlfriends, which he kept at arm's length and then got rid of when they became needy, or harassed him over his long work hours.

This woman was different somehow, and he couldn't touch her. It would completely jeopardise the case to become involved with her, never mind the fact that she was married to a Vin Diesel lookalike.

He turned the car on and checked his rearview mirror. There she was, smoking on the balcony, her red hair shining in the sun. He pulled away before he did anything he would regret.

Winston found Valley Medical Response on Main road in Fish Hoek. When Winston asked the lady behind the counter what services Valley Medical Response offered, she explained that it was a private life-support paramedic service that serviced the south peninsula, while she typed up a form and sipped her coffee, all at the same time. He felt exhausted just watching her busy hands and mouth.

'I see, thanks. Can you tell me how I can get hold of one of your paramedics? His name is Karel Mostert,' asked Winston. 'I need to ask him about an accident he assisted on,' he continued. She actually stopped typing and talking and sipping,

'May I ask why? Mr?' she asked with her quirky little eyebrows rising above her spectacles

'Mr Buswayo, I'm from WSA, a law firm. We are investigating the case of the taxi driver who accidentally killed the woman runner. I'm not sure if you are familiar with the case?' said Winston, covering all possible further questions she may ask.

She pursed her thin lips. 'Of course we are familiar with the case Mr Buswayo. Claire was a wonderful woman and part of this community. What happened to her was devastating.' She glared at him, huffed and continued.

'I'll call in the back and see if Karel is in,' she said, her face red with irritation.

She picked up the phone and dialled. 'Hullo Pete, is Karel in the back? Hmhm. Yes, well tell him he needs to come to the front. There is a lawyer here who wants to speak to him about the taxi that killed Claire. Ya, ok. I'll tell him to wait,' she said, and put the phone down.

'Ok, he is coming through. You're lucky he's here today. Take a seat,' she said dismissively, as she resumed her typing and sipping.

Karel eventually appeared: A medium-build man, in his 30s, in a blue jumpsuit. His hair was shaved to about a centimetre of brown bristle, his receding hairline probably the reason for the close shave. Winston stood up and extended his hand towards Karel. Karel smiled broadly and shook Winston's hand enthusiastically.

'Howzit, I'm Karel,' he said.

'Hi, I'm Winston,' he said, taken aback by the friendliness of the man.

'What's up? They said you want to talk about Claire, the girl that got run over by the taxi driver. What's a lawyer like you needing to know about this case?' asked Karel, looking Winston up and down.

'I'm Mr Dlamini's lawyer. He's the taxi driver in this case. My firm WSA is representing him in his upcoming trial. We have taken the case on as a probono client, for free in other words,' explained Winston.

'Oh really,' said Karel, folding his arms across his chest and taking a step backwards.

'Well as I hear it, that guy got what was coming, lost his leg in the crash, and now is a definite for prison. So, not sure what you want with me?' he shrugged.

Winston dug in his suit pocket and withdrew the card Maureen had given him. 'I got your name from Maureen Klaasen, she was the woman who witnessed the accident. I chatted to her earlier and she mentioned that you may be able to provide some insight as to the scene of the accident. She had your card,' said Winston, showing Karel the card. Karel whistled a long low whistle.

'Now that's a hot chick. I can't believe she gave you my card. I was hoping she would call me. Guess not hey,' said Karel taking the card and pocketing it. 'So, what do you want to know?' said Karel, resigning himself to answering the lawyer's questions.

Realising that he wasn't about to be offered a coffee or a private room to discuss the matter with Karel, Winston indicated the waiting room chairs to Karel so they could sit and talk. 'Can you start by describing what you found at the scene when you arrived?' asked Winston.

Karel sat, slouching comfortably and began: 'We were the first ones there, so we cordoned off the area, put up some cones and things. The girl, Claire, was dead, so we covered her up. We pulled the ambulance up in front of the taxi just to make sure the bladdy vultures didn't interfere.' Winston interrupted.

'The vultures?'

'Ya, the tow trucks. They can really mess up an accident scene. So anyway while I was setting up, Venter, my partner on duty, was hauling the rest of the girls into the ambulance. The one had gone ape shit, screaming at the taxi driver while he was bleeding out all over the tar. Once Venter had got them in the ambulance, we tried to get the taxi driver out, but we couldn't get to him. That taxi was closed tight like a sardine can and we needed the jaws of life.

Luckily the fire station guys are also quick off the mark and they were there soon, so they helped us crack open that taxi. Shit there was blood, bladdy everywhere. We managed to get him to the stretcher and had to tourniquet the leg. Got him sort of stable. Venter took over and called another ambulance from False Bay hospital. He said that the guy would die unless they got him to Victoria, there by Wynberg. So the hospital got the helicopter to False Bay. Venter did that whole thing, but basically he saved that taxi driver's fokken life,' finished Karel.

Winston sensed that if this Venter hadn't been around to manage Tshepo's case, Karel here would have been less enthusiastic to save a taxi driver's life. 'I see. Thank you. At which point did you chat to Maureen?' asked Winston.

'You should have seen her. She was in this like lingerie outfit, barefoot. When I asked her what she was doing there, she told me she had seen the whole thing. She was starting to shake so I gave her a blanket. She seemed freaked out but ok. Once the ambulance had taken the other girls and the taxi driver off, I stayed to watch over the body until the Salt River mortuary came to fetch her. Took a while in morning traffic. So I sent Maureen back inside her house. No point her watching a dead body, right?' he said.

Winston nodded his head. 'Ok, well I think that's everything. Do you think it would be possible to chat with Venter?' asked Winston, hoping to finish up the interviews in one go.

'No way brother. Venter only does night shift. You can try and catch him early one morning, at the end of his shift. He doesn't answer his cell when he's off, so ya, guess you gonna have to try make it here at the crack,' laughed Karel, who found the idea of a polished Winston arriving in Fish Hoek at 5am quite ridiculous.

'I'm sure I can make a plan,' said Winston smiling broadly, having had enough of Karel's low grade wit. 'Thank you so much Karel, that's everything. You've been really helpful. Can I just have your card back please. I may need to call you to clarify your version of the event,' said Winston, putting his palm out. Standing up, Karel dug in his pocket and produced the card.

'Ya sure whatever,' he said, handing Winston the card.

'Thanks,' said Winston taking the card, and then offering his hand to shake.

Karel looked at the hand undecided. Then he shook Winston's hand half-heartedly, nodded and walked into the back room. Winston glanced at the secretary, who was neither sipping, talking nor typing, ears pink to their tips from the strain of eavesdropping in on their conversation. 'Thanks, bye.' he said to her as he left.

Awesome Foursome

It was their first supper club since Claire died. Tanya had taken the lead and messaged the girls, insisting they keep up the tradition of a monthly dinner at one of their homes. The last supper had been at Claire's art deco apartment, their favorite spot. Claire's uncluttered, clean taste had created a home that allowed everyone enough space to feel at ease. Although Kate was by far the superior cook amongst them, her garden cottage could feel claustrophobic on hot summer nights.

The fact that Liz lived right above her parents made all the girls nervous, and they tended to laugh softly and drink far less than usual. Tanya's adequate but charmless apartment was good enough, but held no real inspiration. Tanya decided to have the supper at hers, as it was her turn to host after all. They usually met on the last Thursday evening of the month, but due to Tanya's work they'd had to push it out a week. Her PR job often interfered with her life, but in truth, all the girls had been keen to push it out.

A get together would mean having to face the inevitable reality of their missing friend. They knew they were somehow broken, and if they didn't all get together, or do something they used to do as a group of four, they could somehow avoid the realisation they weren't four friends anymore.

They had seen each other one on one over the course of the past few weeks, and of course at the funeral, but they hadn't all been together yet. Secretly they all dreaded the dinner. Tanya told herself it was the right thing to do - to keep things going as before, but her stomach tightened as she whisked the egg whites for the meringues. She'd hardly spoken to Kate. She loved Kate but found her such hard work, and no matter how she tried to make it right in her mind's eye, she couldn't understand why she had to sleep with all these men. She supposed she couldn't blame her. Kate's mother Zelda certainly hadn't been a good example. You would think that Kate would at least see it for herself though. She knew Kate was really smart, so it really didn't add up or make any sense.

Tanya created mini-meringue swirls with perfect peaks on wax paper and placed them on an oven tray. She popped them in the oven and started to set the table. Tristan was showering in their bathroom. She could hear the water running and knew he was just standing there letting it run over his back. After a long day at the workshop, he liked to come home and clean up, which usually involved standing in the shower for ages. He would then scrub himself down and eventually emerge, clean and fresh. Tanya loved the way he looked after he came out of the shower. It was as if his entire day, the fights with car owners, the disappointment of staff who arrived on site drunk or not at all, were washed down the drain.

Nothing stuck to him. Tanya desperately wanted to be like him, able to lose an entire day down the drain. If she had a rough day, it stuck to her. She'd once tried his method, but as she stood in the shower, her head swirled with the things she wished she could have said to her client.

That client had shouted at her over the phone for a good ten minutes. She'd apologised profusely, and then eventually the client had calmed and she'd put the phone down, her ear ringing as the rest of the PR firm stared at her. Tanya stood in the shower for fifteen minutes that night, eventually realising that she was no better than before. She'd then numbed her mind with murder series and chocolate instead.

As she laid the table, Tristan came through. She could smell soap and cologne mingling in the heat of his shower-warmed body. She turned and smiled at him as he came over to her, enveloping her small frame and kissing her completely. She gently drew herself away, 'I need to finish setting the table,' she said a little huskily.

'Where are you going to go?' she asked Tristan. As a result of supper club, Tristan needed to disappear for the evening and return later once the girls were finishing up. Tristan liked to pretend it was a bit of a drag, but he loved knowing he had a free night to go wherever he liked, with whoever he liked.

'I'm going to meet Johnny and the boys at the Glencairn Hotel. It's burger and pint night, or something. So it should be a goodie. Won't be your cooking though babes,' said Tristan, winking at Tanya.

Tanya smiled, pecked him on the cheek and he left.

He confused her. The other evening, he had lost it over dinner; she'd made a macaroni cheese. Simple enough. She'd tried to reduce the amount of béchamel and cheese, to not make it so rich, but it had resulted in a rather dry and tasteless meal. Tristan had thrown his fork down and called her a stingy cow. When she had tried to remedy the situation, he'd told her he was watching soccer and she should leave him alone. The next morning it was as if it had all never happened. She had just put it down to work stress. Taking over the garage was going to be a big step up for Tristan, so it was probably weighing on him.

He had been so easy going when they'd met. Not quite surfer easy going, but relaxed and charming. Safe in his job, confident, and perfect for her. Tanya had bumped into him at a bar in Glencairn, trying to carry three margaritas. She'd miscalculated her step and ended up spilling half of one of the drinks on herself and on his shoe. He'd grinned boyishly at her and bought her a new drink. They'd hit it off, and after a few months decided to move in together, as it was more cost efficient to live together. It just all made sense.

Tanya smiled at the memory of the old Tristan and put the ice bucket and wine out. She took out the meringues (perfect as usual) and then popped in her chicken. Roast chicken and veg, a good fail safe. All she had to do was make the salad, slice the bread and have a shower. The apartment was spotless, so no tidying required. She smiled to herself, it was going to be ok. They were going to be ok. Her and her girls, her and Tristan; it was all going to be ok.

Liz was early. She parked her car in the street and sat waiting for the half hour to go by before she went upstairs to Tanya's apartment. She'd normally have gone in early to catch up with Tanya and help her make the salad, but today she couldn't face it. Being alone with Tanya would be too hard. Tanya could see straight through her, so she needed Kate as a distraction. She just couldn't tell them what she'd done.

Her visit to see the taxi driver hadn't been what she'd expected. As a professional physiotherapist, who dealt with people day in and day out, Liz had developed an ability to remain calm and collected when people got angry from pain, or complained they weren't getting better fast enough, or moaned about the price of a session. Liz was a well-respected and effective sports physio in the area, and the growing outdoor sports following kept her client list full. As a young physio she'd been devastated when people had questioned her treatment or her fees. As she'd gotten older, her resilience and way of dealing with these circumstances improved. She always managed to distance herself from the emotion, and openly discuss the matter from a professional point of view. Her patients appreciated her approach, and it seemed to calm them instantly and bring them back to her the following week, despite the price or the pain she inflicted.

The meeting with Tshepo Dlamini, had however shown her that she wasn't as cool and collected as she thought. Through her physio network she'd heard that the taxi driver was receiving treatment at False Bay Hospital, to help him learn to walk with the one leg and crutches. His injuries had been severe from the accident, and she found out that he'd nearly died from blood loss. If it hadn't been for the helicopter trip to Victoria over the mountain, he probably would have died.

Liz had felt a sick sort of satisfaction from knowing that the taxi driver had nearly died, and now he had only one leg for the rest of his life. She'd smirked at the news and, in her head, told herself that he deserved it. She'd wanted to tell him to his miserable face that he'd killed Claire and was now going to suffer for the rest of his life. In her imagination, she'd played the scene out perfectly: she would walk in strong and confident, and then she would face him and tell him off. Once she had created this vision of justice, she found out which physio she could convince to take her to him. The physio student had been an easy win; the girl was eager to please Liz.

When the day came to visit Tshepo, Liz was ready. She wanted to see him absorb the horror of what he'd done, and she would be the one to show it to him. When she'd seen him, her anger and strength had evaporated. Before her was a miserable, sad human being, with skin grey and sallow, body thin and deflated, and one leg a stump.

The fact that he'd been driving the taxi that killed her beloved Claire hadn't made her angry, it had made her devastatingly sad. She saw that this man had not wanted to kill Claire. He had just been driving his taxi in the wrong place, too fast at the wrong time, and now his life was a mess.

Liz knew he would go to prison, the state had charged the man. What was to become of this cripple in the prison system? As she had looked at him, the words she spoke had tumbled out of her mouth. She'd felt angry and then sad, and then horrified at her feeling of pity for this man. When her eyes had spilled their frustrated tears, she'd been grateful to Jenny for leading her away.

Once she got back to her car, her tears turned into great sobs and she sat in her car for ages trying to calm down. With a blotchy red face and puffy eyes, she'd gone for a long drive to try and settle her skin. If her mother saw her, she wouldn't let it slide until she told her what she'd done. Her mother would be horrified at her 'unethical practice' and would never have understood the reasoning. This time mother didn't need to know.

Now she had to face Tanya and Kate. How could she not tell them that she had seen him. They had been there too. They were just as involved as she was. What would she tell them? Would they also want to see him? What if they had wanted to see him too, and she had just gone ahead without them? She was distraught that she had forgotten all about them in her crusade to take the taxi driver on personally. It had been all about her, and it had blown up in her face. As she leant her head onto her steering wheel, she felt pathetic; what a mess she had made.

There was a tapping against her car window. Liz jumped and looked to see what it was. It was just Kate. Kate tilted her head to the side and mouthed 'Are you ok? Should we go up?' to which Liz nodded her head, grabbed the wine and her handbag, yanked the keys out of the ignition and climbed out of the car.

Kate hugged Liz firmly. 'Are you ok Lizzie?' she said, concern on her face.

'Ya,' sighed Liz, 'I'm fine I guess,' she lied. 'Long day and week, that's all. Just feeling sensitive,' she continued. 'How are you Kate?' asked Liz, instinctively turning the tables on Kate.

'I'm fine. You know, same old same old. Been busy at the deli, slowly getting into summer and so more and more people are starting to come in,' said Kate nonchalantly. She hooked her arm through Liz's and they walked up together.

Liz had always relied on Kate for extra strength. There was something unbreakable about Kate. As if she had more give in her personality, which allowed her to bend more and absorb less. Liz turned and looked at Kate. She noticed Kate seemed a little less sunny and tanned, and she had bags under her eyes. She assumed that Kate was taking Claire's death badly, as they all were, and that her coping mechanism was less sleep and more sex, or something like that.

Kate felt Liz's eyes on her and turned her head to her; Liz smiled a slow sad smile.

They ambled up to Tanya's apartment, choosing to take the two flights of stairs. They didn't need to talk, as they both slunk back into their own thoughts.

Tanya's doorbell rang across her apartment. She had just put the finishing touches to the salad and placed the bowl on the neatly set table. She threw her apron into the laundry bag and answered the door. An awkward three-way hug took place in the doorway, as the girls tried to hold onto each other whilst clutching handbags and wine bottles.

Once they let go, they all walked into the apartment and the small open plan kitchen. Bags were dumped on the couch, along with spare jackets and scarves, and the first bottle of wine was chosen to be opened. Kate and Liz seated themselves at the bar stools looking into the kitchen, while Tanya brought out some dips and crudité.

'Better than chips guys,' she said, as though she was doing them a health service.

'Thanks' said Kate, I'm starving. 'I think I am finally over the deli food. I just can't stomach working and eating in the same place anymore. Weird, but it's getting to me,' she said, as she dug into the dip with her carrot stick, crunching loudly.

'So, how are you guys?' said Tanya with effort.

Kate and Liz were quiet. Kate chose another carrot stick and shoved more dip into her mouth so she couldn't speak; she nodded at Tanya to acknowledge her question. Liz burst into tears, jumbling her words between sobs. Her eyes streamed as she shoved her hair behind her ears over and over again, her face becoming red and blotchy.

She told them about how she'd gone to see the taxi driver, how it had all fallen apart, and how she hated herself for feeling sorry for him. Finally she breathed deeply and said, 'and I miss Claire so so much. God it hurts every single day. I'm so confused guys. I don't know what's going on.'

Tanya and Kate sat frozen stiff in their chairs. Liz's erratic outburst, her confession and her open sadness, assaulted them. They were shocked and unprepared. 'I need more wine,' said Tanya, and she grabbed another bottle and filled her oversized wine glass to the top. She gulped a long thirsty sip and then looked at Liz.

'You went and snuck into False Bay Hospital and met the guy who killed Claire. Is that what you're saying?' asked Tanya, almost unable to grasp the lunacy of the act and the outburst.

Kate straightened up and stopped shoving carrots into her mouth. She put her hand on Liz's and said 'Liz, are you ok, are you sure you did this. This doesn't sound like you at all?' Liz picked up her wine glass and emptied it, before standing up and pacing the length of the small apartment lounge. 'Guys, that's what I did,' she said, as she began to feel more in control and less burdened now that she had shared her secret. She stopped pacing and faced Tanya and Kate. 'Yes, I did go and see Tshepo Dlamini, the taxi driver who accidentally killed Claire. He is now a cripple, lost a leg in the accident, and he is stuffed because he is going to go to prison,' she stated as a matter of fact. 'He is an amputee,' she said quietly.

'What were you expecting to get from him Liz? He is a murderer. He deserves everything that's coming his way. He is lucky to be alive. I personally wouldn't feel sorry for him, but if that's how you feel... What can I say, you always feel sorry for the underdog,' said Tanya accusingly.

Liz's face fell and her shoulders slumped, and she flopped onto the couch. Tanya watched Liz deflate. 'Sorry Lizzie, I'm not cross, it's just we see things differently and that's ok you know. I mean, well done for going to see him if that's what you wanted to do; I mean that's good. But I can't feel sorry for him, after what he did. I want to see him in prison,' said Tanya, trying to backtrack, but only making it worse.

Kate stood up and went to Liz. Sitting next to her, she placed her arm around her shoulder.

'Lizzie, Lizzie. Don't worry. You were so brave to go and see him,' said Kate, taking Liz by the shoulders and looking her in the eye. 'Tan's right, you're a real softie. I personally don't know how to feel about this guy, what's his name, Tshepo? If you feel sorry for him, that's how you feel. That's cool. He stuffed up in a big way and now look at his life prospects. I suppose I feel bad for him too. One bad decision and everything is now a fuck up. It happens,' said Kate, knowing all too well how it did happen.

Tanya came around the counter 'I'm sorry Lizzie, I didn't mean to get agro; you know I get so hot headed quickly. I'm so sorry' said Tanya, 'I also miss our Claire so much. I have these moments when I'm so on it, and then like a wave I'm a mess, and I lose it completely.' She rubbed her hand through her hair, then fetched their three wine glasses and another bottle of wine

'Let's catch up guys. Liz has offloaded and now it's my turn.' Tanya poured more wine.

Tanya took a long sip, sighed and allowed herself to unbundle the thoughts from her well-organised mind. As if she were standing at a bookshelf, grabbing books and throwing them behind her, she unpacked her thoughts to find a way to stop from going crazy. 'I detest my work,' she began, as she told Kate and Liz in detail about her work. A life they barely understood, and only ever witnessed the consequences thereof. She told them about the long hours, the events she had to attend, the press releases she had to construct and derive, and the pressure she was constantly under in order to meet one or other clients' deadline.

She told them about the snide, derogatory comments from her colleagues to do with where she lived, how she dressed, how she spoke. Basically anything to try and rile her and get a reaction from her. She managed to keep it together most of the time, but this meant that when she came home, she lost it on the smallest things, constantly.

'But Tan, why are they such bitches to you? I don't understand,' asked Liz, who couldn't imagine a place like this on earth.

'My boss. Basically they hate me because of her. She treats us all like mechanical Barbie dolls. We are told what to do and we do it, and look good of course. "We are in PR girls", is what she says to us. So I just happen to do it better than all the others, and this annoys them because then I get the big accounts. That's how it goes. The lazy, slack bitches then get the small accounts with the nowhere brands. This gives them more time to think of ways to undermine me, and actually get in my way. It's revolting!' spat Tanya.

Kate was shaking her head in horror, raising her eyebrows: 'Tan, you have to leave, this sort of work is going to kill your spirit. Surely you can move? I mean you're a great writer, you could freelance or something?'

Kate had always admired Tanya's organisational skills, writing ability and overall togetherness. She couldn't believe that she had landed up in this viper's nest of women who were slowly destroying her.

'Shit, I really want to. But I have good clients, and there is a big project that we just won which I want to see through. Then I'll start looking. Trust me, I can't do this much longer,' said Tanya, rather unconvincingly.

Liz had the sad notion that Tanya wasn't going to actually leave, and it was as though she hadn't even thought about it.

'Ok, enough of me, sorry I just couldn't keep it to myself any longer. Claire used to listen to most of it. But, you know,' trailed off Tanya. 'Let me get dinner out, hope I haven't dried the chicken to biltong,' she said, as she got up and headed into the kitchen. She shouted over her shoulder 'What's up with you Katie? How's your life?'

Kate smiled a wry smile. So like Tanya to steal the floor with her drama, and then flippantly ask you about your life, as if she were asking you what the weather would be tomorrow.

'Fine. All good I guess. As I said to Liz earlier, deli business is picking up, so we are busier in the day. Pretty same old though, but I'm experimenting with some new recipes and that's keeping me entertained,' said Kate.

'Is that all that's keeping you entertained Kate?' said Liz with a naughty grin and one eyebrow raised. 'Oh come on Liz, seriously,' said Kate in a huff of pretense, trying desperately to hide the sick feeling that Liz may know about her and James.

'You come on Kate, you look tired. I was just wondering if the young surfer had been visiting again?' said Liz, always keen to egg Kate on and glean more dirty stories from her.

'I'm not listening to this,' shouted Tanya from the kitchen, although it was hard not to. 'Tell me!' whispered Liz insistently to Kate.

'Seriously guys, and you can listen Tan. I have decided to, well you know, behave,' said Kate. Liz's face was frozen in a smirk. 'What do you mean, behave?' asked Liz.

'Well, it was weird. The other day one of my "kissing peripherals" popped into the deli after his surf and started to ask what time I was closing up so he could pop over. Anyway, as charmed as I was, I was totally not interested. In fact, as he was talking I saw straight past him and read the yoga poster on the wall behind him. So I told him I had taken up yoga and was busy. I didn't even realise the words were out my mouth. It was so crazy. So after work I went to yoga. I haven't been in ages. Remember when I went through my vegan yoga phase with that guy, what was his name? Sky, that's it. Anyway, so I went to the class that night and it just felt so right. I am even thinking of doing the teacher training too,' said Kate. She was resolute, her face determined.

Liz's mouth hung open. 'This is terrible. No, you can't possibly give up rampant sex for something like yoga. I won't have it. Tan doesn't talk about sex and I don't get any. That leaves you, and now you're on a sex sabbatical. I'm devastated,' stated Liz in horror.

Kate laughed out loud. Blushing, she hadn't realised that her sex exploits were important for Liz's fantasy life. 'Go get some of your own for pete's sake, or I'll set you up with someone if you want?' said Kate, once she'd stopped laughing.

Her eyes were even watering. It felt so good to laugh. She hadn't laughed in ages. Ever since the time with James, she had tried to bury all emotions deep within herself. She wanted to feel nothing. She wanted to forget that afternoon had ever happened, that she had slept with the man so deeply in love with her dead friend. She wanted to forget how the guilt on his face had made him pull away from her as if she had leprosy. Had she disgusted him? She felt disgusted by herself.

She remembered standing in the shower washing herself over and over, convinced she could still smell him on her, even after she had climbed out of the shower. Even if the conversation in her head led her to believe that, as two consenting adults, they could have sex with whoever they liked, there had been a breaking of an unwritten law, and they both knew it. This thinking often resulted in her becoming bitterly angry with James. How could he have taken the first step. How could he have played with her like this? Maybe he was a philanderer and had actually been sleeping around behind Claire's back for all these years. He had so casually walked away from her, maybe it was what he did all the time?

The regret, the disgust, the anger, the sadness, and the misery of the whole situation tortured Kate late into every evening. She had even taken to sleeping on the couch. It was as though her bed was tainted. Then, without warning, as she was daydreaming, a sneaky feeling of hot, raw passion would tug at her heart. She'd think of James and their most magical afternoon together, and how he was possibly the most wonderful guy she'd ever met. Then she would shut it down, cover it up, close the box and walk away from the moment. She wasn't allowed to think about it. It was forbidden and it didn't exist.

The sad emptiness, that always came after she thought about James, filled her again. She wiped at her eyes and realised that Liz was watching her. 'Are you sure YOU are ok? You totally spaced out for a minute?' asked Liz.

'I'm really fine, tired, you know and sad. That's why I decided to do the yoga course actually. It covers all the chakras and is actually the only thing that helps me sleep. So that's my plan, I'm going to unblock my chakras and sleep better basically,' said Kate with a smile, desperately working on changing the subject.

Liz took the bait and dropped her inquiry. Tanya brought the dinner to the table and the girls sat down, hungry. The rest of the evening went smoothly and easily. Claire's empty chair was ignored, and they had managed to open up as they used to when Claire had been there, sharing their joys and fears. Well except for Kate, whose secret was too much like a live wire that would burn anyone who touched it.

Kate took her dirty secret and buried it deep in her heart and listened intently to what her friends had to say. As the evening drew to a close, Liz and Kate collected their bags.

'Say hi to Trist for us,' said Liz. 'Where does he go when we come here? Not like Fish Hoek is a buzz of activity at night!' stated Liz.

'He goes out with his mates. Tonight he said he was going to the Glencairn Hotel or something. Think they get very excited when he gets to go out without me, so they go big. He'll probably only be back after one am,' said Tanya, as though this was the usual.

'Ok, well, say hi anyway,' said Liz.

The women hugged each other, and Liz and Kate walked down the stairs to their cars.

'It's weird you know,' said Liz, almost to herself as she was getting into the car, Kate standing holding the door. 'What's weird?' asked Kate, curious to hear Liz's latest slice of insight into life.

'Tan's so organised and rigid about everything in her life, except for him, except for Tristan. It's like he can do whatever he likes. She has a blind spot when it comes to him. I mean, he's a nice guy and all, but I don't know, they just don't seem to gel. Do you get what I mean?' said Liz to Kate.

Kate grew a wry smile across her beautiful lips. 'Yes, I get what you mean Lizzie. I guess you can't control everything hey?' said Kate.

'Night night Liz,' said Kate, as she gave Liz a peck on the cheek and walked to her car.

Dear sweet Lizzie, thought Kate to herself. In her own linear fashion, she had great depth of perception when it came to relationships. Kate would be wise to remember this.

James

James woke up with a pounding headache. He lifted his head and realised he wasn't home. Fuck, he thought to himself. Where am I? He groaned, dropping his head back into the pillow. The room swayed. He closed his eyes, his stomach groaning in self-pity, as he tasted fermented alcohol mixed with stomach juice. He pushed himself up gently so that he didn't have to taste the previous evening, rising in the back of his throat, any longer. He swallowed the feeling of nausea as the swaying stopped. His memory began to kick in.

He had gone home with Amber.

After winning their biggest pitch to date, they had decided to celebrate and go big. It had started at the agency bar with the whole team. After a couple of rounds of beers and tequilas, they'd decided to move to a bar in town with an open rooftop. People stood under the night sky, peering over the roofs of smaller buildings and looking at taller ones. It was a Friday night and the place had been packed. They'd continued drinking until someone had suggested another move to a club, shedding a few more of the team, until it was just James and Amber left, keeping the party going.

Amber was James's junior account manager. She was a real gem and made his life so much easier. She just got advertising and was organised. She also had a knack for sweet talking the designers to push her work through the system, so she always met deadlines with ease. She was going to do really well in the industry.

James realised he was naked, and he could see both their clothes scattered all over the floor. He rubbed his face with his hands, trying to pull the memory of what had happened out of his brain. He groaned softly.

How had he managed to do this? He'd really overstepped this time. He liked Amber, she was a great girl; but she was more than ten years younger than him, and he knew she admired him and looked up to him. He had abused his position. He gently closed his eyes and let his head drop back against the bed's headboard. This was an almighty stuff up, he thought to himself, as his stomach revolted against the abuse he'd handed out the previous evening.

'James?' came Amber's voice hesitantly through James's brain fog. James sat up straight, the room swaying slightly again.

'Woa' said James, as he saw Amber standing against her bedroom door. Her dark chocolate brown hair, usually tied in a neat high pony at the back of her head, now fell down onto her shoulders. Her dark blue eyes were clear and concerned. She wore a strappy top over her full breasts and soft cotton shorts. She was small and delicious to look at, with short, well-proportioned legs.

'So, do you want some coffee?' she asked uncertainly. 'I'll just go grab some downstairs, they make great coffee.' She watched his every move.

James smiled weakly, 'Ya, that'll be great, thanks. Do you have a disprin? My head is killing me,' he said running his hands through his hair.

'Sure,' she said, as she walked through the room to the en-suite bathroom and came back with a foil pack and glass of water.

'I'm just going to grab my coat and boots and head down, see you in five,' she said, as she walked out of the room.

James waited for the sound of the apartment door to close, and then busied himself with opening two extra strength disprins. After he'd glugged the water like a thirsty dog, he wondered what to do next... He briefly contemplated dressing quickly and leaving before she got back. But he had no clue how to get out of the building, because he actually couldn't remember entering it.

He started to pick up his clothes on the floor. Amber's pale blue bra and g-string were also lying on the floor. He picked them up too. They were pretty. An image flashed in his mind as he remembered pulling the underwear off her. Her young full breasts rising and falling as she'd stared at him with big excited eyes. He closed his eyes.

They'd definitely had sex.

Shit.

He put the underwear on a chair, threw his clothes on the bed and decided to shower and clean up before she got back.

Amber stood in the queue of her local hipster coffee shop. Her long hair hid her face, her long bulky jacket hid her pyjamas and her soft fluffy boots kept her feet warm. The queue opened up.

'Hey Amber, what you having today? The usual?' said creepy Jim, his pockmarked face hidden under a less-than-ample wannabe beard. His small watery eyes twinkled against his almost translucent skin. She shivered at the sight of him, and his snake tongue licking his cracked lips.

'Just two caps and two croissants,' said Amber dismissively.

'Two of everything, you thirsty and hungry today huh?' pried creepy Jim.

'Ya, that's right. How much?' said Amber desperate to get out from under creepy Jim's scrutiny.

His jealousy was starting to change his pale skin to a light green. 'Well, was nice to see you last night anyway. Didn't know you went to Apocalypse. I'm always there, so maybe check you there next time,' he said as he handed her the change, winking at her.

Amber shivered and then remembered she'd seen creepy Jim at the club. Who else had been there? It had been James and her and one or two others. Thank goodness she hadn't been on her own with James. She remembered talking to creepy Jim. She must have been so hammered, because she could barely order coffee from him from over a counter without being grossed out. She moved to the corner of the shop, cringing and looking down at her boots; she really hoped she hadn't hugged creepy Jim or anything.

Her order was eventually called. She grabbed the coffee and croissants and went back to the apartment. A part of her wondered if James would still be there. She was so worried about how he would react; he had been so different since Claire had died. He spent hours at work, drowning himself in it. He had also taken to partying with the creatives. This meant he was often terribly hung over at least twice a week, mid-week. He was on a self-destruct mission and it was scary to watch. She had always adored James. He had taken her under his wing and taught her how things worked in the agency. He was amazing with clients and the more she went to meetings with him, the more she was able to emulate his style. All the long hours together plus last night's thrill of winning, bolstered by an enormous amount of alcohol, had led to sex.

She would never have hit on James, ever, but his hands had been all over her, in an overly-friendly kind of way. When everyone else had gone home, she had kissed him and said, 'come home with me.'

He hadn't needed to reply. Her stomach fluttered as she remembered the great drunk sex they had last night. He was great in bed. She had never slept with a guy over 30. Sex with James was mind blowing and she wasn't sure she could ever sleep with a 20-something-year-old ever again. She wasn't going to think about what was going to happen next with James, she was just going to have coffee with him and take it from there.

When she opened the front door James was sitting on the couch. He wore his clothes from the night before. He smelt clean with a whiff of old cigarette smoke from the clothes. He smiled at her, but his eyes were unconvincing.

'Here you go, coffee and croissant,' said Amber brightly.

'Thanks Ambs,' said James as he sipped the coffee. It was perfect.

'Good hey,' she said sweetly.

'Perfect, thanks,' said James as he tugged at his croissant. The silence between them lingered.

'Listen Amber,' began James. 'Thanks for, you know, um, looking after me last night. It was a really cool evening,' he shifted uneasily on his chair, the words evading his foggy mind. 'It really was great, but… look, I'm a bit of a mess at the moment, you know? This was a good thing but well…shit, I don't know what I'm trying to say,' said James eventually.

She could see straight through him and felt a stab of pain in her heart. 'No stress James. You're right. It was a cool evening and thanks for coming over. No sweat. We'll leave it at that. No expectations right. Totally cool with that,' she said, as though consensual one-night stands with colleagues were a norm in her life.

She knew the drill. She had seen herself try and say what James was unable to verbalise, and she had heard it said to her before. She stayed cool and calm while she died inside, her pretense holding up.

'Ok cool,' said James, relieved. He was so obvious. Part of his charm Amber thought to herself.

'Um, thanks for the coffee,' said James as he finished up his coffee and croissant. He grabbed his phone and wallet and looked at Amber, desperately trying to decide how to say goodbye to her. He half halted and eventually bent down and hugged her while she stayed seated.

'Ok, bye Ambs. I'll see you Monday. Let myself out, ok, bye,' he said as he walked out.

He closed the door behind him, took a few steps and then leaned against the cool wall of the passage. He sighed. This was a monumental mistake.

As James turned the key to his apartment, he could hear the soft patter of little cat paws running towards the door. Arora's bell on her collar tinkled like a fairy. He looked down and there she was, the sweetest Siamese with big sparkly blue eyes. She rubbed and meowed her way in and out of his legs.

'You're going to trip me you silly cat,' said James kindly, as he tried to not fall over her. He closed the door behind him, slid down onto the floor and looked at Arora. She meowed at him some more and continued to slither in and around his calves.

'Hey girl. You missed me huh? You're probably starving right, and your poop box is certainly all full up.'

He picked her up and held her close scratching her head.

'Ya, I get it, things have definitely gone bad since our Claire left us. Pretty shit hey,' said James, his voice morose.

He continued to pat and stroke Arora as he zoned out. Arora eventually struggled out of his hold and meowed at him to follow her.

'Ok, ok girl. You need food, I'm coming,' said James. He dumped his wallet and now dead phone on the lounge coffee table, and went through to the kitchen.

Sure enough, poor Arora had a drop of water and no food. 'Shame baby, this is bad. Can't believe Clairey left you to me. Guess she knew I would need someone to look after to keep me on the straight and narrow. Weird hey how she just knew stuff. Here you go,' said James, as he put fresh water and food down for the starving cat.

Arora purred loudly as she gobbled her food. As James stood up, he looked around the apartment and saw it clearly for the first time in weeks.

There were dirty dishes in the sink, the counters were a bit grotty with bits of old food stuck to them and coffee cup marks. Claire's beloved orchids were dying on the window sill.

In a burst of fury and rage, James walked to the orchids and grabbed one, hurling it to the floor. 'Aaargh!' he screamed and then grabbed the next and the next until the kitchen floor was littered with broken ceramic orchid pots, sand and twisted orchid roots. James collapsed to the floor and tried to put the pots back together. 'Dammit Claire, damn you for leaving me here when you know I need you,' he whimpered. He mumbled words to Claire, and eventually left the pots, slouching back against the kitchen cupboards.

Arora returned to the kitchen. She had bolted when the first pot had hit the floor. She gently approached James and purred her bravest purr, rubbing against his arm. 'I know girl. It's a fuck up and I need to clean up. I'll pull it together, I promise I will,' he said to the little cat.

James spent the whole of Saturday cleaning the apartment. The simple activities of cleaning kept his hands busy, while his mind fought the alcohol-induced regret and blues. He eventually climbed into the shower and stood under the water for half an hour. He couldn't rid himself of the guilt. Things would never be the same with Amber. When he came out he eventually felt as though he was awake, for the first time in weeks. He made himself a strong cup of tea and sat on the couch to watch a rugby game. At half time he remembered his phone and decided to plug it in to charge. He also noticed the neat pile of mail he'd made on the kitchen table. He sat down to go through it all: Most of it was bills and junk mail, but there was one letter written by hand with his name on it.

'To Mr James,' it said in childish script. He opened the letter, curious to find out who it was from. It was a letter from the school in Masi where Claire had worked. They were going to be holding a ceremony in honour of Claire. With the donation they'd received from her insurance, they'd managed to purchase and furnish two additional classrooms. They were holding the class opening ceremony on Monday, and asked James to be their guest of honour.

James wanted to throw the invitation away, but he knew that Claire would have been so happy with this development at the school. He had to go.

He stacked the bills and threw the junk mail in recycling. He felt like it never ended. The continuous reminder of how amazing Claire, and life with her, had been. It was as though she was still here, pushing him to keep going and do the right thing, when all he really wanted to do was to lose himself in his pain and misery.

On Monday morning James called his boss to let her know he would be in late. He explained what was happening at the school. She had been annoyed but allowed it, since she was still enjoying the compliments from their big win.

'You may have to put in half day's leave James. But we can discuss that when you get in later,' she said coldly.

He'd called the school early to tell them he was coming to the ceremony, and Mam Tsolo had been thrilled. James had smiled when he'd heard her sweet excited voice over the phone.

'Ooooo Mr James,' she had sung 'we are so happy you can come. That Claire, she was a wonderful woman, neh. This is very wonderful. We will see you at 11. Bye bye Mr James,' she had said in her jubilant voice.

James arrived at the school and was allowed to park inside with the teachers' cars. The gate to the school was locked and managed by a small man with one bad eye. His broken English indicated to James that they were expecting him, and that he was to park inside because he was a very important visitor.

James could see that the school was brimming with excitement. The children who weren't in class were collecting rubbish around the school grounds, slowly and lethargically, as only young adults are able to. The staff had set up a gazebo with a PA system, a tangled collection of cables running from the main building to the gazebo, resulting in a microphone and single speaker. The table, with a flapping white table cloth, had a small posy of flowers and a large pair of scissors on it.

Further down the length of the building, James could see the two new classrooms. They were prefabricated and sat on concrete slabs. The walls of the classes were painted light blue on the bottom half and white above that; they gleamed in the mid-morning sun. Mam Tsolo spotted James and came running out of the building.

'Mr James, you are here, this is very wonderful,' she beamed. 'Come and sit here under the gazebo and then we will start.'

'It is very exciting Mr James. That Claire, she was a wonderful lady,' said Mam Tsolo, as she hustled James under the gazebo and sat him in the front row of chairs. Mam Tsolo bustled off, her small, round body moving quickly.

James was once again left alone, but noticed that the staff were now arriving and seating themselves under the gazebo too. Soon, everyone was in position.

Mam Tsolo returned and took centre stage:

'Today, we are going to be opening up the classrooms that Miss Claire donated. She used to work here with us, but the good Lord has taken her to be with him. We are very sad that Miss Claire is no longer here with us, but the Lord works in mysterious ways as we all know,' said Mam Tsolo, her eyebrows rising as she peered at her staff.

'Hmhm,' came a resounding response from the staff complement behind James.

'Miss Claire, she came to our school many years ago and has helped many of our children to become excellent scholars. She worked with the children, and with me and my staff. Not once did she say a bad thing about anybody. She was a good woman. Even in her death, Miss Claire has continued to give to us. That driver who killed her will be punished by our Lord God the Saviour, for what he has done,' preached Mam Tsolo to all under the gazebo.

She extended her arms out to James. 'Here sits Mr James, the boyfriend of Miss Claire. A lone man now. He is here to be a part of our school. This is now his home, as it was the home of Miss Claire. You are always welcome here Mr James,' said Mam Tsolo, with a kind yet insistent look on her face.

James nodded his head vigorously and mumbled 'Thank you Mam Tsolo.'

'Now the choir will sing before we cut the ribbon,' said Mam Tsolo and she turned and walked out from under the gazebo to stand in front of four rows of children, who all stood patiently in the sun waiting to sing. Mam Tsolo was not only the Deputy Mistress but also the choir conductor it seemed. In an elaborate display of Mam Tsolo's arms, the children began to sing.

The choir had chosen the biblical song 'Morning has broken', and as the harmonies of their voices filled the air, James scanned over each child's beautiful happy face, and acknowledged why Claire had chosen to work at this school. He remembered how she would rattle off names of various children and how she would beam with pride to see the progress in her students.

With a theatrical flourish of arms outstretched and thumb and index fingers pinched together, the song concluded at Mam Tsolo's command. She turned to the gazebo and bowed, to which the gazebo burst into enthusiastic clapping and ululating. Mam Tsolo then walked to the table and raised the oversized scissors like a sword, announcing that they were going to the new classrooms to cut the ribbon. A number of staff members were now positioned to take photos on their mobiles as James and Mam Tsolo each put a hand into the scissors and ceremoniously cut the red ribbon between the two classrooms.

After many smiles and photos with various staff members, James was invited to have tea and biscuits in the staff room. He knew Mam Tsolo was expecting him to stay, so he didn't rush off to his office. Instead he allowed himself to sip his lukewarm tea from a slightly chipped white government-issue teacup, and nibble on a Baker's biscuit.

When the teachers began to disperse, James was able to begin his exit too. Mam Tsolo gave him an enormous hug.

'You must come back and visit Mr James. You are a part of our school now, you know,' said Mam Tsolo, reminding James that he couldn't forget this part of his life with Claire; she would be reminding him no doubt.

'Of course Mam, I will pop in,' he said kindly.

'Good, good Mr James. Let me walk you to your car,' she said and walked with James to the car park.

As they approached the car, a woman dressed in a red, white and black sarong with braided hair and beading on her arms and legs was standing at his car. 'Who is that?' asked James to Mam Tsolo.

'She is the Sangoma. We cannot keep her out of the property. If she wants to come in, we cannot stop her. You never know, she may put a spell on the school,' she said matter-of-factly.

'I see,' said James, raising his eyebrows remembering the speech Mam Tsolo had given, with reference to Lord God the Saviour. Yet the Sangoma still held power, despite the Good Lord.

James stopped in his tracks as he saw the Sangoma pointing at him. In a loud voice, speaking slowly and calmly but with intensity and purpose in her mother tongue, she spoke to James. Once she stopped she looked at Mam Tsolo, indicating with a wave of her hand that she should translate.

'She says I must tell you what she has said,' Mam Tsolo translated, as she looked at the floor, clearly unwilling to continue.

'Sure. Tell me what she said. Please Mam,' said James willing her on.

'She says, the girl with the long white hair, she means Claire, she says she came to her before she died. Claire wanted to learn about the speaking of the witch doctors, because the one boy she saw said he struggled to speak because his ancestors had taken his speech. Claire wanted to find out if the Sangoma could help the boy because she couldn't,' translated Mam Tsolo, now looking intently at James's face.

His confusion rippled across his eyes. Clearly he had never heard this story before. The Sangoma continued. She gesticulated and Mam Tsolo watched her intently. Once the Sangoma had stopped talking she translated again.

'Mr James, while Claire was at the Sangoma she was told her story. The Sangoma threw her bones for Claire. The Sangoma saw that Claire would pass to another life. She told Claire to prepare because her time would be short and she must be ready to leave this place, this life.' Mam Tsolo shook her head, looking at the floor.

'I'm so sorry Mr James. Claire told me she was going to see the Sangoma, but she never told me this. Please Mr James, do not be angry at us. The school, we didn't know anything,' said Mam Tsolo as she nervously looked at James.

James felt dizzy, sick. He held onto Mam Tsolo's shoulder.

Claire had known she was going to die.

He reeled. He had so many questions. 'Does the Sangoma speak English? I need to speak to her Mam,' said James, gently squeezing her shoulder and looking into her eyes. A small droplet of sweat emerged from Mam Tsolo's hairline.

She placed her hand gently on his. She breathed out.

'She does, but she does not like to. I will ask her if she can see you now and if she can speak to you in English,' said Mam Tsolo, easily switching to Xhosa as she turned to the Sangoma.

The Sangoma stood motionless, looking away from Mam Tsolo, as though not listening to her. Mam Tsolo finished, and they waited.

With a wave of her hand, the Sangoma spoke to James directly: 'Come, we go now,' before turning and walking out of the gate, past the gatekeeper who stared in wonder with his one good eye.

James followed on foot. The Sangoma lead James down a concrete road that eventually turned to dust. They passed a mixture of crumbling houses, shacks and containers. They entered the gate of a small free-standing house. A township dog, chained to the door of the house curled its lips as they passed, its large eyes watching them intently.

At the back of the yard were two shacks. The first was bolted closed, but the second was open. The Sangoma walked in and James followed. He blinked his eyes to adjust to the dark interior of the shack. It was mostly empty, except for shelves littered with various roots and bottles along the one side, and it smelt of herbs and old fire. On the other side of the shack, the Sangoma was already seated on the floor with the mat spread in front of her. 'Sit' she said to James, pointing to the space opposite her on the floor. James sat down.

'Speak," she stated. The questions ran through James's head.

Should he ask her how she knew Claire would die, did it matter now anyway? Should he ask her what Claire hadn't told him about their meeting? Should he ask her why she had come to find him? Eventually he heard himself say.

'I am lost without Claire. I don't know what to do. Tell me what I must do?' he asked.

The Sangoma hummed as she reached to the left of her. In a shallow basket lay bones, wood, shells and other items he couldn't decipher. She rattled the items in the basket and mumbled words he didn't understand. She threw the bones on the floor and gently touched some of the artifacts. Eventually drawing herself up, she looked at James carefully, as though seeing him for the first time.

'You must go,' she said.

James couldn't believe it. He had just got here. What was she on about? He sat straight and stared back at her.

'You must go to see the world. You must travel to other places. You do not belong here now. You must find a new life that makes you happy. This work you do does not make you happy. You must go to other places,' she explained. James was relieved, but before he could ask questions she continued. 'But you will come back to your family. You will come to your family when you have travelled enough. They are waiting here for you,' she stated.

Then she gathered the bones and turned her back to him. They were done.

'Thank you,' said James awkwardly as he removed himself from the shack. His eyes squinted in the sun as he stepped out into the day. He walked back to the school, retracing his steps, in a haze of words he didn't understand.

James got into his car. Ten messages on his phone demanded his attention. He scrolled through them, then sent a message to his boss and told her he wasn't coming in after all. He would take a day's leave, then he switched off his phone and drove home.

He needed to think about what the Sangoma had said, but he didn't know what it meant. So he went for a run along the main road that hugs the coastline from Fish Hoek to Simon's Town. As his legs pounded against the pavement, the words of the Sangoma echoed in his mind. As far as he could tell, she had been telling him to leave Fish Hoek and Cape Town and travel the world.

That was insane. How could he leave and travel the world? He had to pay bills, he had a job he was committed to, and he had a freakin cat to look after. How could he possibly just up and leave? Maybe the Sangoma had been right about Claire, but he thought she had maybe lost her touch with him.

The heat of the afternoon, combined with his lack of regular exercise and recent spout of heavy drinking, made his body pour with sweat. His mind however raced on, and he drove his body hard to stop the questions he didn't have answers to.

By the time he got home his shirt was dripping and he felt nauseous. He went up to the apartment and drank hungrily from the kitchen tap, gulping the water to relieve his parched body. He sat at the kitchen table and decided to catch up on his messages before he showered. He switched his phone on. More WhatsApp and text messages pinged through. One message was a phone call. Who left voice messages anymore?

He decided to listen to the message first. An older woman, who sounded as if she had definitely done her fair share of cigarette smoking, explained that she was a rental agent in the area. As the summer season was approaching, they were looking for apartments to rent to overseas visitors for the season. They had James's details on file from a few years back, when he and Claire had let out the apartment, and so wanted to check if he was interested. He actually couldn't believe what he was hearing. He listened to her again and wrote down her name and number. He hadn't thought about that. He could rent the apartment, leave his job and finance his travels using the rental. He actually could do that. Maybe the Sangoma wasn't that wayward, maybe she was right yet again?

One thing continued to bother him: He hadn't understood what she had meant about coming home to his family. His brother lived in Johannesburg and he saw his parents occasionally, but they weren't a close family by any stretch. It was a strange statement and he couldn't figure it out.

Depression, Reflection and Loneliness

Stage 4

A long period of sad reflection overtakes a person and the magnitude of the loss sets in.

Chapter 4

Tshepo

On some days the cell seemed adequate. On other days the bars and grey concrete walls closed in on him. Breathless, Tshepo would huddle in the corner on the floor until he passed out from the feeling of asphyxiation. The medicine from the Dr Naidoo had long since run out.

The stump of a leg became stronger and less sensitive to the touch, and he'd push his finger into it to find areas on the edge with no feeling. When the walls didn't bend in to squash him, he practised hopping from one side of the cell to the other without crutches. He still hoped that he would get the prosthesis from Jenny.

'Don't forget me Jenny,' he called aloud, his voice echoing across the cells. A prostitute whistled back at him. He couldn't even be bothered to respond to her. Stupid slut.

Shaking his head, he sat down on the bench on the other side of the cell. It was all so pointless. He couldn't shake it, this feeling. It was a black hole of nothing that sucked him in. It lived inside him and when he closed his eyes, he felt as though his entire being was falling into itself. Sometime he fought to stay out of the black hole, and other times he let himself be swallowed up. It sucked all feelings away and he felt nothing. No desire, no fear, just nothing.

He stared down at the floor and found himself thinking about his childhood: The hours walking to and from school along the hills of the Eastern Cape, bunking and hiding behind the shebeen until one of the old men chased them away. His childhood seemed like a distant fantasy. How had he ended up here, first as a taxi driver in Masi, and now as a cripple in jail? Why had he left home when life had been simpler there?

He closed his eyes and rested the back of his head against the wall.

His mother.

She'd told him to go to his cousin in Cape Town. She needed more money to look after his sister's children. It had worked out at first. He'd got the job with the Boss, and had sent his mother money every month. Now she was stranded:

'What have you done my son? You have killed a person. This is a very bad mistake you have made this time. You leave us while you eat and rot in jail, and we have nothing but a government grant to survive. What will we do Tshepo, tell me what will we do?' she'd pleaded. He had been unable to answer her.

He could no longer provide for his family, he was useless and alone. So alone, that he hadn't even felt the caress of a human hand since he'd been in this place. Food was shoved along the floor, metal tin scraping along concrete; no one came into the cell. His so-called friends had forgotten him and carried on with their lives. Now that he was here, he had not seen or heard from Boetie. He was probably too scared to visit him in jail, in case the policemen checked his vehicle for fines. Desmond, the Boss man's muscles had also not visited. This was a relief, but it meant that even the Boss man had given up on him. He wondered what had happened to the few belongings he owned in his shack in Masi. After all this time, he was certain his landlord had taken his goods as final payment, and rented the shack out to someone else. He looked across to the other cell. Was he like those hopeless sluts and tsotsis? No, he was just a flea-riddled scrap of a dog that nobody wanted.

'Mr Dlamini,' said a voice interrupting his thoughts.

Winston Buswayo stood outside the gate. The warden busied himself with the noisy lock and let him in, the gate clanging after him.

Tshepo slowly sat up straight and looked at Winston. He had come back. 'Hello Mr Buswayo,' he said.

Winston walked over to Tshepo and sat next to him, the waft of his cologne enveloping him in its rich scent. Winston put his arm around Tshepo's shoulder. 'Mr Dlamini,' he said, 'I have come to speak to you about your trial.' Tshepo's body tingled at human touch. Did this cheese-boy care about him?

Tshepo turned to look Winston in the eye. His sallow skin and ketotic breath assaulted Winston, who carefully let go of Tshepo and sat back to explain.

'We go to trial in the next few days and you must be prepared. I want to explain how things will work. Ok?' asked Winston.

Tshepo continued to look at Winston and eventually replied. 'Yes, tell me what is going to happen to me Mr Buswayo.'

Winston stood up, hands in his pockets, and in three large strides he paced to the other side of the cell. He turned and looked down at Tshepo. The man had become even thinner. He was unkempt and smelt stale. He'd seen this before: clients who lost hope of winning a case would often become depressed and begin to wallow in self- pity. It was common and didn't usually help the case. However, in Tshepo's case, thought Winston, it could work in his favour. He decided to change tact on a hunch.

'I see you're not feeling well my brother, am I right?' asked Winston, the concern on his face concealing his calculated plan.

'Yes, yes Mr Buswayo. I feel very bad and lonely here in this place, and I have run out of medicine from Dr Naidoo who liked to talk to me,' said Tshepo, hands resting on his thighs. Winston stretched out his hand and placed it on Tshepo's bony slumped shoulder.

'I see. Did this Dr Naidoo give you antidepressants?' asked Winston. He could feel the excitement of his new plan materialising.

'Yes, that is what she called it. They ran out two weeks ago and these police, they don't care. They do not listen to my worries, and they do not tell me what is happening.' Tshepo was shaking his head as the tears began to run down his cheeks.

'I will help you Tshepo, you must trust me. I have a new plan. We will ask the court for a psychiatric assessment. I think you are suffering from depression, because you are very sad for what has happened,' said Winston softly.

'Yes, yes Mr Buswayo, I am so sad for killing that lady, and this leg of mine. It is so very horrible to look at,' mumbled Tshepo, his face wet with tears.

'Ok Tshepo, we will ask the court and then you can go to a better place, possibly Lentegeur Psychiatric Hospital, and they will look after you there, see?' said Winston.

'Yes Mr Buswayo please, this is a bad place. I am so sorry, it is all so bad,' said Tshepo through his tears.

Winston stood up in front of Tshepo. 'I will see you in two days, do not worry.'

Tshepo felt slightly relieved as he wiped at his face with the palm of his hands. After all these days in his cell, he was finally going to leave. He grabbed Winston's thigh and sobbed into his suit trousers.

'Thank you Mr Buswayo. You are saving me, you are saving me,' he whimpered. Winston awkwardly patted the back of the man's back, desperately trying to control the feeling of sick rising in his throat, along with the shame of feeling disgust at being so close to this human wretch.

Winston eventually prised himself out of Tshepo's grip and retreated out of the cell.

'Just two more days Mr Dlamini, and then we will see the judge and try and make things better for you,' he promised.

A bleary-eyed Tshepo sat in his human cage, staring at the back of his departing lawyer.

Outside the station, Winston breathed in a gulp of fresh air and got into the car. He dialled his secretary, as there was no time to waste.

'Marilize, listen, I need you to tell the associates they need to prep the paperwork for Tuesday for Mr Dlamini. We need to brief the advocate that we are going to be claiming that the client is unfit to stand trial, and we are angling for a psychiatric assessment for Mr Dlamini. I've just seen him, he's a mess and this could work for a lesser sentence or even none.' He took a breath. 'Ok, got it. Great, I'll see you now; I'm on my way in from Simon's Town.'

As Winston drove back along the beach road towards Fish Hoek, he couldn't help but marvel at the sheer beauty of the coastline; ocean on his right, mountains on his left. Glencairn was dotted with houses down the valley and the small beach was inviting and calm. As he rounded the corner into Fish Hoek, Winston found himself wondering how Maureen was doing. After visiting her at her home, there hadn't been any real reason to contact her again. Her testimony added up. Despite that, he couldn't quite get her out of his mind and the thought of stopping at her house, right this instant, was very tempting. That was, until he realised he had no good reason to re-interview the main witness, unless he wanted to be called in for questionable behaviour. He knew that there was something between them. He hadn't imagined it, but until this case was over, there was no way he would be able to find out. That said, there was a definite concern around the gladiator-looking husband in her wedding photos. Just thinking about encountering a man like that sent a cold shiver down Winston's spine. He turned the radio on to try and distract himself from thoughts of Maureen.

At the office Winston breezed in, confident that his new approach would set the case on an entirely new trajectory. His hope was for an opportunity to place Tshepo in a facility that could deal with his disability, physically, and now mentally. This would look fantastic for the firm in the media. Strutting down the passage towards his office, the head of HR caught his eye and stepped in front of him.

'Winston, so glad to see you, I wanted to chat to you. You mentioned that you had met a woman who you thought may be a great addition to our events team?' she said, smiling to encourage the memory of their discussion.

'Aaah, yes. I do remember. Her name is Maureen Klaasen. Seems like she really knows her stuff,' he said, then added:

'One thing though, she is a witness in a case coming up for trial, although I can't see a problem in meeting her in the interim, just to see if she is what you are looking for. It's not like she is going to change her statement or anything.' He paused in thought. 'I'll send through her details, meet her and then you decide,' said Winston nonchalantly, as though the thought of seeing Maureen didn't make his manhood stand up in public.

'Sure, ok. Could be complicated,' said the HR Director. She twisted her mouth at the corner as she thought. 'But let me chat to her and we can take it from there. Send me those details via email,' she said unconvinced.

'Will do,' said Winston, feeling like he was the cat who'd got the cream. Things were about to get really interesting.

Maureen

The taxi was hurtling towards her. Her body was frozen and she couldn't move out of the way. The taxi was so close she could see the face of the driver. It was Chris; he was laughing loudly and shouting at her, white knuckles gripping the wheel and a look of insane wild intent. Just before she was swallowed by the taxi, she woke up. Sweat made the hair at the base of her scalp wet, and her nightie clung to her damp skin between her breasts and stomach. It had been so real, too real. Her breathing was loud and her heart raced. She sat up.

She got out of bed, trying to find the night stand in the dark. Where was she? She felt panic rising. Her memory kicked in, reminding her that she was at her mother's house in Johannesburg. She felt her way to the bathroom and switched on the bright light. Her eyes blinked, and she squinted as they adjusted to the glare. In the mirror, a pale woman looked back at her, wide-eyed with wild red hair.

'You are fine Maureen, it's all ok. It was just a dream,' she reassured her reflection.

Everything was going to be ok. He wouldn't come to Joburg. She turned on the tap and splashed her face with the cool water, and then slowly wiped her face dry with the hand towel. Sitting on the fur-covered toilet seat Maureen whispered to herself.

'Fuck, I can't do this,' staring between her legs at the pink tiles on the floor, elbows digging into her thighs, with her head in her hands.

'What am I doing?' she continued speaking to herself, desperate to find an answer in the floor tiles. The floor tiles didn't answer.

Maureen's mother had called her just before Chris was due to come back to Fish Hoek. Mother had sprained her wrist in a fall, and in her usual hypochondriacal manner had described, in aching detail, how hard it was to wash, eat and drive. In fact, any task was impossible with a sprained wrist. Maureen had oohed and aahed in all the right places throughout the conversation, while walking around the house, watering plants and plumping her couch cushions. At one point in the long conversation she stood in front of the fridge and looked at the calendar. For the first time that week she realised that Chris was due back in three days.

Her blood had run cold, and her mother's voice had become white noise. She couldn't face him, she couldn't see him. She needed more time to figure out what she was going to do next.

'Ma, would you like me to come and help you for a bit? Take care of you because you are hurt so bad?' she said without thinking it through carefully.

'Ag my darling, that would be wonderful. Yes, I would love to see you and you could really help me,' said Maureen's mother, who no doubt enjoyed the thought of bossing her daughter around for a few days.

'Great, I'll organise it right away, see you tomorrow Ma. Don't want you to have to stress for another day!' she said with conviction.

She hung up, grabbed her tablet and booked a flight to Johannesburg. She followed the booking with a quick email and WhatsApp message to Chris, explaining the dire situation her mother was in and how she had to go and help her. It had all come together. Now Maureen just hoped that she would be able to come up with a good reason to stay at her mother's for more than two weeks. Chris knew that more than two weeks at Maureen's mother would send her to the loony bin, and Chris was back for four weeks, but hopefully something else would come up. Worst case she would have to go home and spend two weeks with him. Worst case.

Chris had responded to Maureen's WhatsApp. Maureen could almost hear him say it: 'Ag for fuck's sake baby, I bet she waited for me to be coming home to fall. Shit, well, you better go and help her out. Try come home as soon as you can. You know I miss you and need you, my lucky charm.'

She felt sick at the mention of her being a 'lucky charm'. Her groin tightened at the thought of him using her vagina as a gambling honeypot, which was what he really meant. Well not this time, she promised herself. This time she wasn't going to be used.

Maureen packed a large suitcase of her favourite clothes and shoes, plus some gym clothes. She scrabbled in the back of her cupboard for her cigarettes and added those in too. She knew she would need them to deal with her mother. She closed the suitcase and sat on the bed, looking around at her life. A beautiful room, full of things and frozen moments in frames, but it was empty and sad. It felt hollow to be here alone, with the tainted feeling of fear etched into everything he owned. It was like he owned her too.

So here she was, in her mother's Edenvale home in Johannesburg. You basically couldn't get more middle class than this life. She hated being in her mother's home. She felt herself instantly revert to her sixteen-year-old self, with her mother at the helm of her life, driving her own agenda.

The house felt smaller than usual, and it hadn't changed since Maureen had lived there twenty years ago. Her old room was the same as it was when she'd left home. Kurt Cobain and Pearl Jam looked down at her as she returned to her bed and put the bedside light on.

She leaned against her bedroom wall and shivered. The nightmare had terrified her.

Chris had called her when he arrived home. She had almost felt sorry for him. He had spoken to her so kindly. Arriving home to an empty house must have been hard for him. He was spoilt and had been used to finding his sexy wife at home, ready to open her heart and legs to him as he walked in the door. Now, all he found was a list of instructions on how to work the Nespresso machine, a fridge full of food and a chocolate on his bed pillow.

He had sounded genuinely upset not to see her, and Maureen had started to wonder what she was doing in Johannesburg in her mother's house. Maybe his last visit had been a one off. Maybe he had just been having a bad time, and wanted to make it up to her. She felt so confused. Chris loved her; he always told her he loved her. In an attempt to get some perspective she had called Alice's offices the previous day.

The receptionist nearly laughed at her, as if the mere thought of speaking to a therapist over the phone was totally bizarre.

'You can send her an email, she will respond to that,' she said.

Maureen wrote to Alice and described the conversation she'd had with Chris. She explained how guilty and horrible she had felt about 'running away' from him when he'd come home. Once she had sent the mail, she reread it.

Her heart had sunk. Who was this person who couldn't understand her own feelings? Maureen had always trusted her gut and instinctively knew what to do next. It was what had made her great at her events jobs. She was quick on her feet and solution driven.

Alice's email pinged through that evening, while Maureen had been sitting watching some mundane cop and pathologist combo series on DSTV with her mother. She'd mumbled some excuse to her mother, and gone to her old room to read the mail carefully.

Dear Maureen,

I understand you are confused. This is a natural side effect of making any drastic change in our lives. When we step out of our normal routine and behave differently, we experience new and sometimes uncomfortable emotions. Do not be alarmed, allow yourself to experience these emotions, and try to write them down each day.

*Describe exactly what you are feeling and why you think you
are feeling this way. Know that the emotions you experienced
and the way you felt after Chris left last time, were true. Do not
deny yourself the certainty of the situation you experienced or the
emotions. Trust yourself.*

Warm Regards,

Alice

Maureen could hear Alice's well-paced voice reading the words to her. It helped, and she felt less confused. She *had* experienced a terrible tragedy during Chris's last visit, and Chris *had* behaved weirdly too. That was real. But maybe it had just been a freak occurrence and maybe Chris had sorted himself out and things would go back to normal. Maybe she just needed to go back to Fish Hoek and chat to him. It had been a big misunderstanding, and the trauma of the accident had blown it all out of proportion.

The past few days at her mother's passed by rather uneventfully. Her mother bossed her around the house, making numerous demands of Maureen, all in the name of her wrist. One afternoon, in an attempt to deflect her mother's attention, Maureen decided to take her mother to Eastgate mall on a shopping trip. Of course this had led to a series of problems as her mother needed her hair done, before deciding on suitable shoes. Maureen found herself playing the role of squire, offering Cinderella six different pairs of shoes to find the perfect fit.

Eventually they agreed on a pair of dark red heels and made their way to the door. As they stepped outside, they saw a man waiting at the gate. They couldn't quite see who it was and Maureen shouted out 'Hello, can we help you?' in an attempt to assess who he was.

'Hey baby, it's me!'

It was Chris's voice.

Maureen froze. For a moment the image of her nightmare flashed before her eyes, a crazed Chris driving towards her with insane glee.

'What you bladdy standing at the gate like a criminal for Chris?' she heard her mother's voice say. 'We are about to head to Eastgate, you gonna come?' she asked.

'Jeez baby, you surprised me. What you doing in Jozi?' said Maureen. Her voice was calm, despite her heart thumping in her ear.

She walked quickly and with purpose to the gate. 'Let me open for you,' she said, fiddling with the large bunch of keys her mother had handed her.

Chris breathed heavily through the bars and whispered, 'fuck baby, you look so hot. I could shag you right here.'

Maureen looked straight at him as he grinned devilishly at her. She found herself aroused, her heart beating faster. 'Shhh Chris, my mother can hear everything,' she hissed.

He entered the gate and drew Maureen into him, kissing her longingly. When he had indulged himself completely, he pulled her away from him, almost tossing her aside as he strode towards his mother-in-law. 'Mom, so awesome to see you,' he said with mild warmth. He hugged her and stood back looking at her.

'You look good. Sorry to hear about the hand,' he said as he spied the bandaged wrist. Before she could respond, he continued.

'I'm glad I caught you ladies. Come here baby,' he gestured to Maureen to join him on the landing outside the front door. He pulled her next to him, his arm enveloping her small waist. 'You see, I have a surprise for Maureen. I booked us a two-week holiday in Sun City. Some sun and fun, a bit of Pilanesberg nature reserve, and maybe a bit of a flutter in the casino,' he said, grinning like a Cheshire cat from ear to ear.

Sun City! She loved Sun City, and a two-week break would be amazing. But why now, she wondered.

Seeing Maureen's puzzled look, Chris continued.

'Aw baby, I know last time I was here it was so hectic, so I thought we could get away. Seeing as you are here already, and I fly out from Jozi anyway, we could spend the last two weeks of my break on a real holiday. It's a winner, right?' he said, bowling her questions out of the way with his absolute certainty.

Maureen's mother interjected; 'So Prince Charming, are you taking her this instant or can I still go with my daughter to Eastgate?' she asked flatly.

'Ag Mom, sorry man, but I need to take my baby now. It's two hours and we need to check in and all that. You know how it is. Sorry man, but you have had her for two weeks,' said Chris. He smiled sweetly, head cocked to one side.

'Fine, go then,' she said. 'Maureen, just lock the door and leave the keys with the neighbour. I'm still going shopping, even though it will destroy my wrist to drive. Go ahead you two, go have a blast,' she said over her shoulder, as she rapidly descended the front steps, climbed in her car and reversed out the drive.

Maureen turned to look at Chris. His eyes were warm and she felt her mistrust dissipate.

'I'm sorry baby, last time was a cock up. But we have now. Live in the now, you know. I love you baby, you're my person,' he said, reassuring her.

Maureen jumped into Chris's arms.

'I've missed you,' she said into his neck.

Holding her off the ground, Chris walked inside the house. Once inside, he kicked the front door closed behind him and put her down. Maureen drew his head to her, kissing him deeply and intently, drawing her body closely into his. She did love this man. He was a good man; it had all been a misunderstanding. She held his face in her hands and looked into his eyes.

'I love you too baby,' she said.

Taking his hand, she led him to her teenage bedroom where they had coming home sex under the watchful gaze of Kurt Cobain and Pearl Jam.

The two weeks at Sun City involved lying on beach loungers, sipping cocktails, eating meals at restaurants and wandering the gardens of the Lost City on warm windless evenings. Chris seemed to have a far better hold on his gambling, sticking to gambling in the evenings and spending the days snoozing in the sun by the pool.

Maureen preferred to stay out of the casino and had ventured in only once. She'd told Chris she wanted to know what games he played. Perhaps if she showed an interest, she would get more of his attention. He'd lit up and gone into a full description of his lucky table and favourite chair. He had taken her to his poker table and she stood behind him, watching over his shoulder, trying to figure out how the game worked.

If she asked a question, Chris hushed her and glared at her. At one point in the evening a young woman, eighteen or nineteen years old at most, had walked up to the table and smiled at Chris, raising her hand up alongside her young lithe body and waving at him in a coy manner, fingers curling in, one by one. Chris sat straight when he saw her and probably said hello too. Maureen couldn't tell because she was behind him, so she leaned into his ear and asked who she was.

'One of the high rollers' daughters. Shame, think she is bored. She wanders around the floor all night. We got chatting the one night. She's ok.' Chris had whispered out the corner of his mouth to her, and then looked down at his cards again, indicating that the explanation was over.

Maureen hadn't gone back into the casino since. Truth be told, the casino gave her the creeps. It was gaudier than she remembered. Mirrored walls along the passages, morose people slouched over the tables and blank-faced croupiers. She hated the sight of the roulette table as the croupier raked thousands of rands' worth of chips into the mouth of the table. Punters with dead-pan faces around the table, eyes glued to the chips as they were dragged away, disbelieving they'd lost a sure thing.

She preferred to stick to Sun City by day - the pools of sparkling blue water, the long forest walks and the gym. To her, the casino wasn't even there. Chris however spent his evenings, from when Maureen went to bed till early in the morning, in the casino.

It didn't bother Maureen. She was used to sleeping alone. Occasionally she would get up early in the morning and go for a run and swim. She loved the cool, crisp morning air, before it became too hot. The hotels and roads were all quiet and the whole complex seemed to breathe easy before the next round of guests got up and started their day. Only the staff bustled to and fro, preparing, fixing and organising.

On their last morning at Sun City, Maureen and Chris would return to Johannesburg International Airport, where she'd catch a flight back to Cape Town and he'd catch his flight back to work.

Maureen had packed the night before, still feeling a little anxious about making her flight on time. She'd slept fitfully, realising that Chris still wasn't back at 5:30am. He always pushed his luck and he was going to be exhausted for his flight back to work. Maureen decided to go for a run, to help her wake up properly and get rid of the gnawing feeling in her stomach.

She dressed and tied her hair up in a high pony, swishing her red hair along the tops of her shoulders. Gently opening the door, so as not to wake any of the other guests, she stepped into the passage.

She could hear her heart beating in her ears again. A few rooms down, Chris was standing half inside another room. She blinked to look again. Yes it was him, engrossed with whoever was in the room. Maureen stepped back into the alcove of the doorway and peered down the passage.

He was smiling, his shirt over his shoulder and his shoes in his free hand. He was pulled into the room and disappeared for a second. Maureen nearly stepped forward, but he began to slowly re-emerge moving backwards.

He slowly drew a woman out of the room. First her arms, then her long brown hair and then her entire body.

It was the young girl from the casino. She was naked and wrapped herself in Chris's arms. She drew his face to hers and kissed him.

Maureen carefully turned and let herself back into her room. She closed the door behind her and leaned against it. The beating in her ears got louder.

She began to breathe heavily and loudly. He'd be coming down the passage soon, so she quickly went into the bathroom and locked the door. Still unable to control her breathing, she sucked in air, pushed it out and her chest tightened.

She heard the bedroom door open. Her breathing stopped and she stared at the locked bathroom door.

'Maureen?' she heard him call. 'Hey baby, are you in the loo?' he said. The seconds ticked loudly in her head.

Her voice responded. 'Hey baby, you must be shattered. I'm just getting ready to go for a quick run. Catch some sleep and I'll see you at breakfast.' She surprised herself with her own voice and how steady it sounded.

'Thanks baby, I'm bushed,' he said, and she heard him fall on the bed.

She flushed the unused toilet and washed her hands. Breathing in deeply, she opened the door. She couldn't look at him and went straight from the bathroom into the hotel passage. She closed the door and looked down the passage, convinced she would see them there again. But all the doors were closed. She was alone.

If it hadn't been her husband involved in the scene, she would have thought it quite romantic. But it had been her husband, and he had obviously enjoyed an evening of fucking an eighteen-year-old. Chris was nearly forty. Asshole. Maureen's face set with determination as she began to walk down the passage.

Room 205 was the child seductress.

She carried on walking until her legs started running. Maureen ran down to reception and out of the hotel to the entrance of the complex and back. Then she ran the length of the Gary Player golf course and kept on running until her legs no longer moved. She walked back to her room, exhausted.

Robotically, she let herself into the room. She showered, got dressed and went to breakfast. Chris eventually arrived and was his usual charming self.

'You ok baby?' he asked her as they packed the bags into the hire car. 'Ya, just sad. We've had such a great time here. I'm sad to be leaving this magical place and you're off again. It feels so short,' she said, putting on her saddest face.

'Ag baby, you're such a softy,' he said, falling for her charade. 'In four short weeks I'll see you again.' He swung the last bag into the car, slammed the boot and hugged her to him.

Her skin crawled.

She pretended to sleep for the entire trip to the airport and luckily had to check in immediately. They hugged and he kissed her. She did her best to kiss him back, but she felt her chest squeeze as he stuck his tongue into her mouth.

'I'll miss you baby. You're the best,' he said as he looked into her eyes. She smiled a shy smile.

'Thanks baby, see you soon,' she said, and she turned and walked through to security. She looked over her shoulder as she entered the queue to the gates. He was standing there, grinning at her. He gave her a wink and turned towards international departures. She watched him walk away. He had no idea she knew. The fear and disgust rose from her belly... the man she married was a gambler and a philanderer.

Awesome Foursome

Liz watched from her practice window as her patient climbed into his navy Audi. His calf sprain was healing nicely, and after a few more sessions she knew he would be able to complete his training, and make it to the Iron Man Triathlon.

Her mind drifted. She'd never imagined that she would be someone who fixed recreational athletes, so they could spend all their time and money away from their families, fighting their bodies to perform great feats. She sighed.

'Liz? Are you ok?' asked Jane the receptionist.

'Hmm?' breathed Liz, as she realised where she was and looked at Jane.

'I was wondering if you are ok? You seemed to drift off for a while,' noted Jane, her eyebrows crinkling. Jane was a young seventeen-year-old who had taken a gap year after leaving school. She was saving money to get to London. She was intelligent and kind. Liz loved having her around and dreaded the thought of having to find a new receptionist at the end of the year, when Jane would leave to go on her adventure.

'I'm ok,' said Liz. 'I, well I am feeling down. I think about Claire a lot. Then all I want to do is call her and chat like we used to, because she always knew how to sort stuff out. She really got me, you know,' she said, slumping down into one of the waiting room chairs before continuing.

'And then I remember. I can't speak to her anymore. She isn't here, and then, I feel crappy again,' said Liz, not realising the weight of her confession.

'Oh,' said Jane softly. 'Maybe you should, you know, go and see a counsellor or something? My mom went and saw someone - a nice lady on the other side of the mountain. It really helped my mom when my dad left. It was someone for her to talk to. Maybe that's all you need, you know, someone to listen,' said Jane. She chose her words carefully and spoke slowly. Liz didn't answer Jane for a while.

Her usual instinct would have been to shut the offer of help right down. She had her folks to talk to. Yet, they just didn't seem to cut it these days. She needed someone who got what she was going through, and who could give advice beyond her parents' limited view.

Jane waited patiently.

Liz stood up. 'Ya, maybe you're right Jane. Why not hey? I could try out this counsellor at least once, and see what it's like? No pressure right?' said Liz, in an attempt to make it sound as if she were making an appointment to have her nails done.

'Exactly,' affirmed Jane. 'No strings. I'll message you her number tonight and you can make the appointment,' said Jane, relieved that she hadn't overstepped the boundary with her boss.

Two weeks later, Liz found herself seated in a sparsely decorated room. She sat in one of two bucket chairs, with a small table in between them and a box of tissues the only decoration on the table. Across from her sat the psychologist. She was a slight woman, white blonde with glasses.

Liz felt panic rise up from her belly to her throat. What on earth was she doing here? She was completely fine, she was coping. She went to work every day and she did her job. She ate, she didn't drink heavily or take drugs, and she didn't even have a boyfriend to complain about. Basically she was a model citizen - perfectly normal. This was ridiculous; she totally didn't need to be here. She opened her mouth to tell the shrink she was leaving, but before the words could come out, Alice interrupted her.

'Liz, am I correct?' asked the psychologist.

Liz closed her mouth and sat back. 'Um, yes' said Liz, avoiding eye contact.

'Great. So Liz, it says you haven't ever been to a psychologist before, however I see you are a physiotherapist, and so must have done some psychology at university, is that correct?' asked the psychologist.

'That's right' said Liz, clinging to something she knew about 'Yes, we all had to do Psych one, but that was ages ago,' said Liz. She smiled nervously.

'Of course,' said the psychologist referring to her notes, primarily made up of the forms Liz had filled in earlier.

'Now tell me Liz, what has brought you here?' asked the psychologist.

The panic rose in Liz again, and before she could stop herself she launched into a tirade. 'I don't know why I'm here. Why does anyone come here? It was my secretary's stupid idea because she thinks I'm losing it, because I stare out of the window and wonder why I am doing what I do. I mean, it's ok for me to think about that every now and then, everyone has doubts and it's not like

I'm the first. Besides, what do you expect? I mean, my best friend was killed by a taxi driver a few months back, right in front of me. I'm allowed to be morose and upset. Why do I have to be ok with anything? It's all so flipping pointless anyway, isn't it?' said Liz, her voice slightly raised, and arms and hands flapping wildly.

The psychologist looked back at Liz, breathing carefully.

'Liz, you said quite a lot of things there that I would like to unpack, if you don't mind. To help me understand better, can you tell me more about your friend who was, as you said "killed by a taxi driver" please?' asked the psychologist, gently opening Liz's mind.

Liz sat back into the chair; her panicked outburst had left her deflated.

The words slowly tumbled out. She hadn't really explained the accident to anyone, not in detail. Not how Claire had looked when she was dead on the ground, or how life felt so vacuous now that Claire was gone. Liz cried repeatedly.

When she was finished, a pile of tissues lay on her lap; her face was blotchy, and she had red-rimmed eyes and wet eyelashes.

'Liz, you've been incredibly brave to come here and tell me about this traumatic event. Your young secretary is wise. What you have been through is severe, and you will find yourself re-evaluating your life and everything you do. We will work together to help you learn more about where you want to go with your life. You don't need to feel freaked out by being here. Be gentle with yourself. Ok?' she said, tilting her head to one side. Liz nodded.

'I'd like you to come back in two weeks?' asked the psychologist. Liz agreed and mumbled a thank you as she walked out of the office. She looked at the floor and went straight to the reception desk to pay.

She heard the psychologist's door open again. As she looked back to see if perhaps she'd forgotten something, she saw that she was just calling the next patient. The psychologist smiled and signalled to a woman with red hair, who was petite with large breasts. She was beautifully dressed and seemed to glide towards the psychologist. She looked so familiar, but Liz couldn't place her.

Liz finished paying her bill and set up her next appointment.

'Ok lovey, Alice will see you in one week. Alright then, bye,' said the receptionist as Liz walked out of Alice's offices.

As she got into her car, the image of the woman in her lingerie, standing and talking to the paramedics came into her mind. It was her. The woman who had just walked into Alice's office was the same woman who had seen the accident. Liz jumped out of her car and ran back into Alice's rooms.

'You forget something lovey?' asked the receptionist as Liz came in.

'No, I, I have to speak to the woman with Alice,' said Liz, taking a step towards Alice's closed door. The receptionist shot up, placing herself almost instantly between the door and Liz.

'Sorry my girl, but you can't go in now, see. You can sit here in the office and wait for her to come out. She will be done in an hour ok. But you can't go in,' she said, her body a wall between Liz and the door.

Liz backed off and walked out of the office and straight back to her car. She'd left the door open with the key in the ignition, so was somewhat relieved that her car was still there.

She slumped back in her car and locked the doors. It was just too bizarre. Liz remembered the papers talking about a witness, but she'd just never realised who the witness was. That woman had been a part of it too; she had seen everything happen. Maybe her life had been affected too, like Tshepo's? It hadn't just been Tanya and Kate and herself. There had been so many people who had been affected by Claire's death: James, Claire's parents, Claire's school, the children she'd taught, this woman, Tshepo and all their families. The enormity of this accident and its impact on so many lives hit Liz like a slap across the back of her head. She had held this so close to her, so convinced it was hers alone to bear, that she hadn't realised she was just one of the people affected. She sat in her locked car and cried, sobbing into her hands.

Kate rubbed her thumb over her fingertips, wiggled her toes, drew her arms over her head, and with her eyes closed, stretched her body along the floor. Her arms pulled in the opposite direction to her toes, and her back arched off the floor. Her muscles felt stretchy and relaxed. Her yoga class had ended with relaxation, and she rolled over and sat up slowly. Sitting cross-legged, she placed her hands at her heart centre, as in prayer, bowed her head and said 'Namasté', along with the rest of her class.

In her head she translated Namaste from the Sanskrit greeting into English: 'The wholeness in me, sees and salutes the wholeness in you.' She loved the simple honesty of the statement, and how it seemed to remove all preconceived notions about another person. She bent her torso over her folded legs and let her head touch the floor. She breathed in deeply and lifted herself up.

It was a Sunday afternoon and she would be spending the remainder of the afternoon in the yoga studio. The yoga course she'd started some months back was nearly complete. Kate had unearthed years of pain, issues and self-hate. It had been incredibly hard to face up to the deluded view of her persona. It wasn't as if she hadn't known that she was somehow faking her life. She did know that she often showed up and put on her party face, no matter how she felt.

Everything she thought she knew about herself had been opened up, and examined with care, love and honesty. Truth, as it turned out, was painful at the best of times. She'd often contemplated throwing her yoga mat at her teacher and walking out of the studio, but when she'd raised her hand to object, there was always another way of looking at a belief. The anger that usually appeared when faced with a difficult discussion had begun to subside, and now she found herself curious. She laughed at her own misconceptions, and enjoyed listening to her classmates, hearing their views and understanding.

She found that her sadness had begun to subside. When she thought of Claire, there was a stabbing pain that hurt, but then it eased quickly. She breathed through it, and came out the other side without dwelling on the pain. As she reflected on James and what they'd done together, she was no longer bitter or angry. It was just the guilt that remained. She'd accepted that it had happened, and maybe one day they would talk about it. She hadn't heard from him. No one had. He'd fallen out of their lives almost as quickly as Claire had.

The worst part of the course had been confronting her loneliness. It had been waiting for her for years. With Claire gone, it was harder to hide from loneliness and it was time to meet it head on. She'd always treated it with sex. It helped her to connect to men easily, albeit only briefly. In that moment of sharing something intimate with another person, she wasn't alone. It was so pathetic, clichéd and obvious, but she hadn't understood herself enough to see it. Now she understood and detested herself for it.

Tanya had been right all along.

She had been abusing herself. As the anger she felt towards herself would rise up, she began to notice it and started to forgive herself too. She didn't have to carry on being that girl that slept around with surfers. She could choose to be someone closer to who she really was.

She could choose.

Kate began to notice how making small different choices would enable her to be more comfortable with her life, and she felt less like she was fighting everything and everyone.

The deli had started to feel claustrophobic. She wanted to create a space of her own - a place that people came to because it was a part of her. She couldn't create that in a place she didn't own and the thought of a book store, combined with a café, had started to form in her mind.

At the end of the afternoon, Kate bundled her rolled-up yoga mat under her arm and walked home. She'd walked to the studio as it wasn't far from home and, as the sun set, she felt calm and almost happy. She smiled to herself, as she thought about the way one of the other women in the yoga class had been complaining about how she felt so out of control as a result of PMS. She explained that she attended yoga daily for the week before she got her period, just to ensure she didn't do anybody physical harm.

Kate rubbed her stomach. She couldn't recall when last she'd had her period. She wasn't particularly regular, but it had definitely been a while. She froze. There was no way she could be pregnant, it was impossible. She was careful, always. Except once. She began to walk, her pace picking up until she was running. She let herself into her cottage and ran to the bathroom. She kept a few spare pregnancy tests in her cupboard, grabbed one and ripped open the packaging.

By 8pm that evening she'd urinated on six sticks: the three old ones she had in her cupboard, plus another three new ones from the pharmacy down the road. They all told the same story. She was pregnant and she knew she was too far along to fix it. She rubbed her belly as she looked at the six sticks on the bathroom counter. How was she ever going to tell Tanya and Liz that she was about to have James's baby? How was she ever going to tell James?

Tanya sat at the base of the sand dunes on Fish Hoek beach. She was still in her work clothes, her smart black trousers and blouse flapping in the breeze. She'd taken her maroon patent heels off and stared across the sea, twisting her dark hair in and around her fingers. It was over, just like that.

Earlier that day, Tristan had surprised her by showing up at work and taking her for a quick coffee. He'd popped in occasionally over the years when he'd come into town to fetch a rare car part, and she'd assumed that this was one of those times. Tanya loved how the other wenches she worked with had ogled at him, wondering how she'd managed to bag him. She checked with her boss and grabbed her purse before taking his hand, and walked out of the office. There was a great little hipster café just down the road, and they ambled along the street.

'So, why are you in town?' Tanya had asked playfully, grinning up at Tristan. He just looked straight ahead.

'Had some work stuff to do,' he stated bluntly, as he quickened his pace towards the coffee shop.

After placing their order at the street-facing window, they hung around a bit further down the street to wait for their order to be called. Tanya began telling Tristan about her new client and was mid-way through her monologue when he placed his hands on her shoulders, looking down at her. Her mouth hung open as she looked up at his stern face.

'Tan, listen. I don't know how to do this, but it's over, you and me. We are done. I dunno what happened, but somewhere along the line we lost what we had. I just, it's just not the same, and I want to move on. I'm busy moving out the flat this afternoon and will be done by six, so don't come home before then, please. I don't want the drama,' he said quietly. His hands were cold and firm on her shoulders.

Tanya had been frozen stiff by his words and had to remember to blink. No words came to her.

'Tanya, do you get it? We are breaking up. I'm here to tell you in person, I'm leaving you, it's over,' he said, squeezing her shoulders. She nodded.

He let her go, walked to the counter, collected his coffee and walked away. She stared at the pavement where he had been standing. The bearded face of the barista appeared through the street window of the coffee shop and called to her. She looked up. He lifted her coffee up and raised his eyebrows.

'Your coffee?' he asked.

She nodded, walking up to him robotically and taking the coffee. She still wasn't sure how she'd ended up getting from the coffee shop in town to the beach in Fish Hoek. After mumbling something to the wenches at work, she'd packed her bag and laptop and left. That was as much as she could remember. When she found herself in the beach parking lot, she texted her boss to tell her that Tristan had left her and she needed some time. She would pick up any emails later.

Her boss had responded quickly. 'As long as you are ok Tan, we were worried about you. Let's catch up tomorrow.'

Tanya left her phone in the car and walked along the beach towards Kalk Bay. On her way back she sat down on the dune, looking out across the water. She couldn't believe it; they'd been together for nearly two years, lived together for most of the time. Tanya had hoped this would be the year that he proposed.

What had happened?

Why had he left her?

What had she done?

She knew she had been down since Claire had passed away, but surely he understood. Claire was one of her best friends and had known her most of her life. How was she going to just get over it? She needed time.

Maybe he was annoyed with her work and how much of her time it took. But why hadn't he said anything? How could he have just broken up with her on a street corner in Cape Town, without an explanation?

What was it he had said about how they'd lost what they had? What did they have? Love. Surely they had love?

The questions without answers continued to swirl around in her head, until all she was left with was *why?*

The sun had begun to set and the wind was picking up. She lifted herself up, her body stiff from the strange crouched-over position she'd been sitting in. Grabbing her shoes, she knew what she needed to do.

Tristan had his back to the road and was closing the boot of his car. Tanya got out of the car as he turned around, his face showing his surprise to see her there.

'Tan, I told you, no freakin drama. It's over and that's it. I told you to come after six,' he said. Standing tall and holding his arm out so she couldn't come to him. Tanya stopped in her tracks, looking at his hand. She folded her arms.

'I know that's what you said Tristan. I heard it all loud and clear, when you broke my heart on a street corner in town. Two fucking years and the reason you give me is that we have lost what we had?' her voice became louder with each word. She glared at him.

'What does that even mean? Did you ever even love me, or is that all bullshit too?'

'Fuck man Tan, of course I loved you. But I don't anymore. There. Is that what you want to hear? I just don't love you anymore,' he said, taking a step back.

Tanya swallowed, his words stung.

'Is that it then, you woke up one morning and BOOM, you don't love me? No talking about it, no counselling, no nothing. You are just moving on, and I must get over it and wait for you to empty out the apartment?' she said, her eyes wild and hysterical.

'It's been coming Tan, even before you went all cold. It's been worse since Claire died, but it wasn't great before. I couldn't leave you after she died, you were a mess. But you're ok now, and you've got your mates. It's just not working for me Tan,' said Tristan.

The words seemed to slap Tan cold and sober. He had wanted to leave her before Claire had died, but he had felt sorry for her and had stuck around. She felt sick with betrayal.

'You stayed with me because Claire died?' said Tanya in a bitter whisper.

'Yes. I did. Look, I'm sorry Tan, but you are bladdy hard work, the sex is minimal, and your job means more to you than you realise. I'm not made for this. This isn't what I wanted. It's over,' said Tristan, as he climbed into his car and drove off. Tanya stood in the road, the wind whipping at her face. He'd done it again. He walked away from her, just like that.

Tanya walked up the stairs to the apartment and opened the door. The place was mostly the same, except for a couch, the TV and TV cabinet. Those were Tristan's. Tanya walked to the bedroom. The cupboards stood open and all his clothes were gone, the bedside table on his side of the bed was clear and his cushion was gone. Tanya slumped on the bed and the tears began to slowly squeeze out of her eyes.

James

James couldn't believe the contents of his work desk amounted to half a box. After nearly five years at the same desk, that was all.

Since meeting the sangoma in Masi to packing up his desk, only a few months had passed. Everything had fallen into place perfectly. He'd met with the estate agent who called him on the off chance that he may want to rent the flat for the summer. She'd walked into the apartment and gushed all kinds of agent adjectives, which helped increase his rental fee.

'Well, that is quite high,' she said in her throaty cigarette voice. James had raised his eyebrows, ready to send her back out the front door.

'But I am sure that for a place like this, right across the road from the beach, we can definitely find the right tenant,' she said. And she had. A young German couple saw the place online and the agreement was signed without a hitch, at the right price. James then sold Claire's car to a young student, who grinned from ear to ear as she drove off in it.

His work resignation had been more trying. He had come in on a Monday morning, resignation letter in hand, hoping to drop the letter into his boss's in-tray, where she'd only get to it after he left. When he'd walked in, she was already at her desk, rearing to go. They were behind on the delivery for a big campaign, and she was going to make sure everyone in the team was pulling their weight.

James realised that the drop-and-run letter approach probably wasn't going to cut it. So once they had finished up the morning status meeting, involving a grilling from the production team, he'd decided to get it over and done with. She was sitting at her desk, typing furiously, as he walked in and closed the door behind him.

She looked up. 'James?' she asked, when she saw the door close behind him.

'Hey Roxanne, can I have a minute? I need to talk to you,' said James carefully as he sat down.

'Ok, but we can't take too long. As you know, we have a lot of work to get through this week. What's wrong?' she said, showing him her best Vampire Queen face.

He could tell she was irritated.

'I've come to let you know that I'm resigning. I can't keep it together any longer and I need a break. I'm selling up what I can, and I'm going to go and travel for three to six months. I'm sorry to do this now, but I just have to. Here, it's all in my letter.' He stretched his hand out to her with his resignation letter.

The Vampire Queen watched him. She had revelled in having James at her beck and call for all these years and, although she was a hard task master, he'd learnt a great deal from her. He respected her, and she never failed to remind him that he owed her his brilliant career growth.

James took a deep breath in as she sat back in her chair. His arm still extended to her.

'So you are leaving the agency, James. Is that what you are saying?' she said.

James nodded. He put the letter on her desk. He could feel her glare melting his face and he didn't dare say too much more.

'Well, that is disappointing isn't it. You're part of a really incredible team, one of the best up-and-coming agencies in South Africa, taking over accounts of global brands' she said, raising her eyebrows, folding her arms over her flat chest. She continued. 'I do realise that you have had a rough time recently, James. But this agency is what you need to, well, you know, move on,' she said, assured in her belief.

James said nothing. Roxanne continued to stare back at him. Eventually in a huff she said, 'shows you, you can never truly tell the mark of a man,' looking him up and down, as though his version of man was not good enough.

'I realise you're very disappointed Roxanne, but this is something I have to do. Claire's death has really taken it out of me. I'm sorry, I will definitely contact you when I'm back,' said James, attempting to keep what was left of the relationship alive.

She laughed under her breath.

'I'm sorry James, but we can't wait for you to come back to Cape Town. This agency is on the up and up, as you well know, and we will HAVE to find a replacement for you ASAP,' she said.

James had been unable to hide the disappointment from his face. All the years and hours that he had put into the agency counted for nothing, now that he'd resigned.

'I see,' he said curtly as he stood up, his chair grating along the tile floor.

'My contract states I have to give a calendar's month notice, so I'll leave at the end of this month,' he said. It was pointless to try and get her to understand his point of view.

'Yes, that's fine. Don't say anything to the team or your clients. You know how clients get when staff members leave. We will just hand over quickly at the end of the month, before anyone has a chance to notice you've left,' she said. 'See yourself out and leave the door closed.' She turned back to her email with renewed vigour.

James returned to his desk in a daze. He wanted to throw something across the room. He would have told Amber immediately but since the night they had slept together, things had been awkward. She'd obviously seen him walk into the Vampire Queen's office and close the door, so she knew something was up.

He walked up to the roof where the creatives smoked, and sat there bumming a smoke off one of the designers until he felt reasonably calm again.

The days since had blurred into the usual work dramas. Late nights, meeting after meeting, briefings with design teams, and on it rolled. He began to count down the days. In the last week of the month he'd confronted Roxanne and asked if he could tell the team and the clients.

'Oh for Pete's sake James. Fine, tell the team, but don't tell the clients, not yet. In fact, I'll deal with it,' was what she hissed back at him. He'd asked the team to meet him for Friday drinks at the agency bar. He had all but stopped drinking since his evening with Amber. Settling for a light beer, James gathered his team around and explained that he was leaving and why.

'Sounds awesome dude, remind me to send you a list of some places to go in South America,' one of designers had offered.

Their positive reinforcement of his decision made him feel excited and less alone. He no longer had to keep his new start in life a secret. He also explained to the team that the clients hadn't been told.

'It's not ideal guys, but Roxanne has suggested that she handle the clients. She doesn't want me saying goodbye as she feels it may upset them,' said James.

'That's weird man,' one of the team commented.

James wanted to say more. He'd built up relationships with his clients and knew about their families, their lives. Roxanne, on the other hand, had an arms-length relationship at best with her clients. The fact that he wasn't allowed to say goodbye to his clients reflected badly on him, and nullified his relationships with them.

'Anyway, try and explain to them when you guys see them, tell them I say goodbye,' said James.

After two or three beers, James called it a night. On his way out, Amber caught up with him. 'James' she called as she walked up behind him.

'Hey, Amber. You also heading out?' he asked.

'No, not yet. Just wanted to say that we are really, I mean, well, I'm really going to miss having you around. You are amazing to work with and it was great learning from you. But I totally get it. I think what you are doing is so brilliant for you. It's cool. Anyway, ya, I'll see you around. I guess?' she said, squeezing her hands. She reached up to James and hugged him before turning on her heel and going back to the bar. James watched her go. Her petite little figure swayed towards one of the other Account Directors who was holding a drink for her, his face beaming at her as she approached. James smiled. Lucky guy, he thought.

The last thing James put in the box was the photo of him and Claire. Their smiling faces beamed up at him from the half-full box. He sighed. He didn't even recognise that guy in the picture anymore. He shut the box, checked the drawers of his desk one more time and went around the office saying his goodbyes. He finished off at the Vampire Queen. He leaned on the door frame and poked his head in. She was engrossed, looking over an advert. He felt the pull to go over and look at it, but gripped the door frame firmly to stop himself.

'Cheers Roxanne, I'm off,' he said. She raised her eyes. 'Well, guess that's it then James. Good luck with your travels. Who knows, we may meet again,' she said, looking at him as if they had met only yesterday.

'Maybe,' answered James, and he turned and walked away. He picked up his box and walked out of the building for the last time. The knowledge that he would probably never again go back into that office made him pick up his pace towards his car. This was it; this was really the end of another chapter in his life.

Kate sat in the back of Tanya's car. Tanya was driving and Liz was sitting in the passenger seat. Kate was glad to be at the back of the car. In the dark, her face was concealed and didn't show how nervous she was at seeing James again. Liz was also feeling chatty and hadn't stopped talking since she'd got in the car. Kate knew her well enough to know that Liz was either excited, nervous or hiding something. They were going to go for dinner after they saw James off, so she assumed she would eventually be able to unearth the reason behind the non-stop chatter.

James had sent all three girls a message, asking them to meet him at the airport to see him off. He'd avoided a large gathering of friends, and had opted for a few smaller dinners. He apologised and said he'd run out of time and that's why he had left their goodbyes to the airport. Tanya and Liz had been accepting of the excuse, but Kate knew that he'd planned it this way - no emotional goodbyes or awkward moments. A quick catch up, a hug, a pat on the back for luck and a swift goodbye at the airport were far easier to deal with. Tanya had insisted that she would drive them there, as it was late in the evening and to be safe, it was better they all went in one car. If she hadn't, Kate would have definitely found a way to avoid this encounter. But she hadn't been able to conjure up anything good enough to avoid being picked up and taken to the airport.

As they got out of the car, Kate quickly checked that her thickly knitted jersey covered her expanding middle. Her face had stayed the same shape, but her belly had started to show. She hadn't told anyone she was pregnant. When she heard that James was leaving South Africa to go travelling, she'd wanted to call him and stop him, and tell him he was about to be a father. But how could she? This was her secret, and if she was going to tell him she should have told him ages ago. Besides, he needed to do this. He'd always been such a together guy. But since Claire's death, he'd been a mess. Kate had heard about all the drinking and sleeping around from a friend of hers, who also worked at the same agency as James. Kate had been upset at first, but realised that this was his way of coping. It wasn't a great approach, but it was what he was doing. When she'd heard that he'd quit, and the subsequent travel plans, she thought he must have finally come to his senses and realised he needed to reflect on his emotions and try and move on.

Liz continued to chatter on as they walked to the international departures terminal. Tanya hadn't got a word in edge ways either. She seemed grey and distant, her hair listlessly hanging down her face. Kate couldn't help wonder what was going on with Tanya. Maybe the wenches at work were giving her grief again?

It was easy to spot James from afar, his height and the way he stood, arms crossed over his chest. He looked like a great modern adventurer with his small rucksack on his back and a larger backpack at his feet. Liz spotted him and waved crazily above the heads of all the people between them and James. He smiled across the departure hall. Kate felt weak and was about to stop, turn and run, when a large piece of luggage bumped her slightly forward and she had to carry on. James hugged all three women. Kate was careful to hold her tummy away. She hoped nobody noticed her ridiculous embrace, which involved her poking her butt backwards away from James, in order to prevent him touching her small bump.

'Hey gals, how're you all doing,' said James, charming, warm and honestly pleased to see them. Kate and Tanya stuck to superficial niceties, and Liz couldn't help herself any longer.

'Well...' she said talking in an excited breath, 'I just can't keep it a secret any longer. I have to tell you guys...So, I've been reevaluating my life and work and everything, and I have decided to close my practice and go and work for the state,' she excitedly told them.

She just about bounced off the floor. Kate and Tanya just blinked at Liz. They couldn't believe it. Liz was by far the most rational and stable of them all, or so they had thought.

'Wow Liz, seriously,' said James. 'That's quite a thing. Are you going to False Bay Hospital?' he asked, curious.

'Nope,' she said, as though she were about to reveal where one could find a pot of gold.

'I'm going to work at Lentegeur Rehabilitation Centre. It's a great facility; there is just tons of work to be done and I'll really be helping people. No more self-absorbed athletes,' she said, visibly delighted.

James digested this information. 'That's fantastic Lizzie, I'm really happy for you. This is going to be a great move for you, and you seem really excited about it. Well done,' said James, giving Liz a high five.

Kate and Tanya slowly processed this information eventually and responded positively to Liz. Liz beamed. Her sessions with her therapist helped her realise what she did and didn't love about her job. This had resulted in much soul searching. When she'd heard about the job at Lentegeur, she applied immediately. The interview had been lengthy, and at the end of it she was certain she had stuffed it up. But she'd been called back for a second and third interview, and eventually she received the offer two days ago.

She hadn't told her parents and had been holding on until this evening to spill the beans. Every bone in her body knew this was the right decision.

An announcement boomed over the intercom, interrupting all their thoughts.

'Ok guys, I better go. Need to check in and get through customs and all that,' said James, 'just one thing I need your help with.' He turned and hauled up his larger backpack over one shoulder. Behind the backpack was another box they hadn't seen earlier. It was a pet carrier box.

'You guys remember Arora, our Siamese cat?' he said looking at the three women. 'Well, I was wondering if she could stay at one of you until I get back. Claire left her to me, but I know she would be ok with Arora hanging with one of you gals in the interim. Until I'm back. Anyone?' asked James, his cheeks turning pink with embarrassment.

The three women stood around the cat box, their blank faces staring at James and the cat box.

'I know this is bad planning, but I totally forgot to organise her a home. I got so caught up finishing work and cleaning out the apartment, that well, she slipped my mind,' he said, looking at the pet carrier clearly ashamed.

'My folks have dogs,' stated Liz.

'I'm so allergic, there is no way,' said Tanya.

'I guess that leaves me,' said Kate with a wry smile on her face.

James smiled at Kate and for a second their eyes met, and it was as if there had never been a time when they weren't great friends.

'Well that's decent of you Kate, and I mean, you are the one with a garden and everything, so ya. Great,' said Tanya, as though she had organised everything.

'All good James. Arora and I have always liked each other. You'd better go,' said Kate, as she gave James a pat and brushed her cheek against his. She then bent down to pick up the cat carrier. The others hugged James and he walked to the check-in counter. Tanya took charge and decided where they would have dinner; she hooked her arm into Liz's and they lead the way. Kate had been peering into the cat carrier. Arora's large eyes had looked out at her, making silent meows with her tiny mouth.

'Poor baby,' said Kate to Arora.

As Kate looked up, she realised that Tanya and Liz had left her and were making their way to dinner. She looked for James; she wanted to see him, just one more time before he left. He was looking straight at her. The colour rose from her neck to her cheeks and she mouthed:

'Be safe' to him, because she couldn't say the words 'I love you'.

'I will,' he mouthed back, before walking through to the other side. Gone.

Arora let off a loud meow which brought Kate back to reality and she quickly turned and chased after her friends with her new cat companion swinging along by her side.

Tanya and Liz were sitting at their table. Kate sat down and noticed immediately that something was amiss.

'What's wrong?' she said to both of her friends.

'Tristan has left me,' said Tanya flatly, as her eyes brimmed with tears.

'Oh my god Tan,' said Kate, sincerely shocked. 'When did this happen?' asked Kate.

Tanya told them how Tristan had broken up with her and moved out in one day. She hadn't had the guts to tell anyone over the past few weeks, and still couldn't actually believe it had happened. She had been in a complete daze since then.

'I just can't believe it Tan, I was expecting a ring, not a break up!' said Liz, as she shook her head oblivious to how her statement pained Tanya.

'What are you going to do? Are you going to stay in the flat Tan?' continued Liz.

'I have to Liz, we signed another year just three months ago. I'm stuck with it and I can't really afford the place on my own,' said Tanya so softly that she was barely audible. Her teary eyes spilled over and she started to cry gently.

'Oh guys, I don't know what to do. I'm so alone. Work is horrible and I'm all on my own against all those bitches. Now I'm all alone at home too. I don't know why my life has ended up like this?' she said.

Kate pulled her chair right next to Tanya, placing her arm around her shoulders. 'Tan, you're not alone. We are here for you. Why didn't you call us?' said Kate, feeling desperately sad for her friend, who always seemed to know what was right and wrong, and the way to go. Yet here she sat, deflated, sad, alone and confused.

Liz tried to solve Tanya's problems and said, 'Tan, it's just a short term thing, everything will come together, you'll see. You just need to…'

'Do what Liz? What should I be doing?' said Tanya, spitting out her words. How could Liz possibly understand what she was going through? According to Tanya, Liz was incapable of connecting with a man beyond a few dates. How could she, this simple physio, possibly understand what the end of a long term relationship actually meant? She had no right to tell her what to do. She glared at Liz, expecting her to back track like she usually did when they disagreed.

Liz raised herself in her chair and calmly responded.

'Tan, you need to get in touch with who you really are. You put on this hardcore chick thing all the time because of your job, and you are completely cold and fake as a result. I'm sorry that I have to say this to you, especially when you are so upset. But actually, you need to hear it.'

Kate felt her jaw loosen and her mouth open. What was going on here? She carefully placed her one hand on Tanya's, and the other on Liz's, as the two women glared at each other.

Tanya eventually turned to Kate. 'Can you believe what she just said?' Tanya was in a state of shock. She didn't have a way to deal with this Liz. But before Kate could answer, the waitress interrupted and shoved plates of food in front of each of them. There was a shuffling of plates, salt and pepper cellars, as well as a handing out of knives and forks. The silence hung between them as they slowly began to push the food around their plates.

'Tan, you've had a tough time. I know Liz has said some intense things, but she means no harm. Please don't be mad,' said Kate, her voice almost pleading.

Tanya carefully placed her knife and fork against her plate. She looked up at both women. Kate sat on the edge of her chair, waiting for Tanya to go ballistic and leave them stranded at the airport.

Liz sat back ready to defend herself, proud of herself, yet slightly guilty for deciding to say what she had said at this time.

'You're right Liz,' said Tanya, tucking her hair behind her ears and looking down at her untouched dinner. 'I don't know who I am anymore. I thought I was a cool, calculating tough PR agent. But the cracks were starting to show even before Claire died,' she said.

'In fact, Claire had said that I should leave and rather do travel writing, like I wanted to do after school, do you remember?' she said, appealing to their memories of a time when she was more true to herself than she was now.

Kate and Liz nodded.

'Wise old Claire. I laughed at her and told her that those were silly girl dreams. I have a proper job that makes me miserable. Who would give that up?' Tanya said, and laughed sarcastically before continuing, 'you're right Liz, I don't know who I am anymore. I'm going to find out though. I am going to quit, try find someone to take over my rental and find something new to do. It's time,' said Tanya. She looked at Kate and Liz, surprising herself with her new resolution.

Liz couldn't hold onto her guilt any longer. 'I'm so sorry Tan, I didn't mean to hurt you. I want you to be happy. You know that right?' she said, the words rushing out of her mouth.

'For sure Lizzie, I know you do. You couldn't hurt a fly. Thanks for saying what needed to be said. I get it, the truth hurts right? But now you are going to have to hold my hand as I take the next few steps. If you push someone to make a shift, you have to hold them as they move along,' said Tanya, eyeing both of her friends, seeking their confirmation of help.

Kate smiled broadly. 'There you are Tan, I can see you now. That's the girl I used to know, who used to love writing and drinking big cups of tea,' said Kate.

Tanya laughed gently. 'Yup, I'm coming back. Maybe Tristan did me the biggest favour yet,' said Tanya, tucking into her dinner.

They all turned to their plates. Kate was initially ravenous, but after a few mouthfuls she felt too full and put her knife and fork down.

'What's wrong with you Kate?' asked Liz. She couldn't believe that Kate had hardly eaten anything. Kate loved her food.

Kate smiled and sunk into her chair. 'I can't keep it a secret for much longer girls, so here goes. I'm pregnant!' confessed Kate. She knew she had to tell them sooner or later and now seemed the best time. She lifted her jumper and showed them her bump.

Tanya burst out 'holy shit!' followed by Liz's 'oh my word. Are you serious?' which resulted in Kate laughing at both of them.

'Seriously Kate, stop laughing, this is serious,' said Tanya, trying to regain order.

Liz's hand was on Kate's belly before she knew what she was doing. 'It's real!' she said, dumbfounded.

'It is,' said Kate rather proudly. She loved her baby bump and was thrilled that she could start showing it off more.

'Who's the father?' asked Tanya.

'Aaah, thought you might ask that. Just a guy. Nothing that would ever work, so I'm not telling him. No point and I'm really happy to do this on my own,' said Kate, using her determined, don't mess- with-me face.

'Kate, we know you are independent and all that, but a kid is different. You're going to need help. I'm going to move in with you when it comes. Nothing will change my mind,' said Liz. She didn't know what had come over her, but she knew that she had to be involved.

'I can help when the child is of school-going age' said Tanya with a wry smile and she laughed. They all knew Tanya wasn't a fan of small children, and the joke was all too true.

'Done!' said Kate.

'Do you know if it's a boy or a girl?' asked Liz, her hand still rubbing Kate's belly.

'Nope, going to be a surprise. Going with the general surprise theme here,' smiled Kate. She couldn't believe how well the girls had taken it.

'Let me call for the bill and go to the loo at the same time,' said Tanya, as she stood up and motioned to the waitress. Liz and Kate watched her walk to the toilets.

'She is going to be great, you know. She's so much better off without Tristan,' said Kate, half to herself.

'She is,' agreed Liz, leaning into Kate, 'it's James's baby isn't it?'

Kate froze.

How on earth could Liz have known? James would never have told her. She sat upright and looked at Liz.

Without saying a word, Liz knew she had guessed correctly. 'It's the way you were all weird with him tonight. I've seen you do that with other guys you've slept with, the ones who brush you off afterwards. You think you're acting cool, but to me, you are see-through,' said Liz quietly, as she leaned over and gave Kate a warm embrace.

'I'm sorry Katie, he probably loves you too. But he is too messed up right now. You should tell him about the baby though. He would want to know,' said Liz.

'No, no way,' said Kate.

'Ok, your choice. Whatever you decide, I'm here. K?' said Liz.

'OK,' said Kate, nodding her head.

'Are you disgusted by me?' asked Kate, searching deeply into Liz's eyes for the truth. Liz smiled, her eyes warm. 'You nutter, I'm not disgusted. Surprised maybe, but you know it takes two to tango. Not like you forced him to have sex with you,' said Liz, 'Right?' cocking her head to the side.

'Seriously Liz,' said Kate, surprise across her face. 'I'm not that bad!'

Tanya arrived back. She seemed better already. Her hair was tied back and she stood straight. 'Ok besties, let's get home. We have new lives to start!'

The Upward turn

Stage 5

Life becomes calmer, more organised as one starts to adjust to life with the loss that occurred.

Chapter 5

Tshepo

The room where Tshepo slept no longer closed in to suffocate him. It wasn't very big, but it fitted two single beds, a small set of drawers and a locker at the end of the bed. The locker doors hung open limply, after years of slamming and kicking had destroyed their ability to ever close again. Tshepo looked around the room once more. The walls were pale green with a number of brown fingerprint smudges, shoe scuffs and other marks dotted along their length. The window above the drawers could be opened, but a set of bars prevented anyone from coming in or throwing themselves out. This was a safe place.

Tshepo had been moved here a few weeks ago, or was it months? It was hard to tell. Mr Buswayo and his clever legal team had told the judge that he was severely depressed and unfit to stand trial - that he needed to come to this place, so that the mind doctors could watch him for a while. They had used long words to say all these things in the courtroom, but Tshepo hadn't really understood at the time what they were going to do with him. Mr Buswayo had explained after the trial, and then he'd understood. He was sick in his mind. The accident, the dead Claire, his amputated leg, being in prison, all these terrible things had made him very sad and this meant that he couldn't answer all the questions in the courtroom. The judge agreed to let him come here and meet with the mind doctor. The mind doctor would then tell the judge what to do next.

In the meantime, Tshepo just had to hang around in this place. It was better than prison and he almost liked it here, as much as you could like a place filled with crazy people. Not that they were all crazy - there were some like him who were sad, and sat around all day, or slept in their chairs. Then there were those who talked into thin air or to the walls. At first he'd been terrified that these crazy people and nurses were going to hurt him. But they didn't, so he started to feel more relaxed. He got fed, and he got his medicine again. It made him very tired for the first few weeks, and he had slept for many days. In and out of the black hole he moved, until one day he felt able to join the others in the TV room. He hadn't felt so tired, and the black hole had held off from swallowing him up. After that day, it had become easier to leave his bed. Some days were easier than others. On the days he made it beyond his bed, he liked to watch the nurses. They gossiped non-stop amongst themselves, and he liked to listen to their stories, which were even better than the soapies on TV. They talked about the doctors and their habits, about the patients and their problems, while they handed out pills or mopped up vomit off the floor. One nurse in particular was his favourite. She was young and smiled easily, her skin smooth and radiant. She would happily chat to patients, whether they made sense or not. Tshepo had explained to her that he was waiting for his prosthesis, and she should look out for it at reception, in case Jenny posted it. With little else to dream about, the prosthesis had become Tshepo's hope for a life beyond this.

He saw the mind doctor often, and he had to tell him all about his life. The mind doctor liked to ask him about how he was feeling and what he thought about his leg. He thought these were stupid questions; wasn't it obvious that he hated not having a full leg? Then the doctor would ask him about killing Claire in the accident, frantically writing notes in his file as Tshepo spoke.

He hated talking about Claire. It was a bad story and he didn't want to have to think about it. He felt angry with himself when he had to remember what he'd done to that girl. The guilt would cover him like a cloak, and he hated the doctor for making him feel that way. Why couldn't he just leave it alone? Yet, as the weeks went by, Tshepo began to notice how the guilt and the black hole didn't cover or consume him as they had before. He began to feel like he could breathe, even when the sadness came. It always came, every day, but now he could see through it. It just didn't smother him like it used to.

Tshepo found himself thinking about what would happen to him after the next court appearance. He remembered that Mr Buswayo had been very pleased with what had happened at the first hearing.

Tshepo recalled how Mr Buswayo had come into the courtroom. A tall, proud man walking towards the front of the courtroom, determined. He spoke to the advocate who was to represent the case, leaving Tshepo wondering why another person was needed. Mr Buswayo clearly knew what was going on. The complexity of the legal system overwhelmed him. He felt small and useless in the courtroom, and the feeling weighed heavy on his back, making his body slump in on itself.

When they moved him from his cell to the courtroom, Tshepo was reminded of his cripple status. He was just another man who would hobble along slowly, while people pushed past and called him names. Would he end up having to beg at the traffic lights to eat, or worse, end up in the gang prisons where they'd push him over for fun and do who knows what else to him. He'd rather die than face that. In fact, death seemed like the best option.

Without the prosthesis, Tshepo couldn't work as a taxi driver, and he knew that the Boss would make him do menial work back in Masi; if he ever got back to Masi. There were no options for a crippled man with no money and no family. Yes, death was a good option and it was how he felt that day in the courtroom.

The advocate had spoken in long lawyer words to the judge and they had all called him Mr Tshepo Dlamini, the accused. The long words bounced between the advocate and the judge. The judge, a puffy man with rolls of fat on the back of his neck, had turned his pinched eyes, which blinked too frequently behind thick glasses, to Tshepo and said:

'Mr Dlamini, do you understand why you are here today?'

Tshepo had nodded.

The judge continued in his resonant voice. 'Your lawyer claims that due to your injuries, as well as being genuinely aggrieved by the accident, together with your remorse, you have sunk into a severe depression. You have no previous records, so I will allow the psychological assessment to take place. You will be sent to Lentegeur for this. Once this is complete, you will return and we will decide if the case will be struck off the roll or if you will stand trial for culpable homicide. Do you understand Mr Dlamini?' The words swirled wildly in Tshepo's head, and he'd hung onto the words which told him he would go somewhere other than prison. Yes, he wanted that.

He nodded repeatedly.

'Please note, the defendant has responded positively,' stated the judge, and continued to mark a date for the next trial. Then he banged the hammer and it was over. Tshepo had been surprised at how he'd been waiting so long for this trial, and in only a few minutes it was finished. He looked across the courtroom, feeling his heart slowly ice over as the faces he recognised came into view:

The one who screamed at him, while he had been lying in his own blood with a smashed leg on the road; she was there, but wasn't screaming now. She was just looking at him, seeing him. He looked away, terrified to be caught by her gaze. He eventually looked up again.

The lady called Liz was here too. She was the one who had come to the hospital. She was also looking at him surprised, but wasn't crying this time.

Another lady stood with them. He hadn't seen her before. She had a round belly. Pregnant. Was she the fourth runner? Had he nearly killed a woman with a baby? He looked at the floor. The thought brought a nauseous wave of guilt crashing over him. What had he done?

Hanging his head like a rag doll, he waited for the court officer to take him away. Away from these women whose friend he had killed.

A pair of perfect Italian leather shoes appeared in his view of the floor. 'Mr Dlamini,' stated Winston. Tshepo raised his eyes to look into Winston's confident face.

'Mr Dlamini, this is very good. You are now going to the place I told you about. They will work with you and help you feel better. I promise this. You don't have to go back to the cell,' said Winston smiling at Tshepo.

'Thank you Mr Buswayo,' said Tshepo, reaching for Winston's hand and placing his forehead onto it. 'You are a good man Mr Buswayo, a good man.'

The humble action touched Winston's cool demeanor, and he was forced to clear his throat. 'You are welcome Mr Dlamini. I will get my people to check in on you at Lentegeur. Go well my brother,' said Winston, as he gently extracted himself from Tshepo's almost desperate grasp.

Tshepo watched Winston walk to the desk to collect his leather satchel. He watched how a small, well-dressed woman, with long red hair had spoken to Winston. She stood close to him and looked up into his face. He could feel the heat rise in his face as he watched them. He wondered who she was. Surely Mr Buswayo had not asked his girlfriend to come to visit him at work.

Maureen

It was easy to get what she needed to set the divorce in motion. With Chris away, and not much else to take up her time, she threw herself into her plan. When she had everything she needed, Maureen contacted the lawyer. One of the gym ladies had been thrilled to share the details of her divorce lawyer. She had beamed at the thought of another man being brought to justice when she'd heard Maureen's story.

The lawyer's offices were in Cape Town city centre, and Joshua Goldstein's office opened up into a spectacular view across the city, with Table Mountain on the one side and the harbour on the other. Expansive and well-furnished, Maureen appreciated that he had decorated the office well.

'Mrs Klaasen, please come in and take a seat,' said Joshua. He was slightly shorter than average in height; his glasses contained bright eyes which took in Maureen, quickly and expertly. His shirt was tailored and his shoes gleamed, his yarmulke rested carefully on the back of his head.

'So, tell me, how can I help you?' asked Joshua, as if there may be some other reason for her visit, other than divorce. He pulled a chair out for her, and walked around to behind his desk to face her, expressionless as he waited on her response.

'Thank you for seeing me Mr Goldstein,' said Maureen.

'Call me Joshua,' he interjected.

'Thank you, Joshua. The reason I'm here is because I want to divorce my husband, who is a gambling cheat,' said Maureen with emphasis on cheat.

'I see,' said Joshua, who had clearly heard it all.

Divorce was his forte, and gambling cheats were obviously more common than one realised.

'Do you have an ANC, an ante nuptial contract?' he asked.

'Yes we do, I have it all here,' said Maureen as she pulled out her folder with all her documents neatly filed inside. She withdrew the ANC.

'Over here it says that we will split our assets equally if we are to divorce,' she said, pointing to a section of the document, before pushing it across the desk towards Joshua.

'I see…' he said as he eyeballed the document. 'Ok, well, it all seems in order from that perspective. Now tell me, does your husband know that you're here?' asked Joshua, looking over the bridge of his glasses, raising his eyebrows.

'No, he doesn't. He works offshore. He doesn't even know that I caught him cheating on me,' said Maureen, sitting up straight.

Joshua smiled a small thin-lipped smile. 'But, do you have proof of this cheating Mrs Klaasen?' asked Joshua, as he sat back waiting for her response.

'I do. Took a little bit of effort on my part, but I do,' said Maureen. Her eyes sparkled and she smiled back at him.

'Go on, tell me what he did and how you have managed to get evidence,' said Joshua.

'We were at Sun City. I woke up early one morning and caught him coming out of the bedroom of an eighteen-year-old. He didn't see me, but I saw them as clear as day. Once I was back in Cape Town, I managed to get the details of the girl. I called her and threatened to tell her father that she was sleeping around with old men. She begged me not to and has written a letter stating she slept with Chris,' said Maureen, as she reached into her folder once again. She withdrew the letter, sliding it to Joshua before continuing, 'the letter says it all. I promised I wouldn't tell anyone, except my lawyer, as long as she told the truth about what was going on. Turns out, the time I saw them wasn't the first. He was really getting lucky in Sun City,' said Maureen, her mouth pursed with sarcasm.

'I see,' said Joshua as he read the letter. 'Interesting, and good for you,' he said, with a nod of his head.

'Tell me, why did you feel the need to get this letter if you already have an ANC?' asked Joshua, curiosity getting the better of him.

'I am worried, Joshua. I haven't worked since I married Chris. He could claim that he has supported me for all this time and so I get nothing, but the truth is that he hasn't allowed me to work. I'm worried that he will put up a really big fight. He likes owning me and thinks I'm some kind of lucky charm for his gambling habit. He could get difficult about this,' said Maureen, leaning in towards Joshua, her voice lowered.

Joshua watched her carefully, as if studying her. 'Has there ever been any kind of abuse I should know about Maureen? Mental or physical?' he asked.

Maureen had known that this question may be asked, and she'd decided that Chris forcing her to have sex was one thing she wasn't prepared to take into a lawyer's office. 'No, he hasn't. But he has a temper and he is strong. He could use it. He is ex-Navy, quite a hard man, and I've always made sure that I keep him happy. Do you understand Joshua, he could get violent?' said Maureen, swallowing hard.

She sat back and met Joshua's eyes squarely. They watched each other for a few seconds. Eventually Joshua responded.

'Yes, I understand,' he said, as he sat up and leaned his elbows on his table, fingers intertwined.

'I will outline the best course of action going forward. Let me call in my assistant to take notes,' explained Joshua, as he pushed the buttons on his desk phone.

The remainder of the meeting provided Maureen with a clear outline of how they would proceed with the divorce. Joshua and his assistant described what would happen in depth, highlighting any areas of concern. They advised Maureen to go home and think about the divorce process, and call them the next day to confirm whether they should go ahead or not. Maureen tried to persuade them that she was certain and they could proceed, but they were insistent that she should sleep on it. She left their office feeling exhausted and scared, overwhelmed by the amount of legal information she needed to digest. After driving home in a daze, she let herself in and went straight to bed.

When Maureen awoke, she lay in her bed and stared at the ceiling. It was late afternoon and the sun had begun to set over the valley, casting shadows across her room. Feeling less overwhelmed than earlier, she played the conversation with the lawyers over in her mind. They'd explained that she could get the divorce even if Chris didn't want it, but he could only be served a divorce summons from the court once he was back in South Africa. She knew it would all go through, her paperwork was organised. Yet her stomach twisted at the thought of seeing him again, the fear of his anger terrified her, leaving her paralysed at the thought.

Unable to do anything but stare at the ceiling, she wondered about the divorce and whether she was making a mistake. Maybe he'd just been confused by the beautiful young girl, seduced perhaps? Her mind went round and round in circles thinking about how Chris could have been drawn into cheating on her, not out of his own free will. She sat up. Had Chris done this before, she wondered. She would call the wife of one of his friends - the same one who had told her about the gambling. Esme would tell her if Chris had slept around before.

Maureen hopped out of bed, still fully clothed and went downstairs. Her bag was still where she'd dumped it on the kitchen counter. She reached in to get her phone, noticing a few messages and emails that she would get to later.

An hour later, Maureen stood on the balcony, a bottle of champagne in one hand and a cigarette in the other. She stared out over the valley and the ocean. The street lights and houses twinkled in contrast to the still, dark ocean. The wife of Chris's friend had tried to get out of telling her the truth, but eventually Esme had buckled.

Yes, Chris had slept with other women while they were married. Some had been local and others had been overseas. Esme knew because Chris had confided in her ex-husband. She'd gone on and on about the details of Chris's exploits, giving Maureen names of previous lovers. Maureen's blood had run cold,

'Ag shame Maureen, this must be hard hey. I tried to tell you, some things you just don't want to know. But you know these flippin' men, they're all the same. Can't fuckin' trust any of them.'

Maureen had eventually ended the call and walked straight to the fridge to get the champagne. Now, as she stood on the balcony, her head fuzzy from the alcohol and cigarettes, she felt as if she could float and almost touch the sea. It was so beautiful, so calm and so silent. The tears began to run down her cheeks as she sank into the chair on the balcony, the bottle of champagne landing on the table with a hefty clunk. She sucked the last bit of the cigarette into her lungs in one long slow draw, feeling the nicotine rush through her veins. As she crushed the red tip of the cigarette into the table, she began to sob from the depths of her diaphragm. She felt so betrayed, used and stupid. Sucking air in desperation, she was overcome by another sob. Surely she should have seen this coming, seen him for what he was. The sobs rolled into one another. How could she have been so blind for so long?

When she could cry no more, she dragged herself back to bed and fell into a deep dreamless sleep.

The next morning, Maureen showered herself awake, washing the previous day away. She watched the water swirl down into the drain and felt it pour down the back of her neck and shoulders. There yesterday goes, she thought to herself, down the drain.

Today was going to be very different from yesterday, she assured herself.

She dried her body and stood naked in front of her bedroom mirror while she dried her long hair. She chose her favorite black dress and tied her hair in a seductive side pony. Today she was going to be strong and in charge. She went downstairs and made herself a double espresso. A rusk and banana would have to suffice as food for the moment. Her appetite had shrunk to almost nothing. As she sipped her coffee, she sat down at the kitchen counter and went through her phone and email messages. Her first email was to Joshua. She confirmed the divorce was going ahead. She hadn't bothered to tell him about the latest information about Chris's infidelity. She knew he would think that her final decision was driven by rage. But it wasn't. This was just confirmation of what she had thought. She now knew for certain that she wanted nothing more to do with the person she called her husband.

He disgusted her. He terrified her.

Maureen felt a shiver run down her spine.

The next email was to the HR Manager at Winston Buswayo's law firm. It seemed that Winston had told her about Maureen as a possible replacement for an events manager at the firm. Maureen had been surprised by the offer to meet, and thrilled at the opportunity to possibly bump into Winston again.

She quickly responded that she was available to meet today. Apologising for the delay in reverting, her response was quickly followed by a meeting request with the HR Manager that afternoon. Maureen couldn't help but smile; must be her dress she thought to herself.

Now she needed to organise an urgent meeting with her psychologist, Alice, this morning.

The delightful receptionist was flabbergasted at Maureen's luck. 'Well, my lovey, it seems you are very lucky. I have just had a cancellation. See you at 12 then,' she said.

Maureen pulled up her old CV and spruced it up. Four years at home, focusing all her attention on her gym contract, hairdresser and beauty therapist made her seem like a lazy slob. She didn't even have children to blame. Thankfully she had worked in a large corporate, before Chris had insisted she become a stay-at-home wife. She hoped that her charm would outweigh her CV's recent paucity. She decided to first meet this HR Manager before she sent her CV. Perhaps she would have to come up with something stronger than 'my husband said I have to stay home,' in order to win some favour with the HR manager.

Maureen completed the last few details on the divorce documents and plans, before closing her laptop and going back to her bedroom. Carefully and meticulously she did her make-up. When she felt satisfied, she stood back from the mirror and looked at herself. Hello Maureen, she said to her reflection, where have you been?

As Maureen pulled out of the car park from her appointment with Alice, she recalled all the times she had left this very same car park. After each session she'd either been in a complete daze or she'd been crying over that stupid man.

Maureen had felt ashamed to tell Alice about Sun City, how she'd fallen so completely and easily back into Chris's arms and believed all of his lies. Alice's rather stony face had actually lit up when Maureen described how she'd seen Chris with the young girl. It was as if she'd been waiting for Maureen to see it for herself all along.

Maureen also detailed her divorce plans to Alice, who had provided the sounding board and support she'd needed to feel justified in her actions. Alice had also offered some insight into what could help her win over the HR Manager at the law firm.

As she stood up at the end of her session, Maureen wrapped her arms around Alice and thanked her for helping change her life. She'd then confidently walked away from Alice and her office, leaving a deeply satisfied psychologist in her wake.

Waters, Shabalala and Associates owned a large glass-clad building in Cape Town. Maureen stood in the reception and gazed across the harbour and the sea. The view was so different to her own, wide open and dotted with large tankers waiting to enter the busy port. 'Maureen?' came a voice from behind her.

She quickly turned around. She couldn't believe it.

'Laura? Is that really you?'

'Oh my word, Maureen! I can't believe it. You've changed your surname!

That's why I didn't know it was YOU!' said Laura as she rushed towards Maureen and hugged her warmly.

'I seriously can't believe it's you. You fell off the face of the earth and we completely lost touch. It's *so* good to see you!' continued Laura, as she stepped away from Maureen and admired her old friend.

'Let's grab a coffee and catch up. This is so fantastic!' Laura purred, thrilled to meet up with an old friend, who she knew would be perfect for this job.

Maureen beamed back at her old friend as she chatted away, their arms intertwined, heels clicking on the porcelain tiles as they made their way to Laura's office.

'So ya, Lar, that's it. The first few years were great and I truly loved him, but, well now that I know who he really is, it's time to move on. So, that's why I'm here, I guess, after all this time. Still can't believe it's you. What's your hubby like?' asked Maureen, curious to find out more about the man who had managed to tame this wild friend of hers.

'Paul's his name. He is great. He worships the ground I walk on. He is so straight laced you would never think we have anything to talk about, but we have so much in common, and....' paused Laura as she widened her eyes and raised her eyebrows, drawing closer to Maureen, 'he enjoys a little bit of experimentation in the bedroom, if you know what I mean,' she said, her voice becoming husky and low.

'I see,' said Maureen raising her eyebrows. 'I so couldn't imagine you with some straight-laced okey. But if he is a dirty dog, then yup, I can see how he has managed to bag you. You filthy girl!' said Maureen winking, all of Laura's past exploits flooding back in a whirlwind of memory.

The two women laughed at each other.

'Ok, so back to work. So after you left corporate, you did nothing right?' asked Laura. Maureen sat up straight 'Yes, that's right. But Lar, I promise I still have it. I would kill to work here. You know how good I am. Remember those events I put together in Mauritius? That kind of experience doesn't just evaporate,' said Maureen trying hard not to sound desperate for the job.

'Listen doll I know how you work. You are freaking amazing. And the fact that Winston, a partner, has recommended you definitely works in your favour. The only problem is this case that you are a witness in. I can't actually give you an offer until it's over, and it could take a while,' said Laura as she sat back. A frown crossed over her face as she thought for a moment. 'Hold on, we could hire you as a contractor. It's not great, but it could tide you over, and as long as there isn't any change to your statement, there is no reason for anyone to start asking questions,' stated Laura, eyeing Maureen.

'What I saw is what I saw Lar, and nothing is going to change that. It's imprinted in my mind and soul forever,' said Maureen, looking down as the image of the accident flashed across her mind's eye.

Laura stretched her hand across the desk and found Maureen's.

'I'm so, so sorry you had to see that Mauzi. Are you ok?' asked Laura.

'I'm fine Lar, thanks. It gets better with time,' said Maureen, visibly saddened by the talk of the accident.

'Ok, I'll sort out the paperwork. Let's start light. Come in as a contractor. It will take a week or so to set you up, but this way we can at least get you in the door. You are so perfect for this job and this place. You are going to love it here. I promise,' said Laura as she smiled broadly at Maureen.

Maureen felt the excitement rise in her belly, and she smiled back. Laura was right. She would definitely love this firm.

'Winston,' called a female voice behind him. He was in a rush to get to his next meeting. One of the clerks had stuffed up some paperwork and now he had to go cap-in-hand to his client; he would have to try and explain why the documents were wrong and that the legal fees weren't going to change. There were days when he wondered if he was actually doing law or babysitting.

In a huff he turned on his heel to see who was calling him. Fuck, he thought to himself, fucking HR, as he spotted Laura shimmying towards him in her grey pencil skirt and killer heels. He could just hear the next staff issue coming.

'Winston,' she said, slightly breathless as she managed to catch up with him. He raised his eyebrows encouraging her to continue.

'Sorry to bother you. I can walk with you, just wanted to let you know I met with Maureen, the events person from the Dlamini case,' she said, as she clicked at high speed alongside him.

'Mmm,' he said, giving nothing away despite his interest in the subject.

'I just met with her now and came to let you know that she is a perfect fit,' said

Laura. Winston slowed his pace and looked at Laura.

'Oh really, I am glad to hear that,' he said, loving the way this conversation was heading.

'Yes, I actually used to work with Maureen years ago, and we lost touch, but she is incredible. Really on top of everything, and comes up with spectacular events. She will be a real asset to that team,' said Laura, her face beaming with enthusiasm.

'So I just wanted to say thank you for recommending her,' said Laura as they came to a halt outside a glass door that led to a meeting room, already occupied by the client. Winston stood tall, impressive and stately. Laura stared at him, a little star struck, and blinked up at him.

'Great news Laura. Well done. I am sure she'll fit right in,' he said, smiling a coy and all-too-charming grin.

After her interview at WSA, Maureen's life hit a virtual sixth gear. Joshua's team kept in close communication with her on every aspect of the divorce proceedings, and the few days that she had left to sort herself out before Chris arrived back were frenetic. She later recalled how he had phoned her and asked her where she was when he'd arrived home:

'Hey baby, where are you? Need some of that lucky charm magic of yours,' he had said. 'And have you done something funny to the house and moved things around?' he'd asked.

She had wanted to laugh into the phone; he was so pathetic.

She had lied and said she would be there in an hour, and he should wait for her.

Of course she hadn't gone back to the house, but the summons for the divorce had arrived in that time. It had taken him over half an hour to figure out what the documents were.

He'd gone ballistic over the phone and called her so many names she had lost count. When he eventually stopped screaming at her she asked, 'so, can I speak now?'

He had grunted in approval, giving her the chance to continue.

'I chatted to a few people and it turns out you have been making some lady friends over the years. Let me see if I can remember their names…Gemma, Anna, AND Faith - that's my personal favourite, and then what was the name of the eighteen-year-old at Sun City I saw you fucking? Oh wait, I remember, Jacqueline.'

He'd started to try and defend himself but quickly realised she was onto him.

'We will deal with this in court Maureen, just you wait,' he threatened.

'We could,' she said, pausing for effect, 'or you could read through those documents carefully and see that court is going to cost you more than you are worth my darling. So have a read and get back to me on that,' she finished, putting the phone down.

She left the phone to buzz on her dining room table as she strolled to the window of her newly-rented Sea Point apartment, gazing out over the expansive, almost infinite blue ocean.

A few days later WSA called her – not about her new contract, but to tell her about the date for the taxi driver hearing. She was to attend the hearing, in case the judge called for her testimony. Her heart sank. She knew this would eventually take place, but was terrified of standing up in front of a whole courtroom of people. She'd never actually been in a courtroom, and wondered whether it would be like the American courtroom dramas she'd seen on TV?

When the day came, she dressed as demurely as possible. Neat and classical, she thought, as she put the finishing touches to her outfit. The courtroom was nothing like the American courtrooms. It was small and pokey and smelt of hot human bodies.

She sat behind the desk where Winston sat. She'd been unable to take her eyes off him; he stood out from everyone else in the courtroom. Before she could concentrate on what was happening, things were tied up and her testimony wasn't needed. She waited in the benches to speak to Winston, and watched the three women – the other runners who must have been the dead girl's friends. The one was pregnant.

Eventually most people had cleared out and Winston returned to his desk to fetch his satchel. She walked up to him, heat rising from her groin all the way up to her neck. She saw how he watched her as she came towards him and her heart rate picked up.

'Winston, can I chat to you quickly?' she asked him, her skin tingling.

'Maureen, how good to see you,' he said, charming and very collected, as though she hadn't made him catch his breath.

'Thank you for putting my name forward for the event's position at WSA. I am hoping it's all going to work out,' she said, her eyes fixed onto his.

'No problem. Perhaps you could pop into my office when you are next in and we can catch up properly,' said Winston, imagining sex on his office desk with this petite milk-skinned goddess.

She breathed in heavily, the bulk of her bosom rising and lifting the fitted jacket. 'I'll definitely do that,' she said, and floated out of the courtroom.

Awesome foursome

The heat of summer seemed to push up from the ground, as the sun blazed down from the sky, creating an uncomfortable middle ground. The meditation garden in the centre of the main building would be hot, but Liz needed to be outside. She'd packed her lunch into an ice cream container: a lunch she had made herself, made with food she had bought herself. The new, simple joy of creating her own packed lunch thrilled her.

For years she had eaten in her parent's kitchen, never having to pack a lunch, or even buy the food for lunch. Now that she had moved out of home, she was forced to actually look after herself. At first she was a little stupefied by what was required to actually live in one's own apartment. But once she realised the freedom of choosing the food she really loved, and eating it when she wanted to, she would start singing to herself as she spread thick dollops of cottage cheese onto her rye bread and marmite sandwiches. She imagined her mother's horror at the excess amount of cheese per slice of bread. She smiled to herself as she added another dollop for good measure. She knew this would end badly for the size of her behind, but she couldn't care less. It was far too much fun to have this small, thoroughly awesome slice of freedom.

Liz had moved to Muizenberg soon after she had got the job at Western Cape Rehabilitation Centre, in Lentegeur. The move saved her an hour's travel a day, usually at peak traffic times, and made logical sense even to her parents. Liz had been really worried about telling them about her change in jobs and closing her practice on their property. She was worried they would feel hurt and think she was ungrateful, so Liz had sat her parents down to afternoon tea, and carefully tried to unpack how she had come to her decision, without telling them about her visits to her psychologist. They heard her out, and when she had finished, her father had jumped in before her mother had a chance to say anything,

'Congratulations Liz. Well done, it sounds like a wonderful opportunity. You must be so excited. We hope you will be very happy with this move,' he said gently, but firmly holding her mother's knee and turning to show her his do-not-argue face. He only used this in cases of emergency, and her mother knew not to push it when 'that' face was used. Her mother was forced to just nod demurely in agreement.

Liz had easily found an apartment in Muizenberg and couldn't deny her mother the opportunity to help out with the decorating. The apartment overlooked Surfer's Corner and had a sea view all the way to the other side of False Bay. It was pricey but worth every cent.

Liz's mom not only redecorated her new apartment, but also quickly turned Liz's old practice and cottage into two AirBnB units. Liz had barely cleared out her belongings before hearing about the new guests expected in the next few days. Liz couldn't help wondering whether her folks had been waiting for her to move out for a while. Or maybe they had just been patiently waiting for her to grow up in her own time?

Her new role at the Centre was more challenging and enjoyable than anything she'd done for years in private practice. Working with other physiotherapists, biokineticists, swimming coaches and trainers had rekindled her desire to learn.

She realised that although she religiously attended her Continuing Professional Development workshops, to earn her required registration points, she hadn't pushed herself very far in gaining new insights in her field. At first she felt very out of her league amongst her new colleagues, most of whom were studying a Masters or PhD in something. Yet during a clinical meeting, and without much thought, she advised on an alternative exercise for a patient, one the other physios hadn't thought about. The physio presenting the case gave Liz a huge smile and acknowledged Liz's idea, adding that they were so glad to have someone on the team whose sports physiotherapy knowledge brought a new perspective to their work. Liz had beamed for the rest of the day. Slowly and in her own time, she began to engage with the various professionals on the team. Some were friendlier than others, but in general, they were all deeply committed to their work, and she admired their commitment.

As Liz unpacked her lunch, she thought about her patient that morning. Many of her new patients had spinal cord injuries, and Liz was working with them to develop the physical strength to use their wheelchairs effectively. She was therefore surprised when she reached for her next patient's file and read that the patient in question was an amputee and required assistance in stability and mobility. A referral from Lentegeur Mental Hospital: 'Severely depressed but not violent,' stated the file.

The admin nurse had already put the patient in one of the waiting rooms. Liz opened the door and spoke as she walked in. 'Mr Dlamini, my name…' The words stuck in her throat, as she recognised Tshepo sitting in the middle of the room. Slowly her mind connected the dots… amputee, no prosthesis, at Lentegeur Mental hospital, Mr Dlamini. It was him. Tshepo Dlamini. The man who'd killed Claire.

She remembered the last time she'd seen him at the hearing. He'd hobbled into the courtroom, and Liz had felt overwhelmed with pity for the man. He seemed miserable and even smaller than when she'd first laid eyes on him in the hospital. The hearing had been short and decisive, and over so quickly that the three friends had gone for coffee afterwards. They'd discussed how they all ended up feeling miserable at seeing what had become of Tshepo. Even Tanya who wanted him behind bars couldn't help feeling pity towards him. He wasn't a criminal.

Liz stood frozen in time. A passing nursing sister snapped her out of her daze. 'Liz? Is everything ok here by you?' she asked in her Afrikaans lilt, sticking her head into the room.

The spell broke and Liz found her voice. 'Yes, yes, everything is fine. I'm sorry sister, please won't you close the door, thanks,' she replied, turning her head back to Tshepo. The man stared back at her, his eyes the size of golf balls. He'd obviously also realised who Liz was and was frozen in fear.

Liz walked to a chair opposite to where Tshepo sat. His wide eyes followed her across the room, not a muscle moving anywhere else in his body. Liz sat down, sighed and smiled, resting her back into the plastic chair.

'Mr Dlamini, we get the chance to talk, properly this time,' she said. Liz spoke for nearly half an hour. She told Tshepo about herself and her three friends, and how they'd been friends for most of their lives. She told him about each of them, their names and what work they did. She told him mostly about Claire, until finally she said:

'You see Mr Dlamini, Claire was an amazing woman and we loved her dearly; that is why I was so cross with you. But, you must not be scared, I am not cross with you anymore. I can see that you hurt too. We are connected by Claire, and maybe this is the universe working in its own crazy way to show us that we are all the same. And here we are, two people who would never have met before, here in this room, trying to find solutions to our problems.'

Liz looked at Tshepo.

His eyes were no longer wide with terror. Tears gently trickled down his sunken cheeks and he sniffed loudly. Liz ruffled through her pockets for a not-so-used tissue and handed it to him apologetically.

Tshepo blew loudly into the tissue and wiped his face. 'I am so sorry Liz. I was only trying to get back to Masi faster that morning. It was a bad, bad mistake,' said Tshepo, once his nose was cleared.

'I will never forget that morning, and even if I could, my missing leg won't let me,' he said, staring at his stump of a leg.

Liz stood up and came over to Tshepo. She put her hand on his shoulder and he turned to look up to her warm, kind face. For the first time in forever, Tshepo felt like there was somebody who actually cared about him. He smiled gratefully.

'We are going to help you Tshepo. I am going to help you to walk tall again, I promise,' said Liz. Her earnest face showed that she meant every word.

'Let me have a look in your file again, I don't remember seeing anything about the amputation. I just want to find out a bit more about the surgery so I have a complete history,' said Liz, as she picked up the file and scanned it once again.

'So, there is no history from False Bay in this file. I am going to need that and also a report from the physios at False Bay. I know them there, so I'll just make a quick call and ask them to email all the info through to me,' said Liz to Tshepo. She turned to leave the room but Tshepo called after her.

'Liz?' he said.

'Yes Tshepo?' she asked, turning.

'Liz, you must ask Jenny at False Bay. She is the one who said she would get me a prosthesis. She said she had ordered it, but maybe she forgot. But she said she would. You must ask her about that please because she said she would,' pleaded Tshepo, realising that he really wanted the leg, maybe even more than he wanted to die.

When Liz returned, she explained to Tshepo that the Jenny had ordered the prosthesis, but these kinds of requests were expensive and required extensive paperwork to be submitted. This all took time. The good news was that the leg had been approved. As soon as it was delivered to False Bay, Liz would collect it and bring it to the Centre for Tshepo, and she would help him become mobile with the prosthesis.

Tshepo couldn't believe what he was hearing. He sat up as Liz explained. How was it that this woman wanted to help a man like him? It seemed curious that she cared about him, even after all he had done.

'Thank you Liz. I'm so glad you are here at this place. You know all about me and I know you are going to look after me,' said Tshepo, speaking quickly and excitedly.

'No problem Tshepo. Now let's do an assessment, across the hallway in the exercise room. I need to see how you are coping on one leg and what your upper body strength is like,' said Liz, as she handed Tshepo one crutch and then clasped his free arm to help him up.

As he rose, his eyes met Liz's squarely. They held each other's gaze for a brief moment, before Liz handed Tshepo his other crutch and they moved towards the door. Physiotherapist and patient stepped out to cross the hall.

After the assessment, Tshepo and Liz walked to the waiting room, where he'd be collected to return to Lentegeur Mental Hospital. 'Goodbye Tshepo, we will see you next week,' said Liz as Tshepo sat himself on a chair. He nodded.

'Yes Liz, I am looking forward to seeing you again too.'

Liz closed her empty lunch box; what a day she'd had, and she was only halfway through. Her mind drifted to something else she'd been thinking about doing for a while. Perhaps today was the day to make that call. It was time, and today was as good a day as any. She walked back into the Centre, empty lunchbox in hand, filled with purpose.

Tanya handed the keys to the new tenants. They were a young couple: he stood tall and strong, with a perfectly trimmed hipster beard. Tanya couldn't help but notice how he had shaved legs in stark contrast to a full head of hair, beard and bushy eyebrows.

His girlfriend was petite and even smaller that Tanya. She had sparkly eyes and seemed almost childlike. She'd shown great enthusiasm as Tanya had walked them around the apartment, explaining to the darling couple about the loo handle that got stuck, and the light switch that couldn't be put on at the same time as the toaster plug.

Once they had finished the not-so-grand tour of the apartment, sparkle-eyes had turned to her bearded boyfriend, clapping her hands together excitedly and exclaiming that it was perfect. Tanya's eyebrows had risen in response to this excited outburst, and she'd turned away so they couldn't see her face. The couple's over-enthusiastic approach to everything and the constant pawing at each other made Tanya feel queasy and old. She continued to do her best to not vomit on them, or break into hysterics like a crazed bitter hag. Finally she was able to land the keys in bearded boyfriend's large palm, put on her fakest smile and close the door on the apartment and memories within.

Tanya's furniture had mostly been sold, and just a few precious items and trinkets remained. She hadn't been able to sleep in their bed since Tristan had left, and it was the first thing she sold. She'd bought herself a futon, in stark contrast to their king size memory foam bed. Her first few nights on the futon had resulted in aches and pains in places she didn't know existed, but eventually her body became accustomed to the bed and harder mattress. Getting up from the floor to stand still took a huge amount of effort, but she was determined to make it work.

Everything needed to change, and getting up out of bed every day reminded her to keep changing.

She'd managed to find a rental in Sea Point, shared with another girl who travelled extensively for work and so was hardly around. The apartment was tiny and at the side of the building, with a sliver of mountain and sea view from either window.

It wasn't ideal but it was affordable at this stage, and most importantly close to work.

The fact that she had the place to herself most of the time was the best part. She was on her own, but not exactly alone, and wasn't surrounded by retired folk either. All in all, it had been a good move.

Her job move had been the best thing she'd ever done. After dinner at the airport with Liz and Kate, Tanya had begun planning how to get out of her job. She couldn't survive without work, so she had thought long and hard about what she wanted to do. The answer was obviously 'no more PR'. That was certain, but then what? She loved writing and travelling, although she hadn't done travel writing for years.

She researched some of the travel blogs and websites, and based on their content she made enquiries about writers. Eventually she received a reply, saying they had one writer leave and were looking for a content writer. They didn't promise the travel, but perhaps in time she could do that part too. The salary had been less than her PR job, but the hours were less and the pressure was definitely halved. By moving to Sea Point she was also close to the travel site's office in Green Point, and everything had slotted into place. It was as if she had been lifted out of her old life by aliens and transported to this new existence.

She felt so disconnected from who she'd been a few weeks back. Her boss at the PR firm had turned sour when she'd resigned. Her once golden girl status was removed, and she was told to hand over her accounts quickly and leave as soon as possible. Tanya had felt hurt and betrayed, especially after all the work she had put in. But as she started to dissociate from work and the people, she realised they had done her the greatest favour by making the process fast and unemotional. She wasn't like them at all and never would be. That was probably why she had never really fitted in, or really loved what she had done. How sad that she had spent all these years doing something she didn't like, with people she had no kinship with.

Now that she was able to get to work quickly and easily, with fewer stressful hours, she found that she had so much free time. At first she had been unnerved and felt like a cheat, like she wasn't working hard enough. She'd called Kate for advice, who always seemed to manage to balance work and play effortlessly.

When she explained how strange she felt with all this extra time, and that she didn't know what to do with herself, she heard Kate smile.

'Tan, you're such a nut! This is amazing. This is called living. What most people call a life! You basically haven't had one in like forever, that's why you're so freaked out. But trust me, it's a great thing. This is the time to figure out what you love doing. Just try everything until you find your thing. Like go to yoga, or art class, or run a time trial and do Tai Chi on the promenade. You know what I mean, get out there already!' insisted Kate.

Her enthusiasm for Tanya's freedom was potentially driven by her impending motherhood and subsequent loss of freedom.

'I hadn't thought about that,' Tanya had responded, sincerely blind to the options before her.

For the past two weeks she'd just come home and sat around the apartment watching series. Once or twice she walked along the Sea Point promenade, but felt spare on her own with no one to talk to or share the time with. Kate's idea of joining some kind of sport class was mildly attractive. Tanya already went to the gym regularly and couldn't be bothered to run a time trial with over-friendly running types.

The art class on the other hand was a very attractive idea. Tanya found a pottery class run by a lady from her tumbledown house a few roads up. The property must have been worth a fortune in terms of location, yet the house was destined to be torn down. The musty smell of the old walls told of years of damp and neglect, but round the back of the house a glass studio sat, in the middle of the garden, like a diamond surrounded by a jungle of green.

The glass studio was a haven of sweet-smelling clay, paints, glaze and all manner of delicious creativity. Tanya joined an early evening class of women - a mix of personas - and immediately fell in love with her group of fellow potters. Classes were held twice a week and Tanya was determined to never miss one.

She threw herself into her plates and pots with enthusiasm, while she listened closely to the stories of everyone's lives. She allowed herself to slowly and carefully unpack her life too, in this safe place amongst kind strangers she never saw outside of the studio. She told her friends about Liz and Kate and how Kate was soon to be a mother, something she couldn't quite wrap her head around. The motherly members of the group had smiled knowingly, explaining that Kate would need Tanya now, more than ever before.

The glass house conversations inspired Tanya to create baby bowls and mugs for Kate's new baby. With every brush stroke on clay, Tanya became more excited about the arrival of this new person in her world.

Kate leaned against the dusty counter and rubbed her belly. Her legs ached and she needed a bath. 'Thank you so much Sofie. I hope it will be. Will you send me a copy of the signed agreement and all the other info too please?' asked Kate.

'Absolutely Kate, will do. Just give me a day or two, okay sweetie. I'm sure it's going to be a hit in the village,' said the estate agent as she stuffed the lease agreement papers into her overflowing paper folder.

Sofie looked Kate up and down once more, and thought to herself how ridiculous it was that this pretty girl was pregnant, close to bursting, and about to open a bookstore coffee shop. There was a high chance of failure for sure, and she'd probably have to find another tenant in six months again. Too bad for Kate, yet more commission wouldn't go amiss.

Kate watched Sofie give her the up and down and nearly told her to get the fuck out of her shop. Her pregnancy had brought on a serious case of honesty, and she had to work hard not to tell everyone what she thought of them.

It had been terrifying to leave the sanctuary of the deli and try to make it on her own. Her uncle had asked her to stay and only take on the new store once the baby was born. But there was something burning in Kate that made her want to start this new chapter as soon as possible, before the baby arrived. She knew she was way out of her depth; she didn't have any idea of what a new baby would do to her life, but she had to start now.

Everything was right, except for her protruding belly.

Once Sofie left, Kate slowly sank to the floor and through the grimy windows of her soon-to-be-opened store, looked out onto the street of Fish Hoek. In a week those people walking past would be her new customers, and she had to remind herself, convince herself, that coffee, food and books in one store, were going to work here.

She drew herself up and scratched through the wood dust on the counter. Finding a scrap of paper, she began to list all the contractors she needed to chase and all the suppliers to pay. She had one month to go until baby arrived, so one week was all she had left to make this shop come alive.

Kate threw herself completely into finishing up the décor. Her days were spent chasing suppliers who either didn't show up, or arrived extremely late without half the materials. She had to remind herself to keep calm because she couldn't afford to have the baby coming early.

As the warmth of the space slowly began to emerge from the empty white shell, she began to feel more and more excited. Two days before the opening, she waved the last contractor goodbye, closed the door and took stock of what she had created. The bookshelves went from floor to ceiling and ran the length of two long walls. A corner of the store housed small child-friendly bean bags surrounded by children's books. Restored tables and chairs were near the counter, on which her food would be displayed, and the coffee machine gleamed on the counter top.

Nearly all of the books had been unpacked by a young student she had hired, and the shelves held their bounty proudly. She'd managed to source old Persian carpets from an antiques dealer and they warmed the wooden floors. The tea and coffee cups were piled on a shelf behind the counter, a hodge podge collection of pink, blue and gold Victorian-style tea sets.

The ensemble of bric a brac, antiques, books, coffee and foodie treats came together to create a unique experience that was sure to please. Kate smiled to herself, wiped down the counter and locked up the store for the night. She beamed as she turned and looked at the store one last time before walking to her car.

She was ready to open.

Kate made her way to her mother's for dinner. This was an unusual occurrence, especially as her mother who hardly cooked, had said to come hungry. Kate was thrilled to have someone else feed her, even if it was her mother. She recalled how her mom had responded to her announcement that she was pregnant.

Kate had dropped in one afternoon and sat down with her mom in the overgrown back garden over a cup of tea. Her mother seemed old. Her eyes still sparkled, but her skin had suffered the years of sun exposure and sun spots gently touched the face of her skin along her cheekbones and below her eyes. Her hair was mostly grey, but still thick and mane-like, hanging around her face in large curls.

As Kate caught up with her mom, she made them tea; she enjoyed the comfort of the old kitchen, knowing where to find everything, old trinkets, a favourite cup, a skew teaspoon and the same old container that her mother kept the tea in. With the tea made, she joined her mother outside in the garden.

'What's up Katie? You don't pop in everyday for a cup of tea. I get the feeling you want to tell me something.'

Her mother looked Kate in the eye, her face questioning.

'You're right as usual mom. I do need to tell you something. Just wanted to say, don't freak out. I've got it under control and I'm going to be fine,' Kate cautioned, in an attempt to set the tone of the conversation.

She wanted her mom to know she would be ok, and wouldn't need to burden her.

Kate's mother raised her eyebrows, but said nothing. She sipped her tea and Kate continued.

'Mom, I'm pregnant and I'm keeping the baby and it's going to be fine, and the father isn't going to feature. It was a mistake and he actually doesn't know,' Kate said, her words fast and rushed as she made sure she covered all the important points with her announcement.

Her mother continued to sip her tea, staring in front of her. She gave nothing away until she eventually looked at Kate.

'Come here,' she said, as she put her cup down and hugged her daughter towards her.

'You aren't upset with me mom?' asked Kate into her mother's shoulder. Zelda pulled her back and held her firmly by the shoulders, face stern.

'Kate, listen to me. You may have heard me call you a mistake, but you were anything but. You regret mistakes, but once you were born, I knew that you were the most wonderful gift I had ever received. I know that motherhood wasn't exactly my strong point, and I left you to get on with growing up while I tried to figure myself out. I want to make it up to you. Let me be a part of your life, of your child's life. Please?' said Zelda.

Her face searched Kate's. Kate couldn't believe her ears. Her mother wanted to help her with her baby? Of all the people in the world. Kate blinked slowly

'Mom, of course. I didn't expect this. I would love you to help me. I need you to help me. I'm so worried and so scared,' said Kate as she embraced her mother firmly, relieved.

The rest of the afternoon was spent discussing the pregnancy and Kate's plans for her coffee shop. Kate eventually left after dinner feeling as though she should probably have fallen pregnant a long time ago, to bring her and her mother closer.

As Kate arrived at her mother's after closing the shop, Kate had to park down the road. There seemed to be an unusual number of cars parked outside her mother's. She slowly emerged from her car. Getting in and out of the car at this stage of her pregnancy was tricky, as she had to heave herself out of the car without toppling over. On a sloped hill, her exit from the car was even more precarious.

Her body seemed to ache from her ankles to the crown of her head. The strain of refurbishing the shop, together with the pregnancy, had taken its toll on her body. She slowly walked to her mother's house. The lights were on and she couldn't wait to get inside and put her bum on a couch and her feet up on a stool. She opened the door.

'Surprise!' shouted a lounge full of friendly faces.

Kate stood paralysed. What was this all about? Her mother emerged from the sea of faces.

'Surprise my love. This is your baby shower. Remember, you're pregnant and going to have a baby?' she winked at Kate, her joke making the room chuckle.

'Mom! How did....I mean, thank you. This is so unexpected. I didn't even think about a baby shower. Thank you so much,' mumbled Kate, as she was led to the couch.

A cup of tea was placed in her hand, and a loving group of friends and mothers of friends surrounded her to touch her belly and hand her gifts in pretty bags. The evening was spent catching up with friends she hadn't seen in a while, who came and sat next to her on the couch and handed her cake and quiche to nibble on, while they squealed with delight at all the gorgeous baby outfits.

Tanya and Liz had clearly been in cahoots with her mother in arranging the event and their faces beamed. At the end of the evening, when most of the women had left, Tanya brought Kate her gift. 'Careful when you open it, it could break,' she said as she handed it to Kate. Kate opened up the gift to reveal a beautiful bowl and mug, handmade and beautifully painted with images of baby trinkets.

'I made it,' said a proud Tanya. 'It was all your idea Kate, and I wanted you and the baby to have the first things I made.'

'I don't know what to say Tan, they're so beautiful. Thank you. You are so clever and talented,' said Kate, as she smiled and realised that Tanya had changed before her eyes. Her new bob made her seem younger, and the dark rings under her eyes were fading. She was finally the person they had all been waiting for her to become. 'Come here besties, I need a hug,' demanded Kate, as Liz and Tanya squashed next to Kate and her large belly.

James

The front of the boat had fewer people. The rush of the water and the sound of the boat's bow breaking through the waves made it incredibly hard to hold a conversation. James was forced to just stare ahead and watch the distant island of Koh Pha Ngan come into view.

It was late afternoon and he was on his way to the Full Moon Festival in Thailand. The festival would only really kick into gear later. As he wasn't staying on the island that night, he'd planned to visit from a nearby island so he didn't have to hang around too long with people half his age.

He knew that this festival was definitely going to play to a younger crowd, but he couldn't resist seeing what it was all about. He'd spotted some travellers his age on the boat already, so he felt comforted in the knowledge that, in a place like Thailand, there was always going to be someone older, someone younger, and definitely someone weirder.

The Aussie Barbie that had been chatting to him while queuing for the boat had given up on him eventually. His vague grunts and head nods obviously had the desired effect. She seemed sweet enough, but the strong accent had been killing him, and all he wanted at this stage of his travels was to be left alone.

Before he left South Africa, he thought he might get lonely travelling on his own, but he'd found there was always someone friendly to chat to, whilst travelling well-worn backpacker routes. In backpacker hostels, waiting to catch a plane, train, bus or boat, he found he was rarely on his own.

He'd begun his route with a quick stop in England to meet some old friends and enjoy London Town. He'd then headed off to South America. Despite the language limitations and death-defying bus trips, he had reveled in the deep green jungles and ancient architecture. India had been his next stop, which had been very intense. Coming from Africa, he thought he was pretty bulletproof in terms of human suffering, but in truth, his life in Cape Town had been very sheltered and hadn't prepared him for what he'd seen in India. It wasn't a violent or scary place, but it was poor, desperately poor, and people lived in terrible conditions.

He'd then decided to head south to the beaches of Thailand to counteract the overwhelming intensity of India. Thailand had been a welcome breath of fresh air. It was absolute escapism and he'd started his trip in Bangkok where he found his mouth hanging open in amazement. The people, temples, colourful and exotic street food, all made him stop and stare. Walking in the streets, he would be suddenly surrounded by a gaggle of school girls in blue skirts and white shirts, chattering amongst themselves, and then they'd be gone and almost instantly replaced by a swarm of German tourists.

He met new people every day, finding himself on new random adventures through the streets of Bangkok, somewhere between slightly drunk, and every now and then stoned. He had heard about the Full Moon Festival from one of the other travellers and knew he'd be able to make it in time if he left the next day. After deciding to use Ko Samui as his base island, he quickly booked a train ride south and boat to the island.

The train ride south had given his mind the opportunity to think about Kate. In amongst a group of other travellers, there'd been a girl with hair like Kate's. Curls everywhere. He remembered feeling excited as he started to walk towards her, until he'd seen her face. She had smiled and looked away. He felt foolish and quickly found a seat in another carriage. For the rest of the trip he'd been unable to think of anything else. The guilt of that night, mixed with something more than friendship, made him feel uneasy. What was it about her? Yes he was attracted to her, but it wasn't just physical, there was more. If he ever went home he would have to speak to her. Walking away from her, and telling her it was a mistake, was the worst thing he'd ever done.

The Full Moon Festival began to heave with bodies the moment the sun set and the moon began to rise above the flat ocean. The festival was a gyrating mass of luminous gear, body paint and buckets of drinks with straws. Gorgeous lithe girls in bikinis and boys in trunks filled the beach. Bodies bumped, sweated, skipped, swam and walked on their hands. After a few bucket drinks, Thailand red bulls and some other cocktail James got handed, he found himself dancing badly and stumbling towards the water.

As his toes felt the cool water, he was able to stop moving and look across the dark blue ocean. It lapped softly around his calves, cooling his body. He stumbled a little and eventually decided it would be better to sit on the sand, before he landed face first in the water. He took a few unsteady steps backwards away from the water and dropped on to his behind.

He looked across the sea, entranced by the moon in front of him: the thud of the music beat behind him, the voices of revelry dimming out as he focused on the moon. Then the moon began to change.

It became Claire's face.

Her skin glowed, mouth stretched into her gorgeous smile. Her kind eyes were looking right at him.

'James,' she said, 'you don't need to beat yourself up anymore,' her eyes sparkled.

James was transfixed.

Claire was here, talking to him.

'You can stop this now; it's going to be ok. I'm happy, you should be too. I love you James,' she spoke into his mind. And as suddenly as she had appeared, she dissolved into the moon's surface.

'Claire!' shouted James as he tried to stand up. He stumbled to his feet and ran into the water.

'Claire, come back. Don't leave me here,' he continued to shout. He was waist deep and thrashed at the water. His splashing hands attracted a group of partygoers who were walking past.

Two of the men ran in and grabbed James, thinking he was drowning.

'What are you doing? Don't take me away. She was here, she was right here,' he pleaded with the men.

'Is your girlfriend in the water too?' one of them asked.

'No, she is in the moon,' said James with conviction.

'Okay mate. I hear you. I think you're just a bit freaked out, right. Let's take you to the chill room. Think you need a cola,' he said reassuringly to James, and firmly took him away from the water and the moon.

James spent the remainder of the evening sobering up on Coca Cola and water and when the sun came up, found himself sitting on the beach waiting for the boats back to Ko Samui. He looked around him at the dregs of humanity left behind after a big party. Everything seemed tacky and smudged. The sky was grey and the humidity was rising. His skin crawled; he was desperate for a shower and bed.

He rested his face in his hands, and the moon image of Claire appeared once more. Her words repeated over and over: 'You can stop this now, it's going to be ok. I'm happy, you should be too.'

The noise of the boat motor drew him back to his reality. He climbed on board and headed to the front of the boat again.

Alone.

As the boat picked up speed, and the wind whipped against his face, tears rolled down his cheeks and were flicked from his skin.

It took James three full days to recover from the Full Moon Festival. He spent them on the beach, being pulverised and twisted by the large Thai masseurs that walked along the beach offering massages. He swam, snorkeled and ate fresh food to soothe his body.

He blamed the image of Claire's face in the moon on the alcohol, but he couldn't let go of her words. They had rung so true. His travels, the sleeping around, the intoxication, it was exhausting. No matter how far he travelled or how many women he slept with, he wasn't any happier. It was as if Claire had died and stolen it all from him, taking his happiness with her.

He floated in the water, his arms and legs spread out like a star as he closed his eyes.

God he missed Claire.

It hurt, like a seeping wound that stung every time he thought about her. Maybe less, since she had spoken to him at the festival, but it still ached. How was he ever going to be happy again?

He opened his eyes as a cloud rolled its shadow over him. Slowly and carefully he swam back to the beach, his heart heavy.

That evening he decided to check his mobile. He hadn't switched it on for weeks. Mostly it was spam marketing SMSes and emails that filled his inbox, but occasionally a friend or his mom would leave a message. Even though he denied himself the pleasure of using his mobile regularly, he couldn't help enjoying the messages when he collected them.

He missed home.

One of the most recent messages was from Liz. She said he needed to call her urgently when he could.

He smiled to himself. Liz had been the most unlikely of the girls to call him, but since Claire's death she had become strong and independent. He had heard about her moving out and starting the new job. He couldn't believe her about turn. Claire would have been thrilled to see Liz take charge of her life.

He texted her to check if she was available before calling and she responded quickly. She'd just finished work and would call him. His phone rang shortly after reading her message.

'Hey Hey Lizzie,' he said in his happy holiday voice.

'James! Oh my gosh. I can't believe I am hearing your voice. How are you?' squealed Liz with delight.

James smiled and chuckled.

'I'm good man Liz. I'm in Thailand at the moment and having a really chilled time here. I've been on the beaches for a few days, went to the Full Moon Festival last week, which was cool. But no waves to surf, so probably need to head across to Phuket island for some waves before I decide where to next. What's up with you?' he said, making sure to stick to the envy-worthy information.

'I'm so good James. The job is fab, and my new apartment is a dream. Can you believe it, I moved out of home! But that's enough about me, I can't blow all my airtime on chit chat. I need to tell you something serious. So, are you sitting down?' she asked.

James was more than amused by Liz's quick debrief.

'Sure,' he said.

In fact he was lying down on his bed. He couldn't imagine what could possibly be so serious.

'So, how do I say this? Ok, let me just say it... Kate is pregnant with your child. There, I said it.' Liz said.

James sat up. 'What?' he shouted into the phone.

'I said Kate is pregnant with your child. That's what I said,' Liz said, speaking more slowly this time.

'Shit! Are you for freaking real Liz?' he demanded, now standing up.

'Yes' he heard her say.

'Why didn't you tell me before? In fact, why hasn't Kate told me before? What the fuck is going on?' He started to pace the room.

'I'm sorry to tell you like this James, but Kate wasn't ever going to tell you. And well, I think it's wrong. I know you are the kind of guy who would want to know,' she said, starting to defend her thinking, and reminding herself of why she was doing this against her best friend's wishes.

'Of course I want to know. What was she thinking not telling me? How far along is she?' he asked as he did the mental maths himself.

'It's nearly time. In fact any time from now,' Liz said. 'I just couldn't keep it from you any longer. Kate didn't want to spoil your travels. She said you needed to do this travel thing and get it out your system, but I know she is going to need help, your help.'

Liz waited for James to respond.

'James?'

James stood still. He looked around his cheap accommodation, at his clothes on the floor, at the unshaven face staring back at him in the mirror. Now what?

'You did the right thing Liz. Thank you. I'll keep you posted. Chat soon,' he said, and with that he put the phone down and started to pack his bag.

The shop was finally ready. Tomorrow would be opening day, and by the universe's good graces, everything had actually come together. Kate looked around her: the floor-to-ceiling bookshelves were full of classics, new fiction, non-fiction, everything you could possibly want. The kids' corner was warm and inviting, to encourage children to scrounge through books for their favourites. Kate had already organised a local author to come through and read from her children's book in the next few days. The post on social media had been a hit, and the shop was bound to be full of mums and kids on the day.

Tanya had written a compelling press release and sent it out to her old contacts, so Kate had found her new shop mentioned across online and print media, without lifting a finger. Tanya had made her sound all woman power, 'mom-to-be mompreneur.'

When Kate tried to resist this angle, Tanya showed her the stern face she used with difficult clients and said:

'Listen to me, I know what works. Just go with it for crying out loud. Do you want the coverage or not?'

So Kate had gone with it and it worked.

She now stood in her shop, her enormous belly wrapped in a beautiful pre-loved preggi-wrap dress she'd found in a charity store down the road.

There were snacks spread out across the coffee tables, which she'd pushed together to create a long table of deliciousness. The champagne was on ice and ready to be popped. He mother was bringing the flowers and she felt excited beyond words. The door opened and Liz and Tanya came in, Liz giving her an enormous hug.

'This is so gorgeous! I love it Kate. Only you could have created something like this. You are amazing!' she exclaimed, as she walked around touching everything and grinning.

Tanya turned into Miss PR and went into 100 questions a minute about all the details. Who was the photographer, when was he arriving, did Kate have the press packs ready, who else was coming? On and on she went, and luckily Kate could answer all the questions to Tanya's satisfaction.

Tanya breathed and gave Kate a hug. Stepping back she looked her up and down 'Hmmm, you know. You actually make this whole pregnant business look quite hot,' she said.

Kate threw her head back and laughed.

'Seriously Tan, of all the ways to describe my situation, you choose "hot"! I feel like a Southern Right whale,' Kate said.

The two women smiled at each other. For the first time in forever they felt as if they were truly seeing each other. The moment slipped away as guests began to file into the shop. From then on, the evening rolled into the clinking of glasses, finger licking, laughter, oohs and aahs.

Kate made a small speech to welcome everyone and said a few thank yous. The evening continued well past your average shop warming time, and eventually the last loud reporter was escorted out the shop and the door locked behind him.

Kate, Zelda, Tanya and Liz all sat around the table. Kate lifted her weary feet onto a chair, her ankles swollen from standing.

'Yeesh Kate, you have cankles!' said Tanya, horrified.

'Yes I know, thanks for pointing that out. All that, you are so hot when you are pregnant stuff seems to have gone from your mind,' quipped Kate, raising her eyebrows in mockery of Tanya's earlier statement.

'I hadn't spotted those earlier,' said Tanya. 'Anyway, it was amazing. What a great opening Kate. Best I've ever been to.'

'Me too,' said Liz, who had probably never been to an opening of any sort.

'Well done my angel,' said Zelda, as she tucked a curl of hair behind Kate's ear.

'Let's go home and I'll help you clean up early tomorrow before you open. Need to get some rest now,' she said, as she helped Kate up and together the four women switched the lights off, locked up and went home.

The first few days in the shop were tumultuous to say the least. Kate's internet was intermittent, choosing not to work each time someone tried to pay. The coffee machine also choked one morning and Kate had to call the technician from across town to come and fix it. Luckily two of her staff from the deli had come with her. They were young and dedicated to Kate, and although their lives seemed dominated by social media, they were friendly and helpful and people never complained about them.

The children's book author reading went extremely well. Kate couldn't believe how much childbirth advice she could receive in two hours, from the mothers who'd attended. She felt terrified by the end of the day and had to take some rescue remedy to calm her nerves. She'd gone to her mother afterwards to ask for her advice and her mother laughed it off.

'Ugh, those women. They are such a drag. One would swear that all they have ever amounted to is a birthing vehicle, the way they go on and on about it. Seriously. Who cares? As long as you and baby are alive and healthy. What does it matter? Stop over thinking it my love. Just get the baby out, because once it's out you can't put it back. And then the real fun starts. Bet those hags didn't tell you anything about parenting, did they?' she said knowingly.

Her mother's disdain for 'those women' had always amused Kate, and in this case, helped her feel much better. She knew she wanted to try for a natural birth, but she was scared and completely freaked out. Liz and her mother were going to be with her at the birth, and this helped her feel safer, knowing that they would be her strength and mind if she needed it. She eventually decided to stop herself from thinking about childbirth. Whatever was going to happen would happen. She had the daily issues with the shop to think about and distract her. That was as good as her birthing plan was going to get.

Reconstruction and moving forward

Stage 6

As a person starts to become more functional, realistic solutions seem possible for life after the loss.

Chapter 6

Tshepo

Tshepo had been practising using his prosthesis for only two weeks, when one of Mr Buswayo's young lawyers visited him. There to collect the report from the psychologist, she'd checked on Tshepo and told him his next court appearance was in four days. He'd tried to ask the young lawyer what would happen next: Where was he going to go? Did he need to pack his clothes? Did they know that he needed to be near the physiotherapy centre?

The young lawyer had listened to his questions with mild concern. She then simply reassured him that Mr Buswayo had everything under control, and all that Tshepo had to do was appear in court on the right day.

Tshepo could hardly sleep after her visit.

He hobbled across his room fitfully that night, until his roommate complained, and the night nurse gave Tshepo a sleeping tablet.

He began to wonder why Mr Buswayo hadn't come to see him. Maybe the news was bad and he was going to go to prison after all. Perhaps he should kill himself now, before they took him away. He certainly knew enough about the workings of this place to figure out a way to kill himself. What about his prosthesis and Liz? She would be sad if he died before he had learned to walk properly. No, he should wait to find out what his fate was, and then he would decide if it was time to die.

On the day of the second hearing, Tshepo found himself dressed in the same clothes he'd arrived at Lentegeur in. Yet this time, he was able to stand without crutches. He still looked foolish because he'd arrived in only one shoe, but now he stood ready to go to court, one synthetic foot sticking out of his trouser leg. He didn't quite know what was more ridiculous: the crutches and half a leg, or the fake foot sticking out the bottom of his pants.

He sighed as he waited at the entrance for his lift. The nurse who had brought him to the reception said: 'You're doing so well with your new leg Mister Dlamini, but I hope you won't be running away,' she smiled at Tshepo, leaving him unsupervised at the entrance to wait for Winston.

Eventually Tshepo saw Mr Buswayo walk through the doors. He couldn't quite believe it was him. Had he really come to fetch Tshepo himself? Tshepo carefully stood up to show Mr Buswayo his new leg. Winston's face went from a warm greeting to shock. 'Tshepo? How are you standing like this?' he asked him quickly, looking Tshepo up and down, clearly in disbelief.

'Mr Buswayo, this is my new prosthesis,' said Tshepo, as he lifted his trouser leg to reveal more of the mechanism.

'I see,' said Winston, as he stepped back to look at Tshepo. His mind worked quickly; how would this look in court? He needed Tshepo to be the downtrodden taxi driver, who had made a mistake and was paying for it through the loss of his leg, riddled with guilt and severely depressed as a result. This prosthesis could interfere with Winston's finely-crafted case. He made an immediate decision.

'You must take it off and get your crutches. We cannot go to court with you like this. The judge won't like this, not at all! You must be the same as last time. Come, where are your crutches? Let's go and get them and take the prosthesis off,' he said, taking Tshepo's arm firmly and guiding him back inside.

In amongst a flurry of nurses, all too eager to please Winston, Tshepo's prosthesis was swiftly removed and replaced with the crutches. Winston stood back once more and looked Tshepo up and down. Order had been restored.

'Ah, there we go, much better. This is better for court my friend. You will see. Thank goodness I came to fetch you myself,' said Winston as he walked to his Audi, Tshepo limping behind on crutches.

Tshepo had never been in such a luxurious vehicle. The number of lights and buttons fascinated him, and it felt as if the car was floating above the road.

'So Tshepo tell me, how have you been?' asked Winston, drawing Tshepo out of his awestruck state.

'I am better Mr Buswayo. Yes, better. I am not like my old person, but I am better. Not so sad. The prosthesis is helping me Mr Buswayo. It is very good. Why did you not want me to wear it today?' asked Tshepo, still confused about Winston's reaction.

'You must not mention the prosthesis in court, do you understand me Tshepo. It is of no concern to the judge. Are we clear?' demanded Winston, his face stern.

'Yes, yes Mr Buswayo, this is not a problem,' said Tshepo, still unclear as to why the prosthesis was such a problem for his case.

'Good, that's good. Everything will go well. You will see,' said Winston. 'The report has confirmed that you are unfit to stand trial. The judge will probably agree and then the matter will be sent to the National Director of Public Prosecution for the final decision, and then the case will be struck off the roll,' explained Winston, as he smiled and looked straight ahead. He sat straighter in his seat, and seemed to expand with confidence.

'This is all much better than we could ever have hoped for, if you had been fit to stand trial,' said Winston, clearly pleased with the outcome he envisioned.

Tshepo understood that he was probably not going to go to jail. For this he nearly wept. Yet the relief was quickly replaced by fear, as he looked out of his window at the world passing by.

Where would he go? Would Lentegeur kick him out? How would he see Liz again? What about the medication? Where would he get his medicine from if he left the mental hospital? The questions bombarded his brain, and he felt gripped by fear and anxiety. He crossed his arms across his body and hugged himself.

'Mr Buswayo, this is good, but I do not know what will happen now? Will they send me away from the hospital?' asked Tshepo, anxiety rising in his voice as his stomach tightened.

'I want to stay there at Lentegeur, I am not well enough to leave yet. You must tell the judge. I cannot go yet, please Mr Buswayo,' begged Tshepo.

Winston listened carefully, silent. His curved cheekbones seemed to harden as he clenched his jaw tighter. Eventually he responded, never taking his eyes off the road in front of him.

'Tshepo,' he said, 'you are about to be a free man. You will be able to do whatever you want. I can request that the judge keeps you in Lentegeur for longer, however this is up to the doctors, not me and not the judge. You are going to be free after being accused of culpable homicide. Do you realise what I have done for you?' his voice became louder.

The Audi purred along towards the courthouse.

Tshepo remained silent, digesting Winston's stern talking down.

'Mr Buswayo, sir, I want to say thank you so much for everything,' said Tshepo, feeling small and inadequate. His words stuck in his throat as he swallowed carefully, trying not to choke. 'Yes, thank you for making me free. I will be a better person when I am free again.' His body shrunk into the leather, the thought of being free terrifying him into submission.

The second hearing, as with the first, was short and to the point. The judge reviewed the report from the psychologist at Lentegeur. Tshepo had been found to be unfit to stand trial, and it was recommended that the case be struck off the roll. The psychologist recommended additional rehabilitation at Lentegeur and the nearby physiotherapy centre, until the final hearing and decision from the National Director of Public Prosecution. The judge did as before and spoke to the advocate in big words, and then there was the hammer and paper. It was all over, again.

Mr Buswayo walked over. 'Well Tshepo, seems you are a lucky man. You will be rehabilitated and you will not go to jail. Congratulations my friend,' Winston said, as he stood tall and proud.

'Thank you, thank you Mr Buswayo, you've saved me,' said Tshepo, as he looked up earnestly at Winston's face. Winston patted Tshepo on the shoulder.

'You are not a bad man Mr Dlamini. You were just in the wrong place at the wrong time' he said, as he took a step back. 'I will see you at the final hearing,' he said, before walking away. Tshepo was escorted to a holding cell, until he could be taken back unceremoniously by a police van to the mental hospital he could now call home.

Winston heaved a sigh of relief when he got back into his car. The trial had gone well, as he'd predicted.

In the meantime, Tshepo would be safe in Lentegeur, learning to walk with his prosthesis. Winston shook his head as he thought about how fortunate he was that he'd gone to fetch Tshepo. He had felt sorry for him, and wanted to ensure Tshepo was still looking as pitiful as he had been, when he had last seen him. He also hoped to see some reporters, as he brought Tshepo to court himself. Fortunately there were a few journalists, and Winston looked forward to some positive media coverage.

He realised now that he'd probably been a bit cold with Tshepo, but he had to act fast to make sure there were no grounds for contesting the psychological assessment and report findings. It had worked, and scolding Tshepo had the desired effect of making the man feel miserable. His sad face and hunched-over body had ensured that everyone in that courtroom felt nothing but sorrow for the taxi driver, who had made a terrible mistake one morning in Fish Hoek, driving too fast.

Winston turned the ignition and made his way back to the office. Once at his desk he switched to autopilot, only surfacing when his stomach growled at him during the afternoon. He took the stairs down to the canteen to see if there was anything left at this time of the day. Worst case, he would grab a chocolate and coke to stave off the hunger.

The canteen was empty, so he grabbed some snacks and headed to the till to pay. As he handed over his money, he noticed out of the corner of his eye that someone else had also walked into the canteen.

He looked up and saw it was Maureen.

He breathed her in and almost instantly she turned and spotted him. Her eyes lit up.

'Winston, you're back from court,' she cooed.

She moved towards him. He felt his spine straighten and abs pull against his fitted shirt. She looked incredible in a deep emerald green pencil skirt and jacket. Costume jewellery sparkled and jangled on her wrist. As she got closer he could smell her perfume. He felt the heat rise up his neck.

'Maureen hello,' he said, in a cool, confident tone, giving nothing away as to how she made him feel. 'Yes, back from court and it looks like we have ourselves a struck case,' he said, smiling broadly at her as he picked up his food.

'Well done,' Maureen said. 'I feel like it's the best thing for everyone. Right?' she looked up at him, her large eyes staring into his for an answer.

'Yes of course,' he said, almost too quickly. Stepping back he continued: 'And how are you getting along?' Winston asked.

'I'm good, just grabbing a coke to get through the arvie,' she answered, as she moved away from him and went to the fridge to get one. He smiled at her misunderstanding.

'No, I meant how are you enjoying the firm?' he said, smiling and trying not to sound patronising. The pink rose in her cheeks as she realised her mistake. She laughed at herself, then paid for her coke before answering him.

'I love it here. It's incredible to be part of a dynamic team and everyone is so friendly. We're preparing for some big client events which will probably be quite stressful, but otherwise, it's all working out really well.'

She looked down at her feet.

'I can't thank you enough, really,' she said.

'It's no problem at all,' Winston said, placing his hand on her shoulder. 'I'm really glad to hear you are fitting in.'

Awkwardly, he removed his hand as they walked out of the canteen together. Winston pressed the lift button.

'I could do with a good meal and a celebration, because of the case and your new job. What do you think about grabbing dinner tonight?' Winston suggested, watching Maureen's face closely, trying to gauge her response.

The lift pinged and they got inside.

'Ok, I think we can do that, but it's on me… We could call it a thank you for putting my name forward for the job, and for winning the case. How's that?' Maureen said as the lift began to rise.

'Deal. Let's go straight from here. I'll book. Let's meet at reception at 7:30?' he said, thinking quickly about which restaurant they should go to.

'Perfect,' she said, smiling up at him as the elevator opened on her floor. He watched her walk away, as he held the lift door open. 'Any weird allergies or foods you don't eat?' he called after her.

She turned around and with a wry smile said: 'I eat everything.'

Maureen

The sun warmed the lounge of her apartment, spilling onto her couch. Maureen snuggled into the sun-warmed cushions on her couch, slowly sipping the steaming hot cup of green tea in the morning sun. The steam curled up from the mug in the sun's rays, drifting through the little flecks of glistening dust. The tea would ease the gnawing headache, but she knew a disprin would be needed, to actually make it go away.

Besides the headache, the rest of her body tingled with delight as she recalled the previous evening. She couldn't actually remember how much champagne she had drunk. She'd gone with Winston to a tiny, funky restaurant in town with ten or twelve tables, overly attentive waitrons and amazing tapas. Winston had ordered a few dishes, and while they waited for the first one to arrive they started to talk. Not as a lawyer and a witness, not as two colleagues, but just as two people who were incredibly attracted to each other.

The conversation flowed easily, and once the tapas were finished, they urgently called for the bill. They'd come back to her place and barely made it to her front door before he'd pulled her suit off. Her hair stood on end as she recalled how gorgeous he was naked. She'd found herself breathtakingly turned on by seeing her pale breasts pressed hard against his dark chest. She loved the look of surprise on his face, followed by absolute delight as they'd explored different positions.

Sex with Winston proved she no longer needed Chris for anything. She finally felt like who she should be: independent, successful and happy. She put her empty cup down and lay back on the couch in the sun. Closing her eyes, she let the warmth envelop her as she drifted back to sleep.

Winston woke up and stretched across Maureen's bed. She wasn't next to him. He sat up with a jerk. What was the time? He spotted his phone and got up to switch it on. He breathed a sigh of relief. Plenty of time to get home, shower and get to the office. Maureen's apartment was close enough to his. He stretched his lithe body and leaned back. His penis began to rise as he thought of Maureen.

He went to find her.

She was lying on her couch, naked and asleep, red hair splayed around her, her skin shining like alabaster in the sun.

He was hard instantly. He walked over to her carefully and began to caress her breasts. His mouth found the tip of her vagina and he buried his tongue gently into her clitoris. She moaned softly as her body woke from sleep. Her eyes flickered open and comprehended what was happening. She moaned until she shook. He then climbed on top of her, rhythmically moving in time with her body.

Maureen and Winston avoided each other at work. It would have been plain for anyone else to see there was something going on between them. In Maureen's mind she felt like there was actual electricity that shot between them. They would go for dinner and it would end at either his place or hers. Or sometimes they just wouldn't bother with dinner at all. Only once they had satiated their lust could they begin any kind of in-depth conversation.

At their first dinner, Winston had asked about Chris. Maureen had skipped over the details and just told him that the divorce was under way. Only over the past few weeks had she slowly unpacked what had been happening with Chris: the gambling, the cheating.

Initially Winston just listened, and then began to ask more prying questions about Chris. He approved of the lawyer she'd chosen for her divorce proceedings. Yet when she told him she hadn't seen Chris since he got back, and only served him with papers, he'd become concerned.

'He's going to come and find you. Does he know where you live?' he asked, jaw tense.

'No way, he hasn't got a clue. Besides he's going to head offshore in a few days anyway,' she assured him, shrugging her shoulders and trying to seem very nonchalant about it. But she knew he was right.

Chris had phoned her a few times wanting to meet, but she was terrified of seeing him face to face. She knew he was capable of hurting her.

'You need to meet him at the lawyer, so he knows it's over. Finalise the paperwork and move on. What you have told me about him worries me that he will intimidate you,' Winston said. He walked over to her mobile and picked it up.

'Here, call Joshua and set it up now. Don't put this off. He is dangerous and you know it,' he said, holding the phone out to her.

She sighed. There was no way she was going to get out of it, so she made the call and Joshua agreed to set the meeting up at his offices.

'There, done. Happy?' Maureen said to Winston, her hand on her hip looking rather coquettish.

'Yes,' said Winston. 'Now, let's take that dress off.'

The meeting with the lawyers was at 9am. She asked her boss for the morning off and as she waited in the reception area, she allowed herself to think about Chris and what they had been. She had been happy for a few years, but the novelty of no work and being kept as a trophy wife for his return had definitely worn off over time.

She also realised that although she'd never wanted for anything from Chris, he'd never actually given her any of the human relationship she craved. The emotional aspect of the divorce felt almost too easy to her, and she often wondered why she hadn't cried about it yet. Had she fallen out of love with Chris before she found out about the affairs? Probably. The accident and everything that followed had merely been the catalyst to knock some sense into her. The truth was that, in her heart, Chris was a man she once loved.

Joshua arrived and took her through to the boardroom. He explained what she could expect to happen, and that she should let him speak on her behalf, unless he asked her to respond.

Chris and his lawyer arrived soon after. Chris seemed leaner to Maureen, but otherwise the same. His powerful personality filled the room as he walked in.

'Maureen, you couldn't fucking meet me without your little lawyer. S'pose you fucking him now hey?' said Chris, looking Joshua up and down.

Maureen's mouth opened, but before she could say anything Joshua put his hand on her arm.

'Please take a seat Mr Klaasen and let's begin immediately,' said Joshua, his voice calm as he slid a file across the table towards Chris's lawyer.

'We will be sticking to the agenda as presented in our previous communication,' said Joshua, shutting down Chris's outburst.

Chris's lawyer and Joshua leaned across the table and shook hands. Chris was slumped in his chair, staring Maureen down. She ignored him and looked in front of her, shifting in her seat to sit taller. As the lawyers reviewed the assets, Maureen focused on breathing. She knew the lawyers were speaking to each other, but she couldn't hear them. All she could feel was Chris's stony eyes, boring into her.

Eventually it was over, and Chris and his lawyer left. Once they were out of the room, Joshua turned to Maureen. 'Are you ok?' he asked, gently. She wilted, her strong façade no longer required.

'That was awful,' she whispered, her voice small and shoulders slumped forward. She looked at Joshua. 'How could I possibly have been married to him?' she asked, face earnest, seeking an explanation.

Gently, Joshua placed a hand on her arm to reassure her.

'Maureen, don't feel alone, this is what often happens with divorce, I see it over and over again. When you have decided it is really over, it's as though the person you married no longer exists, and you're faced with an entirely new person - one you don't even recognise.' Joshua explained. He got up and walked to the water dispenser and handed Maureen the glass.

'I suppose divorce shows you who you've really been married to. It removes the rose-tinted glasses of years of marriage, and everything you've swept under the carpet over time,' he continued, shrugging his shoulders.

Maureen sipped the water. 'I guess so,' she agreed, standing up to collect her things.

'Maureen, can I just check, are you sure he isn't going to try and...' he hesitated, looking for the right words 'hurt you?' he eventually said.

He stood awkwardly, hands in his suit pockets.

'To be honest Joshua no, I'm not sure he won't try something. But he doesn't know where I live at the moment, or where I work. I'm going to try and keep it that way until he cools off. Guess that's the best I can do,' Maureen answered, smiling weakly.

'We could get a restraining order, but hopefully it won't come to that. Keep me posted, ok?' he said, searching her face for a response.

'I will,' promised Maureen as she walked out the door. 'Thank you again Joshua.'

Maureen took the lift to the underground parking. She walked towards her car, starting to think about what the rest of her day had in store. She'd have to catch up on a meeting she'd missed that morning. Lost in thought, she rummaged through her handbag to find her car keys.

'Hello Maureen.'

Maureen froze. She hadn't found her keys. The hand in her bag stopped moving and she slowly turned around.

He was a metre away, standing tall, flexing his biceps as his eyes twinkled wickedly.

'Took you a while to get to your car. You sure you're not fucking your lawyer?' Chris asked.

Maureen breathed in deeply, once, then twice. Time seemed to move slowly as she found the strength to speak. She swallowed hard.

'No, I'm not fucking my divorce lawyer Chris. Are you fucking yours?' she said, one eyebrow raised.

He smiled.

'Still a clever bitch, aren't you?' he jeered, taking a step closer to her.

She couldn't move.

'I remember another time we stood by your car: in the garage, at home, when we had hot sex. What do you say, once more, for old times' sake?' he said, eyeing her up and down. She managed a frantic step backwards, and found herself pushed up against the cold barrier of the empty car park. She was completely hemmed in between two cars, with Chris in front of her.

Her fear started to show on her face, her eyes darting around desperately, looking for a way out as she realised she was trapped.

'Guess that's a no then,' said Chris, as he watched her panic rise. He put his hands into his jeans pockets. 'Don't fret baby, I'm not going to force you. Not here. I know we are done on paper, but just so you know, I'll be keeping an eye on you. Might pop in to your new apartment in Sea Point, when I get back in four weeks,' he grinned.

The colour drained from Maureen's face.

He sniggered. 'Ex-Navy baby, you know I have ways to find you, wherever you are,' he said, in a cold whisper.

'See you around.'

Maureen leaned heavily on the bannister. 'Oh my fuck, fuck, fuck,' she swore softly, looking at her feet. He knew where she lived, and in no uncertain terms, he was definitely going to come and find her.

And do what? What did he have in mind? Was he going to rape her again? Would he beat or kill her? What was she going to do? She scratched in her bag and called Joshua. He answered her call and she frantically told him everything that had happened.

'Ok, this is what I'm going to do. We have cameras all over our parking lot. I'll pull the footage, chat to my team and get back to you. Ok?' he asked. Maureen nodded. 'Maureen, are you ok, are you there?' asked Joshua.

'Yes, yes, that's fine,' she said as she ended the call.

She found her car keys and got into her car, locking the doors once she was inside. Her hands were shaking as she placed them on the steering wheel. There was no way she was going home. She needed to be around people, and work was probably the safest place she could be.

Luckily, the rest of Maureen's day passed uneventfully. Winston had messaged her to say he had a client dinner and wouldn't see her that evening. He asked about the meeting at the lawyers. She told him that it had all gone according to plan. She would tell him about Chris's threat when she saw him. She didn't want to upset Winston, not over the phone.

She stayed at work as long as she could, and then realised she eventually had to go home. She dreaded the thought, and as she arrived home she was on high alert.

She checked to see if there was anyone in the parking lot before unlocking the doors and getting out of her car. Almost running to the lifts, she stood with her back to the door, as she waited for the lift to arrive and open, watching the empty parking lot.

When the doors opened, she jumped in the lift and frantically began pressing the close button repeatedly. The lift closed and began to move up.

The lift stopped at the ground floor. The doors opened and Maureen stood in the corner, holding her breath, waiting. A petite dark-haired woman entered. She was pretty and wore jeans and a t-shirt. She smiled at Maureen in acknowledgement, and then turned to press the number of her floor. Realising it was the same as Maureen, and it had been pressed already, she stepped back and waited for the lift doors to close automatically. Maureen exhaled. She was safe. This woman was with her and she would be ok.

She felt as though the woman was looking at her. Slowly she met her gaze. She was one of the women from the accident, one of the runners.

Maureen blinked, not believing her eyes. Tanya stared back at Maureen and exclaimed:

'It's you, from the trial. You're the witness who saw Claire's accident,' she said with a look of disbelief.

The lift stopped and the doors opened.

'I am,' Maureen nodded.

The doors of the lift began to close again, and the two women stood motionless staring at one another. Tanya quickly pressed the open button and the lift doors opened again. Before she knew what she was saying, Maureen asked:

'Please, do you want to come over and chat? I have tea or coffee. Wine? Whatever you want. It would be really great to chat,' stumbled Maureen, desperate not to be alone in her apartment.

'Yes,' said Tanya. 'I would like that', and she followed Maureen to her apartment.

Awesome foursome

Tanya had been returning from her evening pottery lesson when she had bumped into Maureen. She'd walked home from the potter's house along the busy streets of Sea Point. The warm evening was beautiful, and the full moon was high in the sky.

Her pottery lesson was relaxing, and she'd enjoyed another evening of listening to the women in her group solve the world's problems, over cake, a cup of tea and a lump of clay.

Once she climbed into the lift, it took her a few moments to register who was there. It was so out of context. Fish Hoek, the courtroom, Claire and the accident, all seemed miles away when she was in Sea Point. The past few months had given her the break she desperately needed. She felt as though she'd escaped pain and sadness, leaving it all behind her in the seaside town she'd grown up in. Nobody knew about Claire or Tristan here. They couldn't smile knowingly at her, touch her arm and say: 'How are you Tan?' in that concerned, nosey way.

Here, she was allowed to just be. She wasn't constantly reminded of what had gone wrong in her life. Seeing Maureen had completely floored her. Her mind had ticked through the images of Maureen stored in her mind: a woman in her lingerie in the street, talking to the paramedics; a woman, beautifully dressed in the courtroom, the distinctive red hair. Tanya stared at Maureen, unable to believe she was in the same lift with her.

Still in a daze of memories, she'd nodded her acceptance to Maureen's invitation and followed her to the apartment. Maureen's apartment was beautiful. Minimalist décor allowed the expansive view to own the space. Tanya hadn't realised that on this side of the building, the apartments were definitely much bigger and with real views. Her crummy little view of the mountain had seemed enough. Now that she knew what was on this side, a small pang of jealousy tugged at her diaphragm. She looked down at her clothes and realised she was filthy from the studio. She'd obviously wiped her clay-covered hands on her jeans at some point in the evening, and they were covered in a thin film of dry grey clay dust. She swallowed hard and tried to stand a bit taller, walking over to the glass side of the apartment, looking out at the view of the dark black ocean. The lights of Cape Town's Waterfront twinkled in the distance, and she found herself gazing out across the ocean, spellbound by the moon.

Maureen hardly made a sound when she came back into the lounge from the kitchen. She carried two large goblet-style wine glasses filled with red wine. The liquid sloshed gently from side to side.

She paused and watched Tanya for a moment, before softly announcing her return.

'It's amazing hey,' she said, watching Tanya.

Tanya's slight shoulders sighed.

'It is,' she answered, slowly peeling her eyes away from the glass window to look at Maureen.

Maureen saw Tanya look at the glasses. She smiled and joked, 'I don't have tea, and it's too late for coffee, so guess it's wine.' Tanya smiled, 'sounds good and looks good to me,' she said, walking to the couch. Tanya looked down at her clay-stained jeans and then at Maureen.

'I've just come back from pottery, sorry my jeans are filthy. I can run up and get some clean clothes,' said Tanya, her face showing her embarrassment.

'Oh please, don't bother. It's a couch, it gets cleaned. Sit!' insisted Maureen.

Tanya sat carefully on the couch and took her wine goblet. She hadn't drunk in ages, and the taste of this delicious red ran over her tongue. She felt herself soften into the couch.

'So, what brings you to Sea Point, I thought you lived in Fish Hoek?' asked Maureen. The two women sat facing each other, on the same couch.

Mirror images, comfortable yet cautious.

'I moved here a short while back. I needed to hand over my lease in Fish Hoek, and I thought that Sea Point would be a good change,' said Tanya, glazing over Tristan's rapid exit from her life.

'Well cheers to that,' toasted Maureen, as they clinked their glasses together. 'A change is as good as a holiday, as they say,' she added.

'And you? Why have you moved to Sea Point,' asked Tanya.

Maureen took a deep breath in, followed by a large gulp of wine.

'How do I say this? Basically, I caught my husband cheating on me and I left him and his Fish Hoek house. I never really fitted in there anyway, and I wanted to be closer to work. So ya, that's how I ended up here,' said Maureen, taking another sip.

Tanya took this all in. She couldn't believe that a man would cheat on this woman. She was insanely gorgeous and oozed sex appeal.

'I'm so sorry that happened to you,' she said, looking into her wine glass for better words.

Don't be. He was an asshole and my life is way better without that dickhead,' said Maureen, 'besides, if all the paperwork goes through today, he will be an ex-husband shortly! And then I'll be free of him, forever,' Maureen said with delight.

Tanya realised how thrilled Maureen was to be free of her husband. Yet she, on the other hand, was devastated about Tristan.

'I wish I was as upbeat as you seem to be. My boyfriend just upped and left me after Claire's death, and that's why I couldn't afford the apartment in Fish Hoek anymore,' she said, looking into her swirling wine. 'Just like that, after two years he said he didn't love me and was over me. I hoped we'd get married. Stupid hey?' she said, as she looked up at Maureen.

Maureen smiled gently. 'Well let me tell you, his loss. You are a stunner! Maybe I could set you up with one of the hot lawyers at work. Tell me more about you?' pried Maureen, her casual flattery having the desired impact of making Tanya feel comfortable to open up.

They shared common work experiences, and as the wine flowed, the unease slipped away. It was past midnight by the time Tanya wobbled out of Maureen's apartment. Maureen had promised to lift Tanya to the gym in the morning, and so the two women went to sleep, knowing that they had a person they could connect to in their new lives.

After gym the next morning, Tanya walked back to the apartment as Maureen zipped off to work in her Mini. That woman was a machine, Tanya thought to herself, she had barely kept up with her.

Tanya had to tell Liz about her new 'friend', the coincidence was too bizarre. She really liked Maureen; there was something solid about her that made

Tanya feel grounded.

Tanya called Liz on her mobile, and heard her familiar voice answer. 'Tan, so glad you called. Need to chat to you urgently. Is now good?' bulldozed Liz. Tanya smiled.

'That's why I called, I have something to tell you,' she said. Liz paused. 'Oh really…what?' she asked. Tanya told her all about the lift meeting with Maureen, and their wine catch up and gym that morning.

'Wow, insane. Can't believe it's her Tan. That's cool that you guys connected. I'm dying to meet her. You will have to organise something where we all get together,' said Liz.

'Before Kate pops,' added Tanya.

They both laughed at the ongoing joke. There seemed to be too many things that had to be done with Kate, before the baby arrived; a never-ending list that would probably never be ticked.

'That reminds me about what I need to tell you, and you have to put aside all your issues with Kate,' Liz said, as though she were speaking to a child, who was incapable of listening without throwing a tantrum.

'I'm listening. And by the way I've gotten over caring about Kate's unsavoury sexual habits. Besides, I'm kind of hoping the baby will sort it out,' said Tanya, with a slight smug look on her face.

'Ok, here goes, I think you should know who the father is, of Kate's baby. It's going to be important when he comes back,' said Liz.

'You know who the father is? And you haven't told me. What the hell Liz. Why haven't you told me?' said Tanya, reaching the front of her building and raising her voice slightly.

She paced up and down the steps of the entrance.

'I was waiting for the right time, but I've run out of time, and I want you to be onboard,' Liz added, as though there was some master plan that Tanya needed to buy into, despite the fact she knew nothing about it.

'Onboard for what?' retorted Tanya, her temper rising.

'Tan, breathe or I can't tell you,' said Liz.

Checking herself, Tanya let out a sigh and calmed down.

'Sorry,' she replied meekly.

'The father is James. He is coming back because I called him in Thailand and said it would be important for him to be at the birth. Or something like that. Anyway, I think he's coming home. He totally didn't know,' said Liz, dropping what felt like an atomic bomb into Tanya's ear.

She couldn't actually believe what she was hearing. Kate and James had slept together; obviously very soon after Claire's death, and that had resulted in Kate's baby. Claire's James was Kate's baby's father. It was all too much.

'No way!' gasped Tanya, as she sat onto the steps and held her head in her hands.

'I know, it's weird and maybe sordid, but it's also really great. I mean a baby from James AND Kate will be amazing. This is going to be the coolest baby ever!' babbled Liz, getting ahead of herself.

'Whoa Liz. I am just getting my head around the fact that Kate slept with James, really soon after Claire died. Shouldn't we be mad with her?' she asked, seeking clarity on her emotions from Liz.

'Shouldn't we be mad with both of them?' responded Liz, letting the reality sink in further. Tanya nodded, the phone clutched tightly to her ear.

'You're right. Oh man. That's so wrong. But I won't judge, I promised you. It's in the past right?' Tanya told herself, without seeking an answer.

'Yup' said Liz 'and we are going to be aunties, and Kate and James are going to be parents. They need our support, forgiveness, understanding, whatever. We just need to be there for them, as they sort their stuff out,' said Liz. 'And one last thing, Kate doesn't know I called James and told him. Don't tell her anything yet, ok!' finished Liz.

'Are you insane Liz! She'll kill you. You know she is even more vicious than me if she gets mad,' said Tanya, over exaggerating to make her point.

Liz laughed. 'Yes, I know. But someone had to do it,' said Liz, explaining how she'd guessed something was up between Kate and James, when they'd seen him off at the airport. Kate had folded easily, but asked Liz to keep it quiet so as not to upset anyone.

Tanya accepted Liz's reason for keeping the information to herself. The two friends finally finished their talk and promised to meet the next weekend, unless the baby came. Tanya lifted herself from the stairs, scratched in her gym bag for her access card and headed to the door, shaking her head. Just when you thought things were settling down and normalising, life seemed to throw a few more curveballs to keep you on your toes.

Liz was pleased with Tshepo's progress. His gait had improved immensely since she'd started working with him. For starters, he no longer needed help with his balance, and could walk free of the railing along the side of the room. It had taken some months to get to this point. The hunched-over figure she had first met, was now a man who could walk confidently. Tshepo turned around when he got to the end of the room and saw Liz's face. He smiled broadly back at her, showing all his teeth.

'It is so good Liz. Look, I am a man who is walking like a man again,' he proclaimed proudly.

'Yes you are Tshepo. You make me so proud,' exclaimed Liz as she started to walk towards him. 'I almost can't believe how far you have come. Soon, the limp will hardly be noticeable. Put a pair of long trousers over the prosthesis and 'voila', you are a new man' said Liz, using a gesture with French flair to reinforce the miracle before her.

She sidled up to Tshepo, placing her arm into his and said, 'come, let's walk back together.' As they made their way to the other side of the room, arm in arm, Tshepo spoke quietly.

'Yes Liz, I am a new man. A very different man to who I was. But a walking man, thanks to you!'

Liz smiled and squeezed his arm gently, as they reached the end of the room.

'Tshepo we have a saying in my culture: "There are only a few certainties in life: taxes, death and change." We can't escape any of them. It's ok to change and be new, it will maybe just take time to grow into your new skin,' said Liz.

She raised her eyebrows questioningly and lifted her shoulders up. Tshepo looked at her, digesting her words.

'This is true Liz. I like that saying. I will remember these certainties, and yes, maybe I must just take my time to find out about this new man I am. I guess that's what it will take. Time,' he affirmed.

Liz decided to leave her things and walk Tshepo to reception to wait for his lift. She shook his hand warmly, smiled and said goodbye once he was seated at reception. She returned to the exercise room to collect her files, before attending to the next patient.

As she was organising her folder and gear, one of the biokineticists walked in. He was only slightly taller than Liz, but very well built. This Liz knew, because she'd been taking sneaky peaks at his biceps the one day he'd removed his lab coat. She had hoped that he hadn't spotted her eyes on stalks, bulging like his muscles.

She learned that his name was Garth. He was possibly a little younger than her; not married, according to his unringed finger, but could be in a relationship. Liz had stalked him on Facebook to glean any possible girlfriend information, but hadn't been able to find him. She convinced herself that everyone did a bit of background Facebook stalking, so why shouldn't she? He was definitely good looking, and there always seemed to be some pretty nurse, physio or patient batting their eyelashes at him.

Liz didn't have a chance in hell of getting anywhere near him, and she definitely knew that she was physically incapable of chasing him. She actually just couldn't do it. So she kept her distance, kept it professional, and said hello and goodbye when appropriate. This cute guy, with sandy-brown ruffled hair, had no idea that she wanted to eat him with a spoon. She was way too cool as a cucumber for that.

'Hey Liz,' he said as he walked in. Liz felt the heat rise in her belly as she saw it was Garth. 'Hey Garth, how you doing? Do you need the room? I'm just packing up and it's all yours. Won't be a second,' she said confidently as she finished putting everything away.

Garth smiled a shy smile.

'I'm good hey,' he said casually, shifting from foot to foot strangely, as though on edge.

'So Liz, I just wanted to find out, and I mean, I'm totally cool if it's not your vibe, but some of my mates and I are doing this wine tour thing, and there's a spare ticket and I thought, you may want to join us?' he asked, his boyish face anguished.

Liz was dumbstruck. She had to look away, and repack one of the exercise blocks to compute that he had just asked her out.

'But, hey, if that's not your thing, no worries ok,' he started to say, noticing Liz's hesitation.

'I love wine, I mean, you know, in moderation and all that. I would love, I mean, it would be lovely to come along, if that's still ok?' said Liz, fumbling through her response.

Garth's body breathed a sigh of relief, quickly followed by triumph. He puffed out his beautiful pecs.

'Great. That's great. I'll get your number later, and then I can WhatsApp you the details. That work?' he said. Liz was certain she had a beetroot-coloured face by now, and was desperate to get out of the room

'Sounds perfect,' she responded and nodded her head in enthusiasm.

'Ok,' Garth said, turning and looking back over his shoulder. 'Ok bye,' he reiterated, nearly slamming his face into the door as he turned around.

Liz blinked as the door closed behind him. She stuck her face into her hands and squealed with delight. She had just been asked out by the hottest guy ever. She felt like she was going to overheat and die. No, she couldn't die; that would mean no date and there was no way she wasn't going on that date, even if it was with the mates. Safety in numbers she guessed.

Whatever. It didn't matter, she was going on a date. She had better book a wax, there was work to be done, and wait till she told the girls, they would never believe it!

Liz beamed and floated out of the room.

Kate made herself a cup of rooibos tea and reached into a jar of her delicious, golden honey crunchies. She needed to sit down and think. Arora raised her head from her vantage point on the top counter shelf behind Kate.

As Kate made her way to the corner couch, the sweet little cat padded after her, her little bell tinkling. Dropping into the couch, Kate propped a kiddie's bean bag under her feet to ease her swollen cankles, sipping her tea while ruminating on her crunchie.

Arora climbed onto her thighs and curled herself into a perfect cat ball that hummed. Kate reached around her tummy and stroked the velvet fur. 'Hey pretty girl, have you survived another day in kitty hell? That brat nearly got your tail today,' said Kate to the vibrating cat. She smiled to herself; Arora came to the shop with her every day, risking her nine lives amongst children. Kate tickled behind Arora's ears. She hadn't been able to leave her at home alone and besides, Arora got delicious treats everyday just by being here.

Kate relaxed into the couch, resting her hands on her belly and looking around her. She still liked what she saw: the space was warm and welcoming and it smelt of coffee and cake. As the warm sun of the late afternoon streamed into the glass storefront, Kate allowed herself to think about the arrival of the baby.

After the surprise baby shower, she realised she had to prepare. Tanya and Liz had been helping too, although at times she felt like it was the blind leading the blind. What she wouldn't do for an older sister with children. She had, over the past few weeks, endured many childbirth conversations with the moms who had come in. The horror of childbirth was still clearly apparent in their lives, and some felt it necessary to share their experiences in graphic detail. After one such conversation, Kate had been unable to serve the woman again. She'd made her waitress take the order to her table, because all she could see when she looked at the woman was her "ripped apart vajayjay", as she'd described it.

Kate felt strangely set apart from the women who came into the shop with their children: The mothers who were overly attentive to their cherubs, or the ones who nonchalantly patted the head of their child screaming blue murder. They all seemed so different to her. She wondered if she would eventually become like them, morph into some form of motherhood. Surely she would have to? She needed these other mothers to help her to know what to do.

Her own mother still thought whiskey was acceptable treatment for sore gums, which indicated that she would be of little help. As for Tanya and Liz, they also didn't have a clue.

Kate looked at her ripe belly and rubbed it. 'I am so scared of you little person,' she confessed out loud. She meant it. She had days where she was so overwhelmed by the enormity of what she was trying to do on her own.

After one mother found out Kate was to be a single parent, she'd gone on and on about how Kate would need to find someone to support her, or she'd end up harming her child in the wee hours of the morning. After that, she just smiled whenever someone had declared, 'you and your husband must be so excited!'

It was too hard to explain how she'd ended up pregnant, with a new shop and very little support. She was still looking for a manageress for the shop; her waiters and waitresses were great, but no one was prepared to do the buying, stocking, paying, opening and closing. It was hard work, and Kate was desperate to hand over to someone she knew she could trust. This place was her other baby, her dream.

She sighed and looked into the bottom of her empty cup. No solution there, she thought to herself. Without much grace, Kate nudged Arora off her lap and launched her overburdened form up from the couch, managing to right herself to standing. She had spotted a pile of books that needed to be put back. As she was putting them onto the shelf, she heard the door open behind her. 'Don't let the cat escape,' she cautioned over her shoulder, standing on her tippy toes to put the last book on the correct shelf. Dropping back onto her heels, she turned around to see who'd come in.

It was James: tanned, gorgeous and rugged, holding Arora under his arm.

'Hello Kate, is this the cat you mean?' he said.

Kate blinked, unable to believe her eyes. 'James!' she gasped, staring at him, 'you're home'.

James

After Liz told James about Kate, he'd half-packed his bag, then paced the floor of his small room, until he couldn't bear to be in the room any longer. He decided to go for a walk. Kate was pregnant with his child; beautiful Kate, with her big eyes and infectious laugh.

He walked past the rowdy Irish pub filled with the smell of beer and noise of footie on the TVs. The lady boys, at the dance bar further down the road, waved and whistled at him as he walked past them, his pace quickening. The road snaked through the town, with all the wonders of Thai island life spilling into the road. He had no destination, but the questions pushed him on.

The smell of incense made him lift his head from his footfall. The Buddhist temple was a small, shiny conical structure that glistened in the late afternoon sun. Perhaps he could meditate his way through the noise in his head. The questions, the emotions, the anger and the joy had been swirling around in his mind; maybe the temple would give him peace.

The hum of the monks called to him through the entrance. James took off his slops before he entered. He felt the cool floor on the soles of his feet, in contrast to the heat that surrounded his body and made him sweat. The haze from the smoke made it difficult for him to find a place to sit. After stumbling to a spot, he sat cross-legged and closed his eyes, breathing in deeply. As he exhaled, he began to focus his attention on his breath. His chest rose and fell rhythmically, as the thick incense air filled his lungs. He felt the questions begin to rise, letting them pass and refocusing on his breath: in and out, in and out. He stayed sitting for hours.

When he eventually opened his eyes, he had no answers to his questions, but he knew what he had to do. Calmly and with purpose, he walked back to the hotel.

Within a few hours he'd booked his flight to Cape Town. He would have to travel via Singapore and Johannesburg, but in three days, he would be home. He tried not to think about what he would do when he arrived back in Fish Hoek. He didn't have anywhere to stay, he didn't have a car and no one knew he was coming back.

He liked the last part of that thought. He was glad to be going home without expectation. For this first time in what felt like a lifetime, there was somewhere he wanted to be... needed to be. Somewhere he belonged.

Travelling had let him become anonymous, but he was tired of running from his memories of Claire, and chasing the next "so amazing" place. It was time; he was ready to go home. He was ready to be James, without Claire.

He decided to fly to Bangkok and spend one last night in the city. He stayed away from Khaosan Road and booked himself into a B-grade hotel that had a reasonable room, in an upmarket area with fantastic themed restaurants.

He would have loved to try the Heaven and Hell themed restaurant, but the thought of ordering a meal for one, watching everyone around him chatting, made him feel lonely. So he settled on street cart Pad Thai, and walked the streets for an hour or two. It felt so strange to be in the city, not as a traveller, but just passing through.

The uneventful, long and laborious queues and waiting at check-in counters, overlays and finally passport control all seemed to take forever. He watched the minutes tick by as he stood around, waiting to get to Kate. He couldn't wait to see her face.

Eventually he arrived in Cape Town, in desperate need of a shower and shave. He called Liz and asked her if he could use her place. He could hear her beaming as she told him to collect the key at reception, where security would let him in as she would be at work.

'Thank you James. Thank you for coming back,' she said, before putting down the phone.

James smiled to himself. Good old Liz.

He took an Uber to Liz's flat and peeled his clothes off. He would need to find a laundromat and do his washing. Everything in his bag seemed foreign and filthy, except for a pair of jeans that had seen better days and a t-shirt with red bull branding on it, written in Thai.

He showered and dressed, slowly and deliberately. Then he walked around Liz's apartment. The view of Muizenberg beach and across the bay made his heart want to burst. He was home; he felt his body ache for the cool waters of his ocean.

James rummaged through the kitchen cupboards and found some muesli and milk. He stood in the kitchen and slowly spooned the cereal into his mouth. He knew he was procrastinating, buying time until he could wait no longer. He washed the dish and carefully set it aside.

He sighed, it was time.

The Uber driver dropped James off across the road, and James had time to observe Kate. He watched her potter around, putting books back in place. She looked beautiful: her full belly protruding from her front, yet strangely well-balanced by her tall frame, her long thick hair rippling over her shoulders. He was glad there was no one else in the shop with her. He would have her all to himself.

He spotted Arora through the glass of the door, looking at him as if she had spotted him first. She certainly was a special cat.

He crossed the road.

James had expected Kate to run into his arms. But she didn't. She was shocked and her face left nothing to the imagination.

She tried to ask him when he had arrived and why he had come back. The words falling out of her mouth as she moved to behind the counter, keeping her distance from him. Arora had wriggled out of his arms and followed Kate behind the counter.

Kate started to make a coffee for James, offering him carrot cake, but never once mentioning her very visible pregnant belly. Confused, yet unsure of what to say or do, James watched her flap around her kitchen until eventually he walked around the counter. Gently he held her upper arms and turned her towards him.

'Kate, shhh, I'm here to see you. I've come back for you. For you and our baby,' he said softly.

All the months of trying to be so brave on her own; the confusion, guilt and fear rushed to the surface and Kate began to cry. James held her as best he could, her awkward shape keeping him at a distance. Her body shook, until eventually she pulled away from him and wiped her face.

She looked up at James. 'I'm so glad you're here,' she said, then stepped back, eyebrows furrowed and asked, 'who told you about the baby?'

James smiled nervously, his chest tight with emotion.

'It was Liz. Don't be mad at her, please. She did it for you,' he pleaded, watching Kate's face closely. 'Ahh, Liz, of course,' she said, her eyebrows rising and falling.

James directed Kate towards a table. 'Sit down. I'll finish up the coffee. We have a lot to talk about, and I have a lot to apologise for. Please sit Kate, I'll make the coffee,' he smiled.

They sat at the table for hours. James caught Kate up on his travels, where he'd been, some highlights and lowlights. Kate shared how the yoga course had helped her deal with Claire's passing, as well as her own guilt. It had also helped her stop procrastinating about opening her own place - something she'd been thinking about for years. The conversation between them flowed easily, as it had always done, until they realised the sun had set. As Kate pushed her chair back to get up and clear the cups, James stopped her.

'Kate, we need to talk about what happened. I'm sorry for acting like such an idiot. I was a mess that afternoon, you know at your house, and for a long time after that.' James stumbled through his apology, trying to get the words out as fast as he could. 'I'm really sorry Kate. I should have called you or something. I stuffed up.' He looked away.

Kate's heart sank. She remembered that afternoon. Everything had felt so right and so natural, until he had walked away from her. Ashamed.

The hurt washed over her face as James looked up and saw her eyes begin to fill with water.

She swallowed hard, keeping the tears floating behind her eyelashes.

'It hurt like hell when you treated me like that James. And the guilt, the guilt nearly killed me.' She stared into his eyes. 'It took a long time to forgive myself... and you. But I got through it. And I'm ok. Actually,' she paused, looking down at her hands.

'Actually I'm terrified! I'm so scared of what this baby is going to do to me and my life. Everyone says everything will change. But I've just started a new life without Claire, with a new shop. I can't handle more change. And now I'm committed to this baby, on my own. I'm so scared,' Kate confessed, her voice almost a whisper, her face pale with fear.

'You're not alone Kate,' James assured her. 'I'm here. I'm with you. I want to do this with you. I want to be a part of your life Kate. We have something, I know we do. I'm scared to give it a name, but I now know this is where I need to be. Here with you and with our baby.' He looked at her directly.

Kate's head fell backward and she laughed hysterically.

'Are you telling me you are going to be the hero, walk in, father this child, help me manage my shop, bring me tea in bed?' she said, her eyebrows raised and questioning, the sarcasm thick in her voice.

James sat back.

It was true, he had expected to just waltz in and be the hero. He shrugged his shoulders. She'd seen straight through him.

'I understand Kate,' he said, 'but I want to try, OK?' he leaned towards her. 'Let's just give whatever we are, a try. Don't cut me off. Please Kate,' he asked, touching her hand.

Kate looked at him, her face serious. The silence filled the air. James began to feel that she would send him away. He held his breath.

Quietly, Kate stood up and took the cups to the kitchen, slowly turning around.

'You can stay, if that's what you really want. In fact you can manage this shop when the baby comes. I trust you enough, and you can make a decent cup of coffee. The rest, well, I guess we'll see,' Kate said, her arms folded on top of her belly.

James smiled at Kate. She was gorgeous. Her large brown eyes looked at him intensely, and he couldn't believe she'd given him a second chance.

'We have a deal,' he said, as he stood up.

'Good,' said Kate, as she busily closed up the kitchen and till.

'Home time! I'll just grab Arora,' Kate said as she picked up the cat and put her in the cat carrier. 'Where are you staying?' she asked, curious to know who had the pleasure.

'Well, I dumped my bags at Liz, so maybe there tonight. Don't know otherwise,' James said. 'I didn't really think it through,' he continued scratching his head absentmindedly. 'Still another few months rental on my place, so can't go back there. I dunno.'

Kate listened and said nothing.

They walked to the door and closed up the shop.

'I'll give you a lift to Liz,' stated Kate.

They drove most of the way in silence. When Kate pulled up in front of Liz's building, she said, 'see you at the shop tomorrow. 7am sharp.'

James opened the door, looking at Kate over his shoulder.

'Wouldn't miss it for the world,' he grinned. 'Thank you Kate,' he said, squeezing her hand on the gear lever, before getting out and closing the door behind him.

Kate watched him walk into the building. He had come back, for her.

'James, James, wake up. We have to go,' said Liz urgently. Disorientated, James woke slowly, trying to figure out where he was. Liz's flat.

'Liz, what's wrong?' he asked sleepily. He was on the couch, and he could see that it was still the middle of the night.

'Kate's having the baby. I'm her birthing partner and we have to go. You're about to be a dad,' announced Liz, a wide grin on her face.

Acceptance and hope

Stage 7

The last stage, a person learns to accept and deal with the reality of their situation. A person is more future-oriented and learns to cope

Chapter 7

The ground had soaked up most of the rain from the night before, filling the crisp air with the rich smell of wet earth. The climb from the road up Elsie's Peak was steep at first, but levelled out to a moderate climb. The friends walked in silence as they made their way to the uppermost point of the peak. It had been a year since Claire had died. The four people who walked up the mountain had changed completely in the year since that fateful day, when their lives had been turned upside down.

As they reached the peak, they looked out across rugged mountains and deep blue sea. Simon's Town and the South African Naval base lay to their right, with large grey naval ships docked in the harbour. To the left in the valley lay Fish Hoek, with Muizenberg and Somerset West visible in the distance. The bay stretched to the Hottentot's-Holland Mountains, with Pringle Bay at its tip.

The air rushed past their faces and cooled their warm cheeks as they walked further, in search of a more private and less exposed part of the mountain.

Once they'd settled and found comfortable rocks to sit on, the four friends shuffled closely together. The ocean stretched out in front of them, the wind whipping their hair up in small gusts.

Liz began, 'so one year ago, our amazing Claire passed away. Today, we are going to remember Claire, and tell her how we are doing. You know, in case she has missed something,' Liz smiled sadly, at her poor attempt at a joke.

'We decided we are going to read out a letter to Claire, and update her and remind ourselves about her too,' Liz breathed in, and her body shivered as she exhaled.

'I'll start, if that's ok with everyone?' Liz said, looking at her friends.

All three heads nodded.

'I'm going to start with a letter from Tshepo,' she said, noticing how everyone sat up taller, yet no one stopped her. She continued, 'I asked him if he would like to write Claire a letter. He said yes, and I think it's the right thing. You know, to give him a chance too,' explained Liz.

Tanya clenched her jaw, but said nothing.

Liz dug into her day pack and pulled out a letter. She smoothed the paper out on her thigh before reading it.

Tshepo

Dear Claire,

You do not know me. We never had the chance to meet, to say 'Hello' or to speak to each other. Maybe we would have met in Fish Hoek. Me driving my taxi, you in your car. Maybe I would have pushed in front of you in the traffic, and maybe you would have shouted at me and waved your hand and shook your head. Or maybe we would have met in Masi, because you worked at the school there. Maybe this is how we would have met.

I cannot know.

When we did meet, it was fateful and too fast for anything or anyone to have stopped it.

You were flying across my windscreen. Hair and glass - your long blonde hair - that was how we met. You were made dead and I was made broken. Your brave friend screamed at me, and the men from the ambulance saved me.

For many days in the hospital I wished I would die. The life I had as a taxi driver was over without my leg. My boss sent his Nigerian to tell me this was true.

Then one day your friend, Liz, came to look at me in the face. She came and she was angry, but then she cried. She told me your name. And then I knew the name of the person whose life I stole by mistake.

Claire.

The days only became worse, as I was taken to prison in the courthouse. My guilt about killing you, my leg, it was all so terrible. I didn't want to live anymore. The sadness began to kill me and I wanted to die. Only after Mr Buswayo and the judge sent me to Lentegeur, and I spoke to the doctors, did I start to become less sad. Less sad in a way, but maybe never happy again. It is hard to be happy when you wake up every day and you look at your half leg. And you are reminded that the leg is what I paid for killing another person. For killing you Claire.

Please Claire, please can you try and forgive me. I hope that if you can forgive me, then maybe I can start to forgive myself. But I do not know if this will be possible because, when I speak to Liz and she talks about you, she smiles so much, and says such nice things about you. It is very hard to forgive that I have taken you away from your friends who loved you so much. If I had died, there would not have been so much sadness. But for you, there was so much sadness. I am sorry you died and I did not, Miss Claire. I am so so sorry.

Your friend, Tshepo Dlamini

As Liz looked up, tears streamed down Kate and Tanya's faces. Liz had read the letter earlier and knew what he had written. Her tears had been shed. She swallowed hard and carefully folded the letter, placing it back in her bag. She pulled out a packet of tissues that she passed around.

'He's going to stay at Lentegeur for a while' explained Liz. 'Tshepo. They've given him some odd jobs to do at the hospital, and he is getting stronger. He's going to be ok' she said, 'I think' her voice uncertain.

James had been staring at the ground while Liz had been speaking. He got up and turned his back on the three women. He closed his eyes as the wind blew on his face, breathing deeply.

Liz scratched in her bag again. She pulled out another piece of paper. Unfolding it, she looked over at James. 'James, can I carry on with my letter?' she asked, her voice gentle. James didn't turn around; he just nodded his head and stood with his back to the group.

Liz

Dearest Claire-bear,

I can't believe it's been a year since we last spoke! I mean, really spoke. I still hear your voice in my head all the time, but there are days now when it's a little bit soft, and I'm not sure if it's your voice anymore. But then there are other days, when you are loud and clear. You are usually saying something like:

'Honestly Liz, just let it go,' in that relaxed Claire voice you always had.

Sometimes I hear you also laugh. I miss that laugh. In fact, I really miss you. Like when I think about you and then there is a pain in my chest. Like a tight little squeeze that pinches, just enough to know it's real.

You being gone is so very real.

I used to fall apart when I got that feeling, and would have to go and cry somewhere. Now, I try and remember something about you, us, all of us - stuff we did in high school, things we used to laugh at and then, I usually end up smiling or laughing. Because we always laughed. We had tough times, but most of the time with you was filled with laughter. So when I remember you now, it makes me smile and I don't cry anymore. Thank you Claire. Thank you for all the laughs we had, for being my person who would set me straight. Thank you for being a friend to me, even though I was a bit of a drag for most of my life. Thank you for all the amazing years we had together. I will miss you forever,

Your dearest friend

Liz

The tears that had been welling in Liz's eyes spilled over and she sucked in a gulp of air. The three women hugged, crying quietly as they tugged tissues from the unyielding packet.

James stayed standing with his back to them. He felt his chest close and fought his emotions to control the tears.

Tanya lifted her head. Wiping at her face, she found the tissues and blew her nose loudly, while Liz and Kate wiped their tears away. Tanya leaned over to her backpack and pulled out a piece of paper. She sniffed. 'I would like to say something next, if that's ok?' she said, looking at Kate and James's back. Kate nodded.

Tanya

Dearest Claire,

There are some days when I just can't actually believe that I can't call you, to complain about some absurdity. You were my sanity Claire. You were snatched from me and you left a gaping hole. One that no-one could ever fill. I foolishly thought that Tristan could, but that blew up in my face. And then you weren't here for that. I was actually pissed off with you about that, by the way. I bet you knew he was going to dump me; you always knew these things. I was cross with you for being in the road when that nut job flew past. Why did you, of all people, have to be in the road? Don't get me wrong, it's not like I would have wanted Kate or Liz to be there either, but I can't help thinking that if we had been earlier, or later it would have made a difference, and maybe we would have missed that crazy driver.

Maybe it wouldn't have made a difference.

You were always quite fatalistic, so I guess my wonderings are useless. I can hear you say: "What's meant to be will be. You know that Tan."

You were always so accepting of what life had to offer. I've always been fighting fate, thrashing at life for all its injustices.

Until now.

I've taken a feather out of your cap dear Claire. I'm fighting less these days. I'm letting things go, I'm actually doing a lot of just being. I even go to pottery – don't laugh!

Don't worry, I promise I am not trying to copy you. I could never, but I'm definitely trying to follow your example. Thank you Claire. Thank you for every day we had together; for getting me through maths, for running at a decent pace and for listening. For listening every single time I called on you and your time.

If, for one moment, you think that you are off the hook I'm sure that you've figured out you're not. Dying won't stop me getting in touch with you. I talk to you every day, and just as when you were alive, you listen. Thank you my Claire. Thank you for every breath you gave us. I miss you always.

Lovingly,

Tan

Tanya drew the letter into her chest, covering the paper with her hands over her heart. She hiccupped between tears. Kate leaned across to Tanya and gently squeezed her knee.

The pouch holding Kate's child to her chest, began to move as her little voice complained. Kate stroked her small head and put the soother in her mouth. She sucked hard on the soother and snuggled back into the warmth of her mother's body, content once more.

'I can't say anything Liz. I'm sorry,' said James. His face showed that he was struggling to hold it together.

Liz looked up at him.

'No worries James.'

Liz looked to Kate and asked, 'do you want to say a few words?' Kate nodded as she leaned onto her side and stuck her hand in her back pocket to retrieve a scrunched-up piece of paper. She righted herself, gently holding onto her baby and rocking her ever so slightly. She held up the paper and began to read.

Kate

Wonderful Claire,

Would you recognise me now if we met in the street?

Maybe not.

I am a mother of a little girl now.

She is beautiful and her name is Claire, after you. Everyday when I look at her, I hope that she will be as kind, generous, open-hearted and funny as you were.

Do you remember the last time we spoke? We were laughing at how different we were: How you were probably going to marry James and I would probably stay single for ever, and how that suited us both just fine.

Who knew that you wouldn't live till the next week? Who knew that your death would change me forever? In my heart, my mind and my body. Was there a master plan Claire? Were you always supposed to die and leave us behind, with just your legacy to fill our lives?

The thought terrifies me.

I would never ever have thought of life without you, yet here we are and we continue to breathe every day, without you. We are the same, but we're not. We are a little bit broken, yet a little bit stronger and better. It's all so contradictory and confusing.

I need to tell you something I did. It's pretty bad, but I hope you…. I hope you don't get too cross Claire. I hope you understand.

I fell for James. I slept with him. Very soon after you were gone. I'm so sorry Claire. It just happened, and I have no excuses. I wanted to tell you myself. I can't change it, and to be honest I would never want to. I'm sorry that it happened this way. I love you Claire. Please forgive me or at least try. We need you Claire, to watch over us, to watch over this little girl with your name. You were our guardian angel in life. Please watch over us in death.

Love you so much,

Kate

James sat next to Kate and held her close, his arm around her shoulder. Kate hugged baby Claire to her, her letter crumpled in her hand against the baby's body. Tanya and Liz looked at Kate and James. Liz smiled slowly, looking up behind Kate's head. A faint rainbow had appeared, its colours twinkling gently in the morning sky.

Maureen

Maureen stood in her kitchen, the hum of the Nespresso machine filling the space. She felt a small twinge in her skull. It was probably the three large glasses of wine she'd had the night before, remembering the taxi accident she'd witnessed a year ago. The date was one she would never forget. She knew Tanya had gone to be with her friends for the day; she'd chosen instead to go to work and get through the day, and it had mostly worked. Eventually she'd given up and come home at a decent hour, poured the wine and brooded over her life until she surrendered to sleep.

She switched the coffee machine off and took her cup to the lounge, sipping it slowly as she walked. As she came to the window, she rested her forehead against the cool glass.

He was there, looking up at her.

She stopped breathing and blinked purposefully.

A wide malevolent grin spread across his face. He made the shape of a gun with his hand and pointed it at her, mouthing the word 'bang', then turned and walked away.

She sucked in her breath, stepping back from the glass and spilled her coffee on her toes as she shook. She turned around slowly, half expecting him to be behind her.

There was a slip of paper under her front door.

Slowly she walked over to the door and carefully picked it up. It read: 'You belong to me baby, not that lawyer. I'm going to come and get you. I promise.'

Acknowledgements

I would like to thank the small town of Fish Hoek for being just as it is, without excuses. It keeps things real and entertaining. Thank you to Wendy Waddington of False Bay Hospital for taking time to answer my questions with regard to the hospitals of the area and the services offered. Thank you to my husband, the first person to read the book. You suck as an editor, but your gut instinct was spot on. Thank you to Lee-Anne McQueen and Anne-Marie Greiff, the first people I trusted to read this book. They diligently read through a draft manuscript and deserve medals. Thank you to my wonderful editor Lisa Ferguson, who was so encouraging, kind and just kept giving. I could not have done this without her. Thank you to my clever friend Gail Schimmel, an author of many novels, who Whatsapped advice many times. Thank you to all the Beta readers who gave their time and invaluable feedback: Laura Fisher, Victoria De La Cour, Helen Imrie, Andrea Hoffman, Beverly Houston, Leisl Algeo and Thuli Mncube. You guys rock!

And finally to my children, who sometimes sidle up to me while I'm typing away and speak to me while I ignore them. Sorry my angels, I don't mean it. I just need to get it out, and then we can play. Love you.